A HARVEST OF SOULS

BOOK ONE OF THE GRIM LORE

C.C. EDMONSTON

JOIN THE GANG

For updates, news on forthcoming releases and behind-the-scenes sneak peeks such as character art and offers, see the back of this book for details on how to sign-up to my newsletter.

For Erin, the light in my soul.
(Sorry about all the swearing.)

I have heard sundry men oft times dispute
Of trees, that in one year will twice bear fruit.
But if a man note Tyburn, 'will appear,
That that's a tree that bears twelve times a year.
I muse it should so fruitful be, for why
I understand the root of it is dry,
It bears no leaf, no bloom, or no bud,
The rain that makes it fructify is blood.

John Taylor (1578-1653), *The Description of Tyburn* (Extract)

1

NERVES

I t was early. Too early for Harry to be clomping around the house killing imaginary foes with his wooden sword. Shanklin had heard about enough of it, slouched in his tatty armchair, mulling on why he was so damn nervous about doing this last robbery.

'Son, slow it down, will ya?' he snapped. Not that Harry gave a toss when there were dragons to slay. So on it continued: *bang, bang, bang*, the dusty floorboards taking a pounding and Shanklin's head right along with it.

He closed his eyes, stomach all knotted-up like a ship's log-line. The life of a highwayman could certainly be a short one, and Samuel Shanklin was what one might consider a 'career criminal'.

But there's only so far you can stretch your luck before the noose stretches your neck, and Shanklin was to luck-stretching what Harry was to damn annoying right now.

'Son, I've told ya!' he barked as the lad dashed in and out of the cluttered sitting room like a German cuckoo clock. He might've taken his shoes off first, how many times did he need telling?

Shanklin rubbed at the lumpy bridge of his nose — one that had taken more knocks than a whore's front door. He breathed in, long and slow like it might help settle his nerves. Dancing for the hangman in front of a crowd had little appeal, but then so did bringing a maniac like Bob Creech along for this last planned job. Any one of the others would've been a better choice: Nathan Baines, 'Tall' Saul, even Ben 'Boulder' Bradford. All rum rogues and keen to prove it. But no, Randall had suggested Creech ('cause of his connections) and Shanklin had listened, once again, despite his gut telling him different.

'When you've quite finished daydreaming, maybe I can get some help around here?'

His eyes flashed open. Sarah was standing in the doorway leading out to their hall, holding a wicker basket full of dirty laundry and wearing a frown more creased than the drab dress hanging from her shapeless body. Granted, it was a body that had bore him three children, of which only one was still alive but soon wouldn't be if he carried on stomping around the place.

Shanklin ignored her. 'Harry, if I have to tell ya one more time!'

The boy squeezed past his mother, leaving the room for the fifth time in five minutes.

'Can't a man get some peace?' groaned Shanklin, massaging his temples.

'Not while there's chores to be done,' said Sarah, blowing a long strand of chestnut-brown hair from her face. She'd been pretty once; a diamond of the first water. She used to turn all the heads in a room, now she just turned his stomach. A fading apparition of the woman she once was.

'Things to do,' he said, standing up sharply and pushing past her, out into the hallway. 'Randall's on his way.'

Sarah followed, clutching the heavy basket to her hip.

'Aye, always something else, ain't there, Sam? Something more important than our marriage.'

He pulled a pistol from a cabinet drawer near the front door, primed and ready to pop in case someone he'd upset decided to knock one night unannounced. Best to always have a gun within easy reach when pissing people off was your profession.

'What marriage is that then?' he mumbled as he checked it was loaded and the pan had powder in, despite knowing it had. An old habit that wouldn't die before he did. 'Anyway, you wouldn't have a house to do your chores in if it wasn't for what I do, so don't go preaching at me, Sarah.'

Shanklin snatched his tricorn from a marble bust of Julius Caesar that he'd once stolen from a big house in Peckham. It was chipped now and probably not worth much, but it still gave him a grin some mornings to see the greatest leader of the Roman Empire wearing a hat.

But it was his wife doing the grinning now. More a smirk, in truth. 'Oh, aye, Sam,' she said, 'I'd be nothing without ya. I'd have to sell my body to make ends meet, wouldn't I?'

He tucked two pistols into his belt. 'Aye, and who'd pay for *that*?'

The clothes basket fell to the floor with a *thump* and the grin was gone from Sarah's face. 'You're a callous man at times, Samuel Shanklin,' she whispered, tears welling in her big, brown eyes, 'and I don't know why I put up with it.'

Harry was still darting back and forth between rooms, swinging that little wooden sword like his life depended on it. The life that'd soon be over.

'Makes two of us then,' Shanklin said, placing his hat on and swiping his great coat from its hook just as a knocking was heard at the door.

Bang, bang, bang!

'That'll be your lover,' Sarah said, wiping away a tear. 'Go

3

to 'work' then. Keep me in the life of luxury I'm accustomed to.'

With a battle-cry, Harry weaved around them, oblivious to the real war happening right under his nose. Shanklin's hand shot out, grabbing him by the arm. 'Do as you're fucking told!' he yelled and Harry went stiffer than the bust of Caesar. But nine year olds tend to do that when their fathers are respected rogues with very short tempers and a bite to match their bark. And now Shanklin was feeling that familiar pang of guilt as his son stared up at him with those wide, terrified eyes and that stupid, wooden sword hanging limply at his side. It wasn't fair to take his own fears and frustrations out on the kid. But life wasn't, so fuck 'fair'.

'Come 'ere,' he said, ignoring Randall's incessant door-knocking, kneeling down and clamping a firm hand on his son's shoulder. 'Listen, I don't mind you playing in the house but it's your mother's job to give me a headache, so next time, keep the noise down, eh?'

Bang, bang, bang!

Shanklin shut his eyes once more. 'Christ, if it's not the floor it's the fucking door!' he said, standing up and yanking it open.

Waiting on the step was his one-eyed friend and long-term associate in all things immoral. 'Shank,' nodded Randall, proudly showing off what appeared to be a new eye-patch with a tiny, sparkling diamond set in the centre. He then winked at Sarah with the one still in his skull. 'Sweetheart.'

She said nothing in reply as Shanklin pulled on his coat and stepped outside into Brick Lane, the din of horses and carriages clacking on the cobbles. 'You coming then?' he asked when he realised that Randall hadn't moved from his spot, as if waiting to be asked indoors for a cup of tea.

'Aye,' he replied, looking perplexed as he scratched at his scraggy muzzle of a beard.

'Go earn me my fortune then, Sam!' Sarah cried out as the men walked away from the house. 'Or damn-well die trying!' The door slammed shut behind them.

They made for nearby Stable Yard, walking briskly, early-morning shoppers forced to move from their path. It didn't feel much like spring. The day had started off chilly and Shanklin was glad for his long coat, the tails flapping behind him as he strode.

'Good morning to you too,' Randall said, attempting to crack the stony silence.

'When's it ever?' Shanklin kept his eyes straight ahead as they turned onto busy Whitechapel, the clatter of more coaches and bustle all around them.

'Nice to see you both getting on again.'

'She's a twat.' Knowing that his old friend had a soft spot for Sarah gave Shanklin a little light relief whenever he insulted her. Then he remembered that he hadn't said goodbye to Harry and his mood was right back where it started.

Randall sniffed and wiped at his nose with his coat sleeve, pacing to keep up. 'Well, that may be, but the Lord did not create all twats the same.'

'No, the devil made *that* one,' said Shanklin, looking both ways as he crossed the wide stretch of road, hackney carriages trundling past.

'All I'm saying is that you've got a good woman there, Shank.'

'That so? Then maybe *you* should've married her.' It was barely 9 o'clock in the morning and he was getting the ache with this already. 'Where we meeting Creech?'

'He'll see us there,' said Randall.

'Let's hope he doesn't get lost on the way, then, eh? Wouldn't want him to miss out on all the excitement.'

A fashionable looking gentleman with a polished walking cane side-stepped the pair at the last second as they made no attempt to swerve him.

'You still sore he's coming?' Randall asked, scowling over his shoulder at the aggrieved man who briefly appeared to ponder on whether he should say something to these ruffians but wisely thought better of it.

Shanklin stopped dead in his tracks. 'Aye, it might be that I am,' he said. 'It might be that I'm sore about a few fucking things to tell you the truth.'

Randall's palms were raised. 'Listen, Shank, if ya wanna make it another day for this job?'

'No,' he replied. 'No, I don't.' And he was off again, heading for the stables where his horse, Jess was waiting. 'I just want this one over with.'

2

COUNTRY AIR

Through the hazy lens of the spyglass, Shanklin watched 'em: a young boy and a girl, a little older, silently running through a mist-kissed meadow to the right of the road. More a winding, sloppy, track in truth, with just enough curves to give a heartless highwayman the element of surprise. The road wound its way down from Rousingham House — a big mansion just a couple of miles from Tyburn village — and provided the main route south for Lord Jasper Torne and his Ladyship. Not that Shanklin had ever had the pleasure of their acquaintance but there was a first time for everything. Though sticking a pistol under their already stuck-up noses probably wasn't the best way to introduce oneself, it was the only way he knew how.

He'd chosen the vantage point himself. This part of the wood gave some cover and the hill he was standing on offered a good view of the road and surrounding fields, one of which was currently occupied by these two kids, laughing and leaping without a care in the cruel world. Despite his ruthless reputation, Shanklin liked to think he still had a couple of morals rattling around inside him and spotting 'em here sent a shiver down his spine. They were some way off but a little close for comfort if things turned nasty with a coach guard or even with Torne himself, a former military man and a little hot-headed, so rumour would have it. Though there seemed more chance of the children catching their death from a cold than a stray shot, dressed in flimsy clothes like the fucking sun was hot and high in the sky.

Sweeping the lens across the horizon, a stagecoach came shivering into view, four black horses tugging it along, and at speed too. Had to be Torne's; all the signs of it belonging to someone of quality were there.

'Shit,' hissed Shanklin, swiftly scanning back to the spot where he'd seen the kids playing.

Gone. Good.

Snapping the telescope shut, he adjusted his tricorn, his blue-grey eyes narrowed at the approaching speck while he breathed in a long dose of crisp air. He checked for his pistols — only for the fourth time so far. Felt for his knife too: still sheathed right where he'd left it. Same damn ritual. It didn't matter how many times he did it, he always had that nagging sensation they'd slipped off somewhere, abandoning him like his conscience had many years ago.

Just this one last job. But how many times had he told himself that?

He pulled the collar of his coat a little closer, swallowing the worry that had been creeping up his throat since he'd woken and he turned back towards the clearing.

'It's coming,' Shanklin said, striding past Bob Creech who was busy practising his knife-throwing skills on an unfortunate tree.

Thack! The handle wobbled as the blade buried itself in the trunk.

'So soon?' Creech said, smiling, rubbing at the back of his shaved head while casually retrieving his weapon of choice.

He had a reputation for being a good shot but his throwing skills matched his personality: deadly.

Randall sprang from the log he'd been perched on, yawning, stretching his limbs and scratching his arse. 'About time an' all. My cracker's gone to sleep.'

Shanklin pushed the spyglass into Jess's saddlebag, buckling a strap. 'Well, we're done sleeping, Fluff, so get a move on.'

'And there was I hoping you'd read me a story,' Randall replied. 'And don't call me Fluff.'

'Maybe after I've boned that hole in your skull,' said Shanklin. 'Now hurry up, *Fluff*.'

Creech was grinning, still, gold tooth glinting as he spat something green onto the dewy forest floor. 'Samuel's right, Randall. We can't sit around wanking all day when there's coaches of quality to clean out.'

Shanklin let that one bounce. When it came to Bob Creech, he knew better than to bite. Keep your enemies close, so they say. Five yards from this bracket-faced maniac was close enough. With a piece of ear missing and a scar running the length of one cheek, the man bore the marks of having seen more scrapes than a gravedigger's shovel. He was useful in a tight spot, no one could argue that. But that spot wasn't here, not today.

Climbing up into the saddle, Shanklin gave Jess a nudge with his boot. 'Come on, my whinging crew of rank riders,' he said, turning her towards the road, 'there's work to do.'

The caw of a crow disturbed the cold quiet, only the chink of buckles and the squelch of hooves to be heard as the robbers descended the wood's slippery bank. A kink in the road up ahead gave the gang the element of surprise whilst still allowing a little distance for the carriage to grind to a stop once the driver spotted the ambush. Get the timing right and you had a coachman needing a clean pair of breeches. Get it wrong and you'd be shitting your own before winding up in a tangle of horse and metal.

Randall drew up alongside Shanklin and the pair of 'em stared at the bend, willow branches gently swaying above.

'How many of these we done now, Shank? Fifty? More?'

'Lost count,' said Shanklin. The fire that had once burned in his belly for this line of work was now a very weak flame indeed. And there was something about this job in particular that had lost its appeal entirely. It might've been knowing that it was his last and wondering how he'd break the news to Randall later over an ale in *The Lion*. Or it might've been the fact that Creech was here. Or maybe it was something else he hadn't yet realised, but he remembered how he'd once lived for this; that surge in the blood. The excitement. The anticipation. The power. Like a spider waiting for a fly.

The ground grumbled. A brown puddle shimmered.

'That's the beauty of this game though, ain't it?' said Randall. 'Not quite knowing what's round the corner.'

Shanklin drew one of his pistols. 'I'll tell ya what's round the corner,' he said, as they heard the faint snap of the driver's whip. 'A coach about to get robbed. You know what to do.'

Randall spun his horse round and went trotting back to Creech, both men drawing their guns. Shanklin pulled his black neck scarf up over his mouth and nose. Steam belched from Jess's nostrils, her smooth coat twitching, hooves scraping at the churned earth. Randall and Creech were masked too. For better or for worse Shanklin had two good men at his back. Few better. None worse.

The squeak of wheels on the wind now and Shanklin cocked his pistol as the coach appeared from behind the trees.

'Whooooaaaah!' The driver yanked hard on the reins, all four horses' eyes wide with fright. Shanklin fought to control Jess who was flinching as the carriage lumbered towards them, clumps of mud spinning off in all directions. For a moment, it felt like that bastard crate would keep on coming, looking to flatten anything in its path and Shanklin braced, every muscle taut as it hurtled towards him before finally, with a piercing squeal, it came to a stop just a few yards short of his pistol.

'Show your hands!' Shanklin cried, the order only slightly muffled by his scarf. The stunned driver thrust his arms high as the gang sprang forward, Shanklin moving left, Creech right. No need to look back to know that Randall had his gun trained on the coachman; they'd done this enough times.

The carriage curtains were drawn shut as Shanklin brought Jess alongside. 'Open up!'

Silence, save for the crows and the thumping of his heart.

'Open up now or I'll put a hole in this box, I swear it!'

Click.

The door popped open and a woman's voice seeped out from the gap. 'Please!' she begged. 'Please, sir, don't shoot!'

But Shanklin wasn't letting the gun down. 'Show me your hands, my lady and I shan't!'

It opened further revealing a pair of pretty satin shoes beneath an emerald green, richly embroidered dress. Then two slender, silk-gloved, ringed hands attached to the arms of the most beautiful woman he had ever laid his cold eyes upon. A blast from a guard's blunderbuss might've caused less damage to his pounding chest. She was about five and twenty, so he guessed, powdered hair pinned up high, curls tumbling either side of a face that took the breath from his lungs as if he'd plunged into a lake in winter.

Her sparkling green eyes found his. 'Please, sir,' she said, 'we shall cooperate.'

Tucked into the shadows beside her was another woman; younger, less fair but no less frightened. She yelped as Creech opened the door on her side and began collecting what she owned.

'Hand over what you have and you'll soon be on your way,' Shanklin said, his eyes falling to a thin, silver necklace. 'You can start with that.'

She raised a hand to her breast. 'Please, sir, no! Take what you will but allow me to keep this, I beg.'

'Give them what they want, Eliza!' said the younger of the two women, plucking three rings from her trembling fingers and passing them to Creech.

So it was her. *Lady Eliza Torne. So very pleased to meet you.*

Lowering his pistol, Shanklin slid down from Jess. As he approached the intoxicating smell of jasmine reached his nose even through the face scarf he wore and the ground seemed to shift beneath his boots. All colour had drained from the world. All was grey. All except her. The tables had turned and the spider was now under the spell of the fly.

'You should listen to your friend,' Shanklin said, ''cause mine ain't so smart. Sometimes the pressure of this job ... it gets to 'em, and I don't want any accidents, my lady, believe me.'

She fixed his gaze, her fear doused now by a fire which seemed to swell in her. 'Relieving me of this necklace, *sir*, would be no smart move on your part either.'

Shanklin frowned. He admired her spirit but he preferred her frightened. 'Then for you, I'll play the fool,' he said. 'Hand it over. We're running out of time.'

'Sister, please!' begged the younger girl as Creech swiped a bracelet from her and placed it into a leather pouch.

Lady Torne's glare burned into Shanklin for a moment longer before she finally unclipped the chain from behind her neck and pulled from her breast, a tiny, white stone twirling on one end.

Her countenance then softened. 'There is a kindness in you, sir,' she whispered. 'I see it. You don't have to do this.'

'I may be a fool but you've mistaken me for another,' Shanklin said.

Taking the necklace, he closed the carriage door before giving Randall a nod to allow them onwards. The driver didn't need telling twice, cracking his whip and jolting the coach back to life. As it rolled away, the curtains were parted and Eliza Torne stared back with eyes of a fierce, green fire, until finally she was out of sight.

'Shank?'

The voice came from some place far off.

'Shank!'

Shanklin blinked, pulling the scarf from his face and catching a whiff of something that definitely wasn't jasmine. Looking down, he found that he was standing ankle-deep in horse shit.

Randall too had removed his mask, frowning from up in his saddle. 'We're leaving!'

Creech was also now back on his horse, grinning again while Shanklin scraped the heel of his boots along the ground. 'Well, I've done some shit jobs in my time ...,' he said.

Dropping Eliza's necklace into his coat pocket, Shanklin climbed back up onto Jess. 'Aye, ain't we all?' Then he turned her back towards the clearing.

The little white stone swivelled as Shanklin held the necklace up.

'That's it?' Creech asked. 'That's all ya got from her?' He let out a laugh but clearly wasn't amused, puffing his cheeks as he paced the clearing, hands on his hips.

Shanklin's frown followed him. 'Something wrong, Bob?' he asked, slipping the necklace away and already knowing where this was heading.

Creech turned. 'I'll say there is, Samuel! I could see from where I was standing that the tart had more on her than you've got there! We sat in these woods for two fucking hours waiting for that coach and you walk away with *one* poxy necklace?'

Randall was rubbing at his beard and gazing at the ground like he hoped it'd swallow him up.

'Well, you did all right by the other one, so let's just leave it there, eh?' said Shanklin, making his way back towards Jess.

'Leave it there?' Creech said, looking more confused than ever. 'Like you just left whatever silver that ton bitch was carrying? It's *left* when I say it is, Samuel.'

Shanklin turned to find Creech posturing; arms splayed wide like he was inviting him in for something other than a cuddle. The signs were all there. No going back now.

'When you're on the gallows doing the Tyburn Jig,' Creech went on, 'just ask yourself if it was worth it for all you're holding there.' He was jabbing a finger at his chest now. 'I've got goals, Samuel, and they don't involve standing in horse shit while some bluestocking flutters her eyelashes at me.'

Creech was right, of course. There was no explaining what had happened. The woman had been dripping in lard; sparkly rings on her gloved fingers and probably more chink in her purse than they could swipe in a month. But somehow she'd stolen his silly heart before he'd had the sense to steal anything else from her. And now he was paying the price for it. Samuel 'Soft To The Touch' Shanklin, that's what they'd call him. Infamous highwayman of England, tossing his credibility aside.

Just like his hat which landed softly on the damp grass. His pistols he placed gently alongside.

'No, no, no ...,' Randall was protesting, but it was too late for that. Shanklin and Creech were taking long strides towards each other and soon met in the middle of the clearing, swiftly swapping blows, the clap of knuckles on jawbones disturbing the peace.

Creech went for the clinch and the two men tussled, grunting while Randall simply groaned, vainly waving his arms around. A headbutt from Creech glanced Shanklin's cheek and he tucked a foot behind Creech's calf, tipping them both over. They hit the ground, hard, rolling in damp leaves and snuffling like pigs at a trough far too small for sharing.

Shanklin was on his back now, arms wrapped round Creech's thick neck, keeping him in close while he tried to catch a breath. Creech's fingers clawed at his face, digging and scraping, pushing Shanklin's head into the forest floor before he squirmed free of the hold and began raining punches down like hammers on an anvil as Shanklin swerved left and right, elbows together, blocking what he could but tasting the metallic tang of blood in his mouth. Having had enough of the beating, he thrust his hips skyward, toppling Creech and forcing his hands out to break the fall. Shanklin reached up above him, wrapping his arms round his opponent's and pulling 'em in tight, flipping himself over so that he was on top now and—

Being pulled backwards onto his arse.

Shanklin scrambled to his feet to find Randall with his palms raised. 'Shank, no! Enough, eh? Enough!'

'Stay away from me!' Shanklin shouted, surprised to find he was pointing a knife at his old friend.

Creech was back on his feet now too, wiping blood from

his nose, thin eyes fixed on that gleaming blade. 'It's like that now is it, Samuel?'

Shanklin spat out a blob of bright blood, re-sheathing the knife beneath his torn coat. 'If I'd wanted to kill ya, Bob, I'd use my gun,' he said. But he wasn't convincing himself let alone anyone else.

'Gonna tickle me with it then, was ya?' asked Creech. 'You lost your fucking mind?'

Stooping to pick up his hat and his pistols, Shanklin brushed leaves from his coat, struggling to bring his eyes up to look at either of 'em. 'Don't play the saint with me, Bob,' he said. 'Telling me you ain't ever thought it?'

Creech's hand moved inside his own coat as he came forwards like he still had some fight left in him and Shanklin lined himself up for whatever was coming. But Creech stopped when their noses nearly touched and his voice dropped to a gravelly whisper. 'I've had more than my chance, Samuel,' he said, pushing the pouch of stolen jewellery into Shanklin's chest. 'And you're *still* here.'

Taking the pouch from him, Shanklin watched Creech walk over to his horse and swing up into the saddle before heading from the clearing, towards the road.

'Time we were back in London, ain't it?' Randall said, somewhat unamused. 'All this country air's killing me.'

THE DEADLY NEVERGREEN

The two children tightly held hands as they weaved through the gin-pickled crowd of Tyburn Fair, basking under a sizzling sun. Jack was being pulled along by his older sister, squeezing through gaps amongst the sweating mass of drunks. He kept his eyes keenly focused on the black ribbon that was tied in Charlotte's fiery, auburn hair, bobbing like a beacon at sea.

All around him the people pressed in, twisted grins turning to angry objections as his sister shoved her way through the heaving throng. Whenever Jack was scared, his tongue would often prod and poke at his loose back tooth, the last of his baby molars to go. It was strangely comforting somehow and he wondered what he'd do to calm his nerves when it was finally gone. He prodded at it hard now.

They were not too far from home — a large, four-bedroom house they shared with their mother in Tyburn village. Jack disliked it there, yet he hated this place more. He hated the suffocating smells and the noise. He hated the merriment and the ale-stained shirts and the stuffing of cheap pies into mouths. He hated seeing the prostitutes push themselves up against men who looked like they had money, while pickpockets and pedlars did the same, albeit more discreetly. And he hated that Charlotte had made him come when he'd much rather be enjoying the sun, running with her in the surrounding fields.

But most of all, he hated that he was being made to watch people die, something he'd never witnessed in his ten years of being alive even though his sister's morbid fascination with gallows day had only grown.

They finally emerged at the front of the audience to a sight that made Jack's heart sink and Charlotte smile as broad as the River Thames. He swallowed as he gazed upon it; a large wooden triangular structure, comprised of three crossbeams bolted atop three tall stilts.

'There it is, Jack,' Charlotte said, gazing in awe. 'The Triple Tree! Isn't it a sight?'

Jack said nothing. He had no words for this. His mouth was dry and there was a sick feeling in his tummy. Behind the gallows, the scorched Middlesex hills rolled off into the distance like glazed buns in a baker's shop. The sun flashed brightly upon the tips of the long pikes carried by the horse-mounted constables who'd formed a line to keep the crowd at bay. The sheriff himself, in his colourful uniform, was sitting upon his steed, sternly watching the mob for any signs of trouble.

Then Jack saw them: the condemned. Eight men and one young woman, standing in two separate carts, one of which was already positioned in the centre of the great structure. The condemned. Their tied hands were clasped in prayer, halters draped around their necks while the Ordinary, in his flowing robes, received their final words. Above them, two men secured the ropes to one of the beams, the hangman himself leaning lazily against a cart, a long clay pipe protruding from the corner of his mouth, white smoke curling up into the sticky-warm air.

Shielding his eyes from the sun, Jack squinted up at a huge wooden stand; a semi-circle of seats where the *quality* were sat, wearing tall wigs and stupid hats, chattering and smiling down on the proceedings. He wondered how they could be so excited by this.

'How I wish to be sitting up there one day,' said Charlotte, catching him stare. 'Mother Proctor's Pews, the best seats at the most famous gallows in all of England!'

'Die well!' cried someone in the crowd and a cheer went up for a well-known criminal, grinning like this was the day he'd been waiting for all his rotten life. But the young woman standing next to him in the same cart was not smiling. Not one bit. Pretty she was, her skin as white as milk, her wet eyes blinking up towards heaven, her bound hands trembling while she spoke silent words. And, quite suddenly, she met Jack's eyes, causing him to flinch and avert his gaze.

'She looks even more frightened than you,' said Charlotte in his ear.

'I'm not frightened,' lied Jack.

'Are too!' His sister's smile was thin and spiteful. 'I almost feel sorry for her, being that she's innocent.'

'Innocent?' he asked. 'How would you know that?'

'Because, my dear brother, as I have explained to you before, we each have a halo; an arc of light that crosses from one shoulder to the other. Call it an aura, if you will.'

Charlotte knew only too well that Jack struggled with this ridiculous idea but it didn't stop her from trying. 'Halos are not simply reserved for saints, no matter what they teach you at school,' she continued, then looked up at the condemned as the Ordinary listened to their final words, not that he seemed particularly interested.

'We all have them,' Charlotte went on, entranced by those

standing before her. 'Some are like blood-red rainbows, like those wicked people have up there. But some are...' His sister's scrutiny returned to the terrified girl. '... *golden*, as is hers.' She smiled. 'Yes, pure as snow that one!'

Jack was dizzy. This wasn't his idea of fun and he didn't appreciate Charlotte's silly games.

'Now *him*,' she added, her eyes had narrowed and she pointed at a gaunt, expressionless man with whom the Ordinary was now speaking. 'He's as rotten as old apples! Beat his own children to death with an iron bar, apparently.'

Jack shuddered despite the heat. If ever there was a look of pure evil in someone then this man had it. Many of the condemned were dressed in their finest clothes for this day, but not *him*. His filthy shirt hung from his thin body and his sunken cheeks were pitted with pockmarks.

'I want to go,' Jack said. But Charlotte wasn't listening.

A fight had broken out somewhere in the crowd, probably involving one of the criminal's friends or family, and just as a stone creates ripples in a pond the mob surged and the children were shunted and shoved like sheep in a pen. Jack's heart raced as he clung to his sister's arm. The constables stuck out their chins and gripped their pikes that bit tighter, sitting more upright in their saddles to get a better look. But none made an attempt to intervene. They were here to prevent any attempt at saving a prisoner or to retrieve their body, once dead, from the surgeon's men.

Though the day was hot, the atmosphere was turning cold.

'Please, Charlotte, can we go?' Jack asked again, tugging at her sleeve as the drunks pressed in and the children's place at the front of the audience was beginning to slip away. But his sister seemed so utterly drawn into this macabre spectacle that she was not really there with him at all. As though her mind had wandered to some other place.

A priest was standing in front of one of the carts now, a large Bible held aloft in one hand while attempting to recite holy words above the noise of the increasingly raucous mob. Except that no-one cared to hear him. Helped by the hangman, he clambered up into a cart and placed white caps on the heads of those about to die, giving them each a hasty blessing before moving on to the next. The terrified young woman finally found her voice and began desperately screaming her innocence but the agitated crowd responded by pelting her with whatever they happened to have in their hands at the time. Pieces of pie and bits of fruit began raining down on the sheriff and his constables, their horses nervously shuffling. A half-eaten apple bounced from the priest's head as he hastily climbed down from the cart and the hangman brought his hand down hard on the horse's rear. The wagon jerked forward and, one by one, the prisoners dropped from the end, nooses taut at their necks as they writhed and kicked at the empty air, mouths opening and closing like freshly caught fish.

Jack gasped. A hush finally descended upon the crowd as they watched the accused hang. He saw the life drain from them, one by one, their tongues bulging between blue lips, their eyes rolling back into their heads so that only the whites were visible. They thrashed and kicked, hopelessly flailing their legs until, after what seemed an eternity, the young woman and her companions in death became still.

But the gaunt-faced child killer was holding on, twisting and jolting, until the hangman began to pull hard on his legs in an attempt to end his suffering.

'No!' cried a woman close to Jack. 'Let the bastard suffer!'

'Aye, leave him be!' called another.

The crowd roared their approval of this, wishing that the man take as long as possible to be turned off. Jack's bladder was fit to bursting. He placed his hands over his ears and he wanted to run away from this place as fast as he could. To escape the madness and hide under his bedsheets and hope never to witness such a horrid sight ever again.

Then, after what felt an age, the killer appeared to be quite dead, one shoe hanging from the end of a twitching foot.

Jack removed his hands from his ears and looked around. Charlotte was gone! A panic surged through him and he spun in desperate circles, calling her name over and over. Then he spotted her, several feet away having edged nearer to the gallows. In all the commotion and the uproar, his sister had slipped free of the mob and had managed to get herself very close to the cart without the sheriff's men noticing. She was now standing just yards from the dead murderer and she appeared to be frozen to the spot. Jack sprang forwards to join her.

'Charlotte, let's go!' he said, yanking at her arm. But his sister's eyes were squeezed shut and her fingers were pressed hard to her temples.

'I have a headache,' she mumbled, swaying.

'What's wrong?' he asked, but she wouldn't respond.

Suddenly, her eyes flashed open and Jack recoiled. They were white to the corners! Charlotte's body shook and trembled before dropping to the ground like a stone, her rigid elbows tucked to her sides and her fingers bent like the claws of an animal, locked in spasm as she began to convulse. Jack looked on, helpless, while nearby a group of young men laughed.

'Seems as though these two ain't cut out for all the drama!' said one. 'Best get her home, lad, she don't look so good.'

With tears running down his cheeks, Jack crouched to touch his sister's face. 'Charlotte! Charlotte, wake up, please! Wake up!'

Then, without warning, she arched her back, frothing

saliva from her mouth whilst clenching her teeth before rolling onto her side and being sick on the grass.

'Jack?' Charlotte whispered, confused and dazed as she lay on her back, blinking up at her brother who was kneeling over her.

A horse-mounted constable appeared, pointing his pike down at the children. 'Get her out of 'ere!' he ordered. 'Move!'

'We need to leave,' Jack said, and he helped his sister struggle to her feet.

Holding her hand it was now *his* turn to lead; to navigate their way through the crowd and take them home to Mother, where it was just a little safer. A little.

BAD ALE AND GHOSTS

S hanklin was sitting in his armchair, gazing at the little white stone attached to the necklace, dust motes dancing in the sunbeams which streamed through the curtains. Seemed he couldn't take his eyes from the thing, nor his mind from the woman he'd robbed it from. In his other hand was Creech's leather pouch containing the jewellery he'd swiped from Lady Torne's sister. The necklace belonged in there too, along with the rest, ready to be handed over to a receiver for moving on. A man with a reputation for giving a good return on stolen items. A man like Levy Kremer.

But something was holding Shanklin back from doing that one thing. From simply dropping the necklace into the pouch and passing it to Randall who'd then pass them on for pawning. Something was blocking him. It wasn't like Shanklin was short of stolen goods; the sitting room was full of 'em. Clutter, that's what Sarah called it; scattered all about the house. The place was like a museum of thieved artefacts, full to bursting with items he'd acquired down the years. All manner of decencies he hadn't got round to shifting yet. Oil paintings leaning against every wall. Pretty, patterned plates stacked up. Crates of this and boxes of that. *Clutter?* It was this damn 'clutter' that kept a roof over Sarah's damn head.

His pride and joy though was a duelling pistol he'd taken from a coach guard and which now sat mounted above the study fireplace. A pretty thing too; filigree curling up the handle and lock plate. To have the pair would've been nice, but he took what was going at the time. Seemed a shame that it was left stuck up on a wall above the mantelpiece and he vowed one day he'd breathe some life back into it, even if it meant taking someone else's. Someone such as Bob Creech.

Sheathed in its scabbard in one corner of the room was a military sword an old war veteran had refused to give up. Pathetic really. The old fool was no hero that day as he'd stared down the muzzle of a pistol. Shanklin had thought it might fetch a fair price at the time, but seeing as Harry had taken such a shine to it he hadn't the heart now to sell it on. Not that the boy was allowed anywhere near it yet. If he wanted to be a nuisance and swing swords around he could stick to wooden ones.

He closed his eyes and there she was again: Eliza Torne, a face so divine, burned into his brain like he'd been gazing at the sun for too long. Two days had passed and it was all he could think of. All he wanted. To see her again. To catch a glimpse. To smell that jasmine perfume once—

'I won't ask where you got it from but I'm doubting it's a gift for me.'

Shanklin's eyes opened and he moved the necklace from sight, curling a fist round it. Sarah was leaning in the doorway with her arms folded.

'Seems you spend more time dozing than doing much else,' she added.

Getting out of his chair, Shanklin made for the hallway, squeezing past her.

'Off out again, are ya?' his wife asked. 'Where to this time? Let me guess; *The Lion.* Or you going to see *her*?'

'What you on about?' asked Shanklin as he pulled on his coat.

'That necklace you haven't stopped staring at,' said Sarah. 'D'ya think I'm stupid, Samuel?'

'No, I just think you're losing your mind,' he replied, holstering a pistol in his belt. 'It's not a gift. I stole it.' He plucked his tricorn from Caesar's head.

'I don't know how much longer I can do this,' Sarah blurted out, bottom lip quivering. 'Not knowing where you're going or if you're coming home. Not knowing when they'll catch up with ya. Worrying that one day I'll have to watch you hang! You've got cuts and bruises on your face and I don't ask how or why or bloody-well what! You think I'm so used to seeing 'em that I don't care, is that it? That your *son* doesn't care?'

Shanklin sighed. Maybe she had a point: that Harry had seen his pa come home with black eyes so often that to not have them would seem strange. Deep down he knew his family didn't deserve this; this life he'd carved out for them. For *her*. Always looking over their shoulders, careful who they spoke to in case some thief-taker decided to 'cry beef' to the authorities just so he could claim a little blood money. Part of him wanted to tell Sarah that he'd already quit. That the necklace he'd stolen represented his last ever robbery. That this was a turning point for them. That he'd be looking for honest work down at the timber yard or the docks tomorrow and praying hard he'd be lucky enough to get some. A part of him still cared — it must have — otherwise why would he feel the guilt like he did now?

And part of him just wanted to darken her daylights for having the nerve to make him feel anything at all.

'You done?' Shanklin asked as he watched her wipe a tear from her cheek.

Sarah smiled, shaking her head in disbelief. 'Aye,' she said. 'I'm done, Sam. You go to her, whoever she is, and maybe I'll still be here when you get back. And maybe I won't.'

Even now, knowing that he should apologise, he just couldn't stop himself. 'Oh, you'll be here,' he said, holding up the pouch of jewellery Creech had handed him. ''Cause without these moveables you'd be nothing.'

As he opened the front door, the clatter of a passing carriage filled the hallway.

'Here's the door if ever you feel like using it,' Shanklin said. 'I'm sure your half-wit cousin in the country would welcome you in with open arms.'

He stepped out into the street, checking both ways as people walked past, always aware that someone he might've upset would feel like taking the opportunity to stick him with something sharp.

'Maybe I'll take that advice then!' Sarah called out after him as he began walking away.

They were like ghosts of their former selves: a few afternoon drinkers scattered around the gloomy tavern, trying to take the edge off the bad hand life had dealt 'em. Shanklin was standing in the doorway of *The Lion,* watching through wispy pipe smoke strewn about like cobwebs. He'd seen more life in a bowl of rotten fruit than in these punters, hunched over their tankards like they might see someone else staring back in the reflections. Even on a warm day like it was the sun didn't shine in here, certainly not since that fat bastard Tom had decided to brick up the windows due to the tax. Yet here was Shanklin, once again; treating this shit-hole like a shabby waistcoat he couldn't bring himself to throw away.

Randall was propping up the bar with his back to him, a couple of little rats leaning in on either side and sniffing for the latest gossip. Shanklin's blood was still bubbling from the argument with Sarah but it was like lava now he'd spotted these two. A sign of the times maybe. He'd once known everyone that came into this place, but not anymore. The pair caught his eye, burning 'em like ants under a magnifying glass. The one with curly hair, a sharp chin and pointy ears turned a shade of pale, tugging at his friend's arm before they both scuttled off into a dark corner. Shanklin might not have known them, but they knew *him* all right.

Randall twisted round, wondering who'd just spooked his audience, but Shanklin was at the bar before he had time to stand up straight.

'The usual, Samuel?' asked Tom, waddling over, jowls wobbling like an oversized turkey's. Shanklin wasn't keen on the new bluffer from the moment he took over management and assumed the feeling was mutual. It was just that Tom had a way of hiding his disdain whereas Shanklin gave no shit for disguising who he hated.

'Aye, and the same for him,' he replied as Randall rubbed nervously at his jaw like it was about to get a fist planted on it.

'We all right then, Shank?' he asked while the landlord made busy pouring two pints of small-beer from a barrel.

'Was it you and me fighting?'

'No, but—'

'Then I guess we're all right.'

A frothy tankard appeared and Shanklin scooped it up, guzzling down the ale, more out of thirst than pleasure. A puddle might've tasted better but water was in short supply here.

'Well, this place has gone downhill,' sighed Randall, sipping his beer and attempting to fill another awkward silence. He never could appreciate a bit of quiet.

Shanklin glanced sideways at the two lads he'd scared off, perched on stools in the far corner and nattering like nothing had happened. 'I'll fucking say.'

Randall might've only had one eye in his thick skull but he could spot trouble a mile off and Shanklin could tell he was making an effort at keeping things civilised. 'Remember being that age?' he said. 'Running errands out of here for the Butler brothers. We cut our teeth here.'

'Back when you had teeth,' said Shanklin, focusing on his beer again.

'Back when I had two eyes.'

'Now look at ya. I've seen flotsam less washed up.'

'Speak for yourself,' said Randall. 'There's tarts all over London that'll testify I got some life left in me.'

'The ones you're digging out the ground, y'mean? Shame, there's no life in *them*.'

''Oi, I've done some dirty deeds in my time,' Randall said, 'but don't be thinking I'm gonna get my hands filthy using a shovel.' He nodded towards the two lads in the corner. 'I'd get one of those pricks to do it for me instead.'

Shanklin nearly laughed. God knows he needed to.

'Anyway, I've got years left,' added Randall. 'I'm in this for the long haul.'

Setting his beer down, Shanklin pulled the leather pouch of jewellery from his coat, dropping it on the bar. 'Well, I'm not,' he said. 'I'm done.'

Randall wiped froth from his beard. 'You just got here!'

'No, ya nocky. I'm done thieving. I'm finished.'

'What you talking about?'

'Get that lot moved on to Levy Kremer,' instructed Shanklin. 'Split the money with Creech. Leave me out of it.'

'Finished how?'

'Finished robbing. Coaches. Houses. All of it.'

A pause then as Randall's brain caught up with the new information. 'So what else you gonna do, bake cakes for a living?' he asked. 'Bang straw? I never really saw you as a farmer, Shank, to be honest. You're a fucking highwayman; it's in your blood. It's what you do. It's what *we* do! Christ, some might even say you're good at it.'

'*Good*?' replied Shanklin, turning his face to him. 'Like the other day?'

Randall lowered his voice like no one in the damn tavern already knew who or what they were. 'Well, if you'd just stuck to using your fists on Bob then I don't think there'd be much of a problem. But pulling a blade? Jesus, if that ain't inviting trouble...'

'Y'know what, Randall,' Shanklin said, shaking his head, 'for a man with one eye that's very fucking observant of ya. I don't need telling what happened, I was there. And Creech *shouldn't* have been.' He sipped his foul ale like it might wash the fouler taste from his mouth.

'Look,' said Randall, 'I appreciate it's either honey or turd with you two, it always has been. There's nothing in-between and there's no doubting you've both had your moments. But as far as rogues go, he ranks right up there. He'll have your back no matter what.'

Aye, by sticking a knife in it, thought Shanklin. No more than he deserved now though.

He was staring at the bottles all lined up along the back of the bar. He reckoned a whisky might go down a little smoother than the stew Tom served as small-beer. Besides which, suffering Randall's increasingly drunk rambling required something a little stronger.

'When I was a young lad,' Shanklin said, 'there was only

one rogue I really respected. Just one man I aspired to be like.'

Randall's frowned eased up a little and he had another sip of his ale. '"Gentleman" James McCabe,' he said, reading Shanklin's mind. 'A knight of the fucking road if ever there was.' He sloppily raised his tankard as though toasting the legend.

'All class without a silver spoon up his arse,' Shanklin went on. 'There was something special about him. Garnered respect from all he met. Nothing short of a hero.'

Tom had reappeared, busy wiping down the other end of the bar with a dirty rag like it'd make any difference whatsoever.

'Never caught up with him, did they?' said Randall. 'Though I'll never know how they didn't; that tattoo of his was a bit of a clue as to his occupation.'

'If I'd slain three high-ranking members of the aristocracy in one blundered robbery, I'd make sure they never caught me neither,' Shanklin said, staring into the middle distance. 'But, if they *had* caught him, and *if* they'd ever brought him to Tyburn, then I swear the crowds would've flocked in their thousands to pay their respects.'

He sensed Randall's beady eye on him again. 'And you don't want for that? Tales told about you by the fire when you're gone? You're still the Upright Man round here so don't be telling me you're quitting, Shank.'

Shanklin looked sideways at his old friend and longest-serving colleague in criminality. 'Men like us retire from this game at the end of a rope, Randall. That's not how I'm going. They're not turning me off while I swing, pissing my breeches up there in front of my son.'

'Whether I go to the gallows or I don't,' Randall replied, 'I'll make damn sure there are a few stories about me left behind. 'Cause that's all we are once we're in the ground. A story. A memory. Better to make it a fucking good one.'

'A memory? Hero to my Harry or not, I'm no good to him dead now, am I?' Shanklin rubbed his thumb against the handle of his mug, scratching at it with his nail. 'I'll make Creech half right about one thing: I won't be dancing for the hangman over a poxy necklace. I'll die for something worth dying for.' The two lads in the corner were sniggering over a joke. 'Like murdering those two,' he said, finishing his drink and slamming the tankard on the bar, startling those still sat around.

'Same again, Samuel?' asked Tom, licking his dry lips and looking about as pasty as a freshly peeled potato.

'No, make it a whisky.'

Randall chimed in with some more words of wisdom. 'Well, just so ya know, one of those two — the one with the sharp chin and pointy ears to be precise — happens to be a very fine buzz-cove. He's a natty lad, Shank. What he doesn't know about picking pockets ain't worth knowing. So, before you go doing something silly, I'd suggest that a sneaky little diver like that could prove useful to us.'

Shanklin's whisky arrived in a tumbler. He swirled the glistening amber round in the glass and tried to refrain from hurting anyone. For now.

'I see you included your lovely lady's necklace,' Randall added, peeking inside the pouch with that lop-sided grin he always wore when he started getting top-heavy drunk.

But Shanklin didn't see what there was to smile about with a remark like that. 'What d'ya think I was gonna do, keep it?'

'Well, you might've got off on the wrong foot by robbing her,' he said bringing the tankard to his mouth, 'but I'd bet my other eye that Lady Torne will be attending the next spring ball in Vauxhall on Saturday.'

Before Shanklin even had a sniff of the spirit hovering under his nose, he lowered the glass. 'Say that again?' His heart was thumping just hearing the mention of her.

'Good with faces, ain't I?' said Randall. 'I spotted her and the husband there last year. He's known for giving generous donations to charity schools. Makes a real fucking song and dance about it too; climbing up on stage to do his speech.' He sucked air through what was left of his rotten teeth. 'But if it's helping out the poor and deprived, right?'

Shanklin knocked his whisky back in one but his mouth was now drier than when he'd walked in here. A chance to see her again? Perhaps. An opportunity to get a glimpse, if only from a distance? Maybe. A moment to get so close to her that he could smell that sweet jasmine once more? Madness.

'And every bluestocking in London will be attending.' Randall was still talking, apparently, while Shanklin's head spun with more thoughts of Eliza. 'Aye, they'll be there, the perfect couple in front of their adoring crowd. And I can tell what you're thinking, Shank. I've known you too long.'

'That so?' Shanklin said, trying to keep his nerves from not showing. 'Then what's your crystal ball saying?'

Randall scratched at the ragged hair on his chin. 'You're thinking it'll be rich pickings down there in Vauxhall. And you're thinking that if we pay a little visit to that charity stall, once 'Lord and Lady of The Manor' have collected what they can during the event, then we hit 'em hard and take whatever they've made before slipping off into the night.' He was beaming from ear to ear like he'd just found a cure for tuberculosis.

But Shanklin only frowned further. 'Well, I hate to disappoint you, my mystic friend, but you've been in the sun too long ... I might steal for a living but I draw the line at robbing from a children's charity.'

Randall chuckled. 'Ah, but I'm not thinking we do that

neither,' he went on with a new-found smugness. 'I'm thinking that if you feel like you've got one more job left in you before you take up baking cakes that, while our perfect couple are drumming up support for such a worthy cause, we head to Rousingham House and finish what we started back there on the road.'

Shanklin stared. 'Crack-lay the crib?' It seemed that not only did his friend lack an eye but he lacked ears as well. 'Have you not heard a word I've said? I'm *done thieving*.'

Randall's crooked smile sloped lower than the empty book shelves angled around the tavern. 'We've robbed houses before, Shank, but nothing like that place!' he said. 'I'll bet there's paintings in there that King George would cream himself over!' He wiped a hand across his mouth like he was trying to hide what was coming next. 'Besides which, it might help smooth things over with Bob.'

What Randall lacked in brains he made up for with heart, but he was pushing his luck with this. The thought of doing anything to appease Bob Creech wasn't worth thinking on at all and suggesting that they rob the very house belonging to the one woman Shanklin hadn't stopped dreaming about since they'd encountered each other only added to the insult.

'I'm not going near Rousingham House, Randall, and neither are you,' he said.

But the lack of enthusiasm for the thrills they'd shared in times past took the wind right out of Randall's sails. 'Well, I hate to tell ya,' he said, 'but I'm pretty sure Creech already has his eye on the place so—'

Shanklin's tumbler came down with a thump, spilling whisky on the bar. 'So tell Bob Creech from me that he's to leave it alone, that clear?'

Randall was leaning back like someone had just opened the door on a baker's oven. 'Creech ain't gonna listen to a word I say, Shank, you of all people should know that! And after your episode with him the other day, I don't think he'll be listening to *you* either.'

Tom was hovering around again, drying another squeaky glass with that rag he couldn't let go of, like a child might cuddle a blanket for comfort.

'If I wanted another drink, Tom, I'd fucking-well ask for one!' Shanklin barked. 'So go and change a barrel or something, eh?'

The landlord took his cue to leave, shaking his head while the men watched him waddle off out of sight. He'd held his tongue, as well he should. It might have been his tavern but this was none of his business.

Yet Randall clearly still had something on his mind as he sloshed what was left in his glass. 'If you're so keen on quitting, what's it matter what Bob does from here on?'

Shanklin's cheek was twitching like there was a maggot crawling under the skin. Once more he had to force himself from not doing something stupid. Wouldn't be the first time. A fight with Creech was one thing, but another with Randall was a line he didn't want to cross. Friends were getting hard to find.

'It matters,' he said. 'That's all.' He wanted out of this game, but now his head was full of black thoughts involving Creech and Lady Torne. The man was a maniac and didn't do things by halves. Simply robbing Rousingham House wouldn't be enough; he'd use violence to get what he wanted for no more than it being a thrill.

Shanklin's eyes roamed back to the two lads in the far corner before he finished what was left of his whisky and swiped the pouch of jewels back from the bar.

'I thought *I* was moving 'em?' asked Randall.

'Not this time,' said Shanklin. 'I'm off. Tell Tom to stick the drinks on my tab. I'll meet you back here in a couple of days with the money from Kremer. You can arrange splitting it with Creech.'

Slipping the pouch back into his coat, he made for the door.

'Y'know something, Shank?' Randall said to his back. 'I'd give my other eye for what you've got.'

Slowly, Shanklin turned. 'And what exactly have I *got*?'

Randall shrugged, swaying. 'You're so hung up on that beau monde bitch we robbed that you can't see what's right in front of ya,' he said with a slur. Then he raised his glass. 'So, here's to family. And friends.'

'You want to talk about family?' asked Shanklin. 'I lost two kids to the pox before either of 'em were four years old. I'd give more than my eyes to have 'em back.'

Finally, Randall looked like he'd run out of things to say.

Shanklin took one last glance at the pair sitting in their dark little corner and he approached, watching the colour drain from their cheeks as he towered over them.

'What's your name?' he asked the curly-haired one with a reputation for picking pockets. 'I don't think we've met.'

'Skim,' the lad replied, shakily, jutting his pointy chin out like it'd fool Shanklin into thinking there was a pair of bollocks on him somewhere.

'Well, *Skim*, I'm Samuel, but I'm sure you already knew that.' He thrust a hand out. 'Pleased to meet ya!'

Uneasily, the lad reached up and Shanklin gripped as tight as a snake coils its prey. 'I'll be seeing you,' he said, keeping the hold there longer than was needed. Then he made for the door again, casting a final glance at Randall who was back to leaning on the bar and waving a hand at Tom to fetch another drink.

5

ENLIGHTENMENT

Jack was running as fast as he could through the meadow, warm air whistling in his ears and sunlight blinding his eyes. 'Charlotte, wait!' he was shouting, trying to keep up with his sister and not for the first time that morning. But she wouldn't. Most likely it was that she couldn't hear him as she ran too, screaming so loudly with joy, her arms outstretched as if she were a bird in flight.

On they went, charging happily through the barley fields, until they reached the top of a hill overlooking bright grass where a herd of cows were lazily grazing.

Breathless, Jack finally caught up with Charlotte, lying exhausted under the shade of a tall oak. He dropped to the ground beside her, panting, smiling and feeling about as happy as could be for the first time in as long as he could remember. Happy to be out here in the fresh air, away from the damp house and its dark, dingy rooms. Away from Tyburn village. Away from Mother and her twisted tongue and bitter words. Happy to be alive and believing all that mattered was this moment, right now, here with his sister, playing like they used to when long days really meant something.

'We haven't done this for so long,' Jack said, as he rested his head on the soft grass. He treasured these days, yet only wished that Mother's influence was not so deeply ingrained in Charlotte. Her visions of 'halos' were becoming more frequent and the seizures were a new occurrence altogether.

She was sitting upright now, guzzling water from a leather flask that she'd fished from her bag. Cupping a hand to his eyes to block the glare of the sun, Jack watched it trickle down her chin before she wiped her mouth with a sleeve and handed it to him. He sat up and he drank in great gulps and when he finished he gazed at her, sat with her back propped against the oak, her eyes closed and bathing in the peacefulness of this blissful moment.

Yet, despite the tranquility, there was something bothering him.

'Are you all right?' Jack asked.

'Meaning?' Charlotte replied, her eyes remaining closed.

Jack felt silly for mentioning it but it needed saying. 'Yesterday, when you collapsed at Tyburn fair ... I was worried.'

His sister blinked, looking to the field below them where the cows were feeding. 'I'm fine, Jack,' she said, taking the flask back from him. 'Besides, you wouldn't understand.'

And, in that instant, his perfect bliss was gone. She was right: he didn't understand. He couldn't fathom her Gift, as Mother called it, and couldn't bring himself to believe she even had one. Nothing beyond being talented and clever and pretty, which of course she was. He was sure that she was making it all up, encouraged by their mother who praised her and scolded *him* in equal measure. Jack's dream was to be a physician when he was older. To study medicine and science. He believed in logic and reason. This was a time of Enlightenment. Of great minds. He was not interested in any notion of the spiritual or the supernatural. To him, it was all superstition and nonsense and belonged in the Dark Ages. But this didn't stop his concern for Charlotte's well-being.

'Don't take it personally, Jack,' she said, sensing his frustration. 'I wouldn't expect you to appreciate or indeed entertain such ideas.'

'Ideas of what?' he asked, hoping more than anything that some insight might help him better appreciate her condition, or at least allow him enough of an understanding so that he could tell someone who did.

Charlotte appeared distant then, watching the cows chewing slowly on the cud. 'There are so many species upon this rich earth,' she said, more to herself than him. 'So much ... diversity. Each and every animal with its own consciousness. So many varying layers of life. Such complexity.' She turned her face towards him. 'Quite ... *magical*, wouldn't you agree?'

Fascinating, yes, but magic it was not.

His sister's eyes returned to the scene below them, like the serenity of this place was a part of her very soul. 'I *see* sounds,' she whispered. 'I *hear* colours and I *taste* smells and ... and I *feel* things that I am sure others cannot.'

Jack's frown was heavy. 'Colours?' he repeated. 'Auras?'

'I prefer the term *halo* myself.' Charlotte smiled at him. 'And yours is particularly bright today.'

'Is that so?' He hated hearing her speak like this. He worried as to what was happening in that brain of hers. Such talk only suggested there were things going wrong. Like a clock that still ticked but had lost all sense of timing.

She was watching a Red Kite hover high on the wind, scanning the ground for its prey, its wide wings fluttering. 'Such magnificent, opportunistic birds,' Charlotte said. 'Once persecuted to the point of extinction, did you know? A tragedy so closely avoided. When they are chicks in the nest, the older and larger sibling will peck the younger ones if they attempt to eat before it's had its fill. Quite often the younger will be killed.'

Jack swallowed. Charlotte's smile was unsettling. 'I didn't know that.'

'Then never say I don't teach you anything,' she replied.

He also observed the bird. 'And does *it* have a halo?' he asked. 'And those cows down there, what of them?'

'Yes, but unlike ours.'

'Because we have ... souls?'

His sister tutted at him. 'I do not *see* souls, Jack! No more than you can.'

'Then what? What are these halos you speak of?' He was desperate to understand.

'I don't know,' Charlotte sighed, frustrated. 'Not exactly. Not yet.'

Moving a fallen oak leaf a little closer to them, she uncorked the water flask. 'Here, let me show you something,' she said.

Jack sat up straighter as his sister allowed a tiny drop to fall upon the leaf. Carefully, she dripped another, very close but so they were not touching, and the children watched as the droplets gravitated together, merging to form a whole.

'You see?' asked Charlotte.

Jack's face was scrunched up. 'No,' he replied.

'It's the law of attraction!' his sister said. 'When two things are close enough so that they combine to become one. If I had put the other droplet on to a different leaf altogether, then of course they wouldn't have been able to merge like that, would they? It can only come to be when the two are extremely close.'

Jack scratched his mop of blonde hair. 'Like how a magnet works?'

'Yes, exactly!' said Charlotte. '*Everything* is connected.

And everything is *energy*. When something dies, the spirit leaves the body.'

Jack felt as though he was following this, to a point. 'Our souls go to Heaven,' he said.

Charlotte was looking a little annoyed. 'Do you think *they* have souls?' she asked, pointing to the grazing cows. 'Ignorant animals, bred only to be eaten.'

'No, I don't believe they do,' said Jack. 'But they have sensations. Physical feelings. They experience pain and—'

'Because they are *alive*!' Charlotte said. 'They live and they breathe. Cows, birds, bees, goats, dogs, cats; these are not mechanical automatons. So, what keeps them … what keeps *us* alive?' She watched Jack as though he might have the answer, which of course, he did not. 'An unseen force!' his sister went on. 'An energy that resides in every single living thing. You cannot feel the blood flowing in your veins but if you cut yourself you'll see it's there!' She stared while her brother struggled to make sense of it.

'And yet I *see* it,' Charlotte continued. 'I see halos; the very energy that is in us. And where does it go once the body is deceased? Does it evaporate into the air like mist? Does it return to the source from whence it came? Back into a void? Back to God?' She smiled at him. 'Or does it find another path? One of least resistance?'

Jack blinked. 'You?'

His sister relaxed back against the tree trunk and breathed in, deeply. 'I am a vessel, Jack,' she said, 'nothing more. But the universe is an ever flowing stream of consciousness of which I shall have my fill.'

He watched her close her eyes, a satisfied grin upon her lips. And so it appeared that his sister was quite mad.

'Not all streams are for drinking from, Charlotte,' Jack said, 'especially if something dead lies floating in it.'

'Oh, Jack,' Charlotte exclaimed, shaking her head. 'How

we fear that which we do not understand. You have so much to learn.'

That made him cross. He was young but he was no fool and he was tired of being treated as such. 'And does Mother know that you attend the gallows days?' he asked.

'No, she does not,' scowled Charlotte, 'and you shan't tell her!'

'Why not? What are you afraid of? You told me yourself that she knows of your *Gift*; your ability to *see*, or whatever you—'

'She's frail, Jack! Until she regains her health then I'd rather she knew nothing more.' Charlotte gazed at the horizon. 'I don't know why I even took you along.'

'Nor I!' said Jack. 'You're not well, Charlotte. You need help. A physician could—'

'No!' She was pointing a finger at him, her face flushed scarlet with anger. 'No No!'

He had never seen her quite so upset, and it shocked him, turning his blood cold.

'You're just jealous!' she spat. 'It's pitiful and it's pathetic!'

'I'm not jealous! I ... I just want you to be well and I'm worried that—'

'Worry for yourself, Jack Hunter! Worry that you don't have abilities like I have. Because the world is full of cruelty and to see it first, to truly *know* before it strikes is a gift indeed!' She was breathing fast and her nostrils were flared.

After waiting so patiently for its prey, the Red Kite quietly swooped down from the sky and carried something off in its beak. An awkward silence followed and when Charlotte's temper appeared to have finally cooled and when all he could hear was birdsong once again, Jack made an attempt to change the subject.

'Why does no one come to visit Mother?' he asked.

'Because, like I told you,' Charlotte said, still shunning

him in her own way, 'the world is cruel and full of callous people.'

'And was Father cruel to Mother when they were married?' He was studying the leaf his sister had used for her demonstration.

Her eyes were closed and dappled shadows from the tree above them danced on her skin. 'He ran off with Aunt Ruth, Mother's very own sister. He couldn't have treated her much worse.'

Jack was worried for Charlotte. For what might become of her if people knew how broken her mind was. Would she be thrown into Bedlam? Or would she be the first person in a hundred years to be tried as a witch? He had to speak to Mother. He wasn't happy about it but who else did he have to turn to? He needed to convince her that what was happening to his sister was not normal. He could not lose her to this madness.

Her head was tipped back against the tree trunk and for now it appeared the storm inside her had passed. Jack had no choice but to play along.

'The people whom you watch hang,' he said. 'Those whose ... *energy* you say you can absorb ... for the most part they are cruel and wicked people, are they not?'

'They are on the gallows for a reason,' Charlotte said.

He continued with caution. 'So, if their *energy* is evil, then ...'

Her eyes flashed open. 'Then I shall become evil like them?' Charlotte asked. It may have just been the sun or it may have been something else, but Jack saw a glint in her gaze as though the thought may have crossed her own mind before now. 'It's a chance I'll take to feel like this.'

A fly buzzed somewhere close by.

'And how is it you feel?' Jack asked.

'Enlightened, of course!' she replied. Charlotte studied

him. 'When was the last time you did anything wrong, Jack Hunter?'

His cheeks burned. She'd always thought of him as being such a little saint and he hated it. 'I once called Tilly Jones a fat whore,' he said.

Charlotte laughed. 'Good! Though it will hardly get you hanged.'

Jack shuddered at the thought. For him, it had been a horrid thing to do. He'd felt awful that day as Tilly cried whilst running home and the others who were there had laughed and jeered at her. But he'd only really done it to impress them and he'd felt terrible about it ever since.

He crumpled up the silly oak leaf his sister had used for her demonstration and tossed it away.

'You're a good soul, Jack,' said Charlotte, 'but don't believe everything they teach you at school. Christ will only get you so far.'

'He'll see that I get to Heaven,' Jack replied. 'Where will *you* go?'

His sister stuffed the flask back into her bag and sprang to her feet. 'Home!' she said. 'I'll race you there!'

And then she was off, running and jumping without a care.

Jack scrambled up after her. 'Wait!' he cried. 'That's not fair, I wasn't ready!' And he ran too, laughing again with the warm breeze in his ears and wishing he could hold this moment in his heart forever, forgetting that his sister was utterly insane.

6

A PROPOSITION

The rain dripped from the three large gold-painted balls hanging above the shop's sign that read: *Kremer & Sons.* It tapped at Shanklin's tricorn too, fat drops clinging to the brim. So much for spring.

He pushed open the pawnbroker's door, a little bell tinkling as he stepped inside, removing his hat and shaking London's finest weather all over the floorboards. A stocky Jewish man in his mid-sixties was leaning on the other side of a counter, inspecting something bright under a magnifying glass. His bushy, white eyebrows formed a thick frown above the rim of his half-moon spectacles perched on the end of his nose.

'Shower, is it, sir?' the man asked without looking up, his slippery cockney drawl sliding across the wet floor like an adder.

'More a tidal wave,' replied Shanklin, gawping at the trinkets and all manner of decencies gleaming from inside glass cabinets. He flicked more rain from his collar as Levy Kremer slowly unfurled until he was standing up straight, glowering at his latest customer's ability to soak his floor. But Shanklin was too busy thinking he'd wandered into Aladdin's cave to even care and wondered why he'd bothered robbing stagecoaches half his life when he might've just cut out the middleman by coming here. Except that anyone with half a brain knew you didn't rob from Levy Kremer, not unless you wanted that very brain plastered up a wall.

Yet it wasn't only shiny things that were in this shop. Piles of clothes were stacked high on shelves alongside shoes and boots and anything else someone desperate enough for a little balsam in their pocket might trade with an untrustworthy Jew.

'And how may I help you, sir?' the pawnbroker asked, smiling as he gently put down his pliers and magnifying glass before placing two large liver-spotted ringed hands on the counter. 'I'm guessing you didn't pop in simply to make a puddle upon my floor?'

Ambling over, Shanklin dropped Creech's leather pouch on the counter. 'How much for these?' he asked.

Kremer rubbed at his broad jaw, opened the bag and tipped out the contents, clearing his throat while picking up one of the silver rings.

'Hmmm ... right now ... well, it's difficult to say. I'd need to—'

'So when can you say?' Shanklin wasn't forgetting where he was but time never seemed to be on his side these days.

The creased ochre skin around Kremer's eyes creased further. 'Well, I'd have to—'

'Hours? Days?' asked Shanklin.

The pawnbroker was smiling again, pushing his barnacles higher up the bridge of his nose. 'You are an impatient man, Mr ...?'

Shanklin was doing his best to remain polite, given whose shop he was in. Kremer's reputation for running a tight network of receivers was well-renowned within London's underworld. Women mainly, married to gang members and responsible for the redistribution of stolen goods. There were never any questions asked and he paid well, but he was Randall's man and up until now it was Randall who'd always dealt with him.

'Robert Knight,' Shanklin lied. 'I have a friend who comes to see you regularly. Wears an eye patch.'

'Ah, Mr Randall!' Kremer replied. 'I can't forget a face like that.'

'He says you know stones better than most, so I'll get right to it.' Taking Eliza Torne's necklace from his coat pocket, Shanklin laid it on the counter. 'The rest can wait but how much will you *loan* me, right now, for this?'

Kremer picked up his magnifying glass and hunched over the little stone. 'Unusual,' he mumbled after a few moments.

'Meaning?'

The old Jew was poking at it with his pliers as though dissecting a rare insect specimen. 'I see many items come through this shop, Mr Knight,' he said, bent double so that his nose was nearly touching the work surface, 'but this one, it would appear, is quite ... priceless.'

Shanklin's stomach flipped. 'Priceless? How priceless?'

The pawnbroker took the little stone firmly between finger and thumb and, using the pliers, popped it clean out from the necklace's silver clasp.

Every muscle in Shanklin tensed. 'What the—?'

'Priceless, I suspect to whoever once owned it, sir, but of little value to anyone else.' Kremer offered up the stone. 'I do believe it is a child's tooth.'

It was Shanklin's turn to frown now as he took it back from him. 'A *what?*'

'That clasp there,' Kremer said, 'has been expertly made to fit the root of the tooth. The 'stone' has been filed and shaped, but if you look close enough you'll notice tiny bumps typical of those found on a child's tooth. Hardly distinguishable at first but those indentations lead me to believe this is indeed what you have there, Mr ... *Knight*.'

Shanklin's head was whirling. *A tooth?*

'Feel free to have it inspected elsewhere, sir,' Kremer added, 'but I've been looking at stones all my life.' He held out his hand to take the tooth back for a moment. 'And, if you'll observe,' he said, clicking it back into its clasp, 'it will re-house rather snugly.'

Shanklin tried to weigh up what he was hearing. That stagecoach had been his last robbery and he'd wanted nothing more than to finish his long and lucky career on a high note. Instead, he'd fallen in love with a woman who wore teeth as fashion accessories. His week was getting stranger.

'Do you have children, sir?' asked Kremer, retrieving a small wooden box from under the counter.

'What?'

The pawnbroker placed the box down as softly as though it was the most delicate thing his large hands could ever hold. More precious than any pearl or diamond. He unclipped a tiny latch and opened the lid, taking from within a fragile-looking piece of paper that had been neatly folded in half. Shanklin watched the old man gently unfold the paper and press it flat. There was a crude charcoal drawing on it, as though created by a child's hand. It looked to be that of a dog.

Kremer smiled as he looked down at it. 'This was a picture my daughter made not long before she died,' he said. 'I keep it with me, always. Either when I'm working here or when I'm at home.' The smile on his lips was evidence enough of the times they'd shared. 'It's all I have left of her.' He looked up and Shanklin was certain that his eyes were glistening behind those spectacles. 'A grieving parent will hang on to what they can.'

But Shanklin didn't need lessons in anguish. He'd felt the pain of losing his own kids as keenly as anyone in a city with such a high infant mortality rate.

'You have my sympathies, Mr Kremer,' he said. 'But we have no way of knowing if that tooth belonged to a child who's dead or still alive. It might just be a keepsake. Or belong to the very woman it was taken from.'

The pawnbroker carefully placed the drawing back into its box and closed the lid. 'Of course, sir,' he said, 'But, for the right price, I can ensure that it's returned, if that's what you should choose. You won't need to lift a finger. They will not know who took it or whom had the ... 'decency' to sell it back it to them. I am certain that we would all benefit from such a transaction as this.'

Shanklin rubbed at his forehead. This shop was an established channel within London's criminal fraternities. It wasn't difficult to see how a grieving mother might pay handsomely to have her child's tooth returned, if that's indeed what it was. Under normal circumstances it wasn't a decision at all, and, if Randall were here right now, he'd be wondering what the delay was all about.

'Shit,' hissed Shanklin under his breath as he turned his back and tried to think. Of all the things to steal! He'd taken some items from folks in his time, objects that no doubt meant a lot to them. Desirable, yes. Expensive, certainly. Diamonds and pearls and pretty things soaked in significance for those that owned them. But *this* ... this was different. Lady Torne had objected so openly. Not that he wasn't used to hearing the pleas of those he robbed, but this ... *this* ...! He'd ripped her heart out and now perhaps she deserved it back. Perhaps there was an opportunity to do something right for once. A chance to prove he had something resembling a heart of his own before it one day stopped beating altogether.

Shanklin took back the necklace. It may have been no more than a tiny tooth on one end, smaller than the nail of his little finger, but there was every chance that it was bigger than a boulder to a heart-broken mother. A chance he wasn't willing to take. Slipping it back into his coat pocket, he left the pouch of jewels with Kremer.

'I'll have Mr Randall stop by tomorrow to collect the money for the rest,' he said.

'Very well, sir,' the pawnbroker replied, looking a little disappointed nonetheless.

Shanklin left the shop, the bell tinkling above his head. He'd be needing some help if he was going to return the necklace to its rightful owner, free of charge. And he knew just the rat for the job.

A weak fire was hissing in the *The Lion's* hearth. Skim was grinning from ear to ear, reclining on an old velvet sofa with a tart draped across him, her thin, white arm wrapped round his neck while she whispered in his ear and twisted her curly red locks around a finger. Candles burned on a low table that separated them from the same lad Skim had been speaking with the other day. He was sitting on the sofa opposite, a hand wedged between the legs of some other moll and moving it up and down like a ship's bilge pump. To her obvious delight, it was noted.

Too engrossed in their cavorting, they hadn't spotted Shanklin watching them from the doorway and wondering how these crafty fuckers had somehow managed to make a home for themselves in here without him really noticing. It seemed like every time he went outside to take a piss these days there was someone in his seat when he got back. He'd been young once; you couldn't knock 'em for getting their thrills from a tart or two. But this was *The Lion*. This was his church. Hallowed ground. Sacred fucking space. This was where the Butler Brothers made a name for themselves. Where the Dowlings carved a reputation by carving the faces of those who crossed them. These were people Shanklin had looked up to. Men he'd respected. He wouldn't have taken a liberty like this.

'I hate to break up the party,' he said, unbuttoning his dripping wet coat while he watched them flounder, 'but, go away.'

After the initial embarrassment there was some hesitation on the part of the 'ladies' present; a little rebellion, fumbling with their frocks and looking at the boys like they should say something to this fiend who was towering over them. But the lads had lost their tongues all of a sudden and all that met Shanklin was a wall of silence.

'I won't ask again.'

Everyone stood to leave.

'Not you,' said Shanklin, aiming a finger at Skim. 'We need to talk.'

'Mr Shanklin, I—'

'Shut up, I want these three gone first.'

The other lad was puffing his chest out now like he even had one. 'Skim, if you want me to hang about?'

But this left Shanklin a little confused. 'I didn't catch your name the other day, son?'

'Jonah,' he replied, fidgeting. 'Jonah Oakes.'

'Well, Jonah Oakes, I need a quiet moment with our mutual friend, Mr Skim, so if you'll excuse me ...'

Shanklin could tell the lad was weighing up the right thing to do. Stay or go. Live or die. Simple really. Admirable but it was about to get him hurt.

So he made up his mind for him. 'You've got three seconds before I break your fucking jaw,' Shanklin said, and Jonah Oakes made for the exit, the two girls stumbling along after. The strawberry flavoured one shot a glare over her shoulder that might've knocked Shanklin dead if it was loaded.

'And don't get too wet!' he called out as the door swung shut behind them. He turned back to Skim. 'Heh, heh. Oh, she's wet enough for ya, that one, ain't she?'

Skim tried to smile.

'Right, where were we? Oh, aye, sit back down.'

The sofa seemed to swallow the young thief up as he lowered himself into it, looking far more uncomfortable than he had five minutes ago. Shanklin took his place on the one opposite, still warm from its previous inhabitants. He was eyeing Skim like a wolf that hadn't eaten for a week.

'Thought I might find you here,' he said, glancing around at the flaking walls and the rotting beams and rotten faces, hunched over their small beer. 'Y'know, when I was much younger than you are now, I spent more time in this place than I did at home. Probably because my Pa would kick the hell out of me as often as he could and coming here was something of a safe-haven for me. Somewhere I could feel protected and be amongst my peers, knowing that bastard I'd been blessed with as a father couldn't come within three feet of the place or he'd be skinned alive.'

Skim swallowed.

'These men that I speak of,' Shanklin went on, 'these *real* men, they took me under their wing. Protected me. Gave me proper work. Kept me fed and sheltered and secure.'

The thief appeared close to tears but Shanklin reckoned it wasn't on account of his story.

'And yet,' he continued, leaning forward so that he could

be heard very clearly, 'I never took those men for granted. I was always grateful of the kindness they'd shown to me.'

'Mr Shanklin, I—'

Shanklin raised a hand. 'So, I'm giving you a chance. Just one. An opportunity to show me that you ain't the disrespectful little cunt I'm starting to think you are.' He smiled, warm, friendly. 'Because everyone deserves a chance, right?'

The puzzled-looking pickpocket said nothing.

'Randall tells me you're all right,' Shanklin continued, 'and for some reason that I am yet to fathom, that counts for something. He also tells me you're a very good diver and that counts for a bit more. So, here's my proposition: I want you with me at the ball in Vauxhall on Saturday. I want you to show me you've got what it takes to earn a place on that sofa you're sitting on. To be *here*. In *my* tavern.'

Skim was blinking like a frog in a hailstorm as he realised that the beating he was convinced was coming, now wasn't. 'Er ...'

'And you tell no-one you're working for me, you understand? Not Mr Randall, not that fat prick Tom over there. Not your friend Jonah 'Arse-Wobbler' Oakes and nor the two tarts getting wet outside. *No-one*.'

'Sure, Mr Shanklin. No problem.'

'Good.' Shanklin reclined into the tatty sofa again, stretching his arms out. 'Now, I have a particular gentleman in mind that I want you to rob while we're down there. He's quality. He'll have a guard or two with him so you've gotta be nimble. You take what you can and you're gone. I'll be watching how you get on. Think you can do that?'

A little colour had returned to Skim's face. 'Aye, 'course.'

'All right then!' Shanklin said, clapping his hands and standing up. 'Meet me at *The Fisherman's Arms*, six o'clock, Saturday evening. We'll head down there together.'

He made for the door, pausing to turn when he was halfway. 'Oh, and bring a mask to wear.'

'A mask?' asked Skim.

'Aye.'

'What sort of mask, Mr Shanklin?'

'One that covers your face, how the fucking hell should I know? It's a ball, use your imagination.' He waved a hand with a flourish. 'Be ... *creative*.'

'Right.'

Shanklin nodded. 'Good. I'll see ya Saturday. Don't be late. If you want to keep those bollocks that tart was looking for, you'll be on time.'

He opened the tavern door only to freeze as he was greeted at the threshold by a smiling Bob Creech, gold tooth glinting beneath a dried cut to his lip.

'Hello, Samuel, fancy catching you here. I hear this place is very popular.'

Shanklin's pulse was racing like a coursed hare. *The Lion* wasn't Creech's watering hole. 'Only with arseholes,' he replied.

Creech laughed, streaks of rain running down his scars and bouncing from his shaved head. 'Funnily enough, I'm looking for one. Randall in?'

Shanklin shrugged. 'Not here.'

'Oh well,' Creech said. 'I'll just drop by for a quick drink anyway. Can't hurt, can it? Dry my bones by the fire. Make myself at home.'

Brushing past him, Shanklin stepped out into the street, getting wet again.

'Shame you're leaving though,' Creech said from the doorway. 'We might've talked a few things over.'

'Nothing to say, the way I see it. What's done is done. Randall will have your money from the jewels soon enough. Take it up with him.'

'Well, there's always next time, ain't there, Samuel?' Creech said. 'I ain't going anywhere.'

'Looking forward to it,' replied Shanklin as he walked away, his back all tensed up like there was a target painted on it.

7

A MOTHER'S LOVE

The chopping knife *click-clacked* on the cutting board, slicing through the carrots with ease. From the kitchen doorway, Jack watched Mother prepare supper: a thick stew bubbling in the pot above a good fire in the far wall. His mouth should have been watering, but it wasn't. It was as dry as the bunches of herbs hanging from the hooks in the ceiling and he'd lost his appetite knowing that he needed to talk about Charlotte. Knowing how Mother might react.

Her greasy auburn hair was streaked with grey, her cheeks pale and drawn and there were dark circles around her eyes. But, despite her illness, she carried on, unwilling to seek help or even employ a servant. Mother was stubborn and Jack had no doubt as to where his sister acquired the same trait from.

'Why are you staring, child?' she asked, without looking up from her slicing. 'We'd all be better off if you helped around here rather than simply staring.'

Jack straightened up. 'I ... I was just—'

'Just what?' Mother snapped, the blade moving at speed. 'Just being idle, is what. Idleness will rust you, boy.'

Shuffling over to the pot, she scraped in the vegetables and reached for a jar from a cluttered shelf before coughing so hard that her whole body shook and she was forced to plant her hands on the work surface for support. Jack looked on as she pulled a handkerchief from the pocket of her apron and pressed it to her mouth.

'Are you ... all right?' he asked.

She was wheezing and Jack noticed that there were specks of blood on the cloth.

'I'm fine,' she replied. 'Stop fussing and fetch me the parsnips.'

Taking them from a basket and handing them to her, Jack watched the sharp knife go to work once more.

Clack, clack, clack.

'What's on your mind, child?' Mother asked. 'Or are you just standing there waiting for me to die?'

'No!' he said. 'I ... I only wish to speak of something.'

'Then spit it out or lose your tongue to this stew!'

Jack tried to summon what courage he had. 'It's Charlotte. I'm worried for her.'

Clack, clack, clack.

'Worried? Why?'

'She's not herself. She speaks of seeing ... *halos*. Of *seeing* sounds and *tasting* colours!'

The *clacking* came to an abrupt stop. Slowly, Mother turned to him. The broth bubbled and the fire popped. She looked tired. Too tired for his nonsense and he wished already that he hadn't spoken of it.

'And you think her ... *mad?*' Mother asked, frankly.

'No!' Jack said. 'Not at all. I ... I'm unsure what to think, Mother. I'm just so frightened for her and I thought that you might be able to help and ...' He trailed off, stumbling over his words now even though he'd recited the whole thing in his head a hundred times.

She placed the knife down on the worktop and shuffled towards the dining table. 'Come,' she said, beckoning him to her and pulling out a chair that squealed on the flagstones like a piglet being dragged to slaughter. Carefully, she eased herself into it. She looked far older than her actual years.

Jack approached and she took his soft hands in hers, hard and callused from a life of of demanding work. He was suddenly very hot and uncomfortable, far from feeling safe like a son should when in his mother's counsel. She had never been one for holding him close or comforting him in times of need. He'd always relied on Charlotte when he was scared or unhappy. Now Mother was staring into his eyes more deeply than she ever had, as though searching for something hidden inside him. As though trying to find it, so that she could pull it out by the root, like a weed. It alarmed Jack. Now that he had her undivided attention, he wasn't so sure that he wanted it. Surely they both knew what was best for Charlotte? But now he was concerned that they had different ideas of what that might be. And he couldn't tell Mother of what he'd seen at Tyburn. Of how Charlotte had collapsed straight after those people were hanged. Or of the things she'd said to him on the hill the following day. So he waited, nervously, as she filled her fragile lungs with a long, rattling breath and then spoke.

'Your sister is a very special young lady,' Mother said, gripping his hands. 'She has been through so much since … since your father left us here, alone.'

There was a tightness in Jack's throat. An anger welled up in him. Hadn't they all been hurt by Father leaving? Jack missed him also! Who was concerned about that?

'But I'm worried that she's so unwell,' he said. 'And that if we don't find her help then she'll only grow worse.'

Mother briefly closed her tired eyes, as though she'd had

quite enough of his questions already. 'Then what do you suppose we do, child?'

The moment had arrived and Jack had no choice but to seize it. 'I have a friend at school; his name is Alfie. His father is a physician; a clever man! Perhaps we could speak with him? We could see if he might visit?'

Mr Kilne was indeed a physician, but Alfie was no friend. Not in the true sense of the word. Jack occasionally teased him and made his life a little more miserable in order to relieve the misery of his own.

'Maybe Mr Kilne would prescribe her something?' he went on. 'Maybe he could help *you* too—'

Mother's dark frown silenced him faster than a slap to his face and she'd delivered a few of those in her time.

'Child,' she said, sighing, 'you have so much to learn. So many lessons that life will teach you. And your first lesson begins now.' She pulled him closer, her skeletal fingers tugging at his shirt sleeves. Her stale breath was in his nose as she leaned forward. 'If you utter a word to anyone about your sister's Gift, your punishment will be severe. Is that understood?'

Despair. What little hope Jack had held on to drained away as her words echoed those of Charlotte's. They were so alike. With every beating she'd dealt him he'd grown more accustomed. But now, here in this kitchen, as she held him so tightly and her eyes bored into his ... now he *did* understand. And he simply nodded, only wishing to escape her clutches and run, his doomed attempt at helping Charlotte having shattered like a glass on the flagstones.

'Now go from my sight,' Mother hissed, as though blowing away a dandelion in an icy wind. She smiled and it was so like his sister's smile. 'But not too far, for supper shall be ready soon.'

Outside of the house it was warm and somewhere a Woodlark sang. Jack was sitting against the wall that surrounded their overgrown front garden and overlooked the fields which stretched for miles around. His tongue pressed at his wobbly tooth, pushing and prodding. He only wished to feel pain in order to feel something other than misery. On the horizon, beyond the barleycorn and the rich meadows drenched in happy memories, stood Tyburn gallows, a dismal blot against the perfect sky. He wished so hard that it wasn't there, pulling Charlotte nearer to it and further from him each day.

He was picking at grass when he heard a purring to his right and saw that Tilly Jones's cat, Acorn, had decided to join him. He brushed his soft, ginger body against his leg and Jack ran a hand along his fur as the cat slunk beside him, twisting and turning and purring with delight.

'We all need a little love at times, don't we, boy?' Jack said.

Back and forth Acorn moved, arching his spine with each stroke.

'Well, we'll show *her*. If Mother won't help Charlotte then I'll just have to do it myself.'

The cat quickly grew bored and turned away, more interested in licking himself than listening to Jack's woes. Gazing out across the fields, he wished that there was a way he could stop time, if only for a while. Some way that he could freeze those moments he spent with his sister. A way of living the rest of his days like that, care-free. And idle!

'Booooy!'

Mother's voice split the humid air like thunder, startling Acorn who promptly darted off. Jack sprang to his feet and turned to see her standing there; a withered shape at the porch of their house, coughing and struggling for breath.

'Yes, I'll show her,' he said, as if the cat were still listening. 'That's if she doesn't die first.'

8

DIVIDENDS

hack!

T Shanklin's axe split the log clean down the middle. He pictured it cleaving Creech's skull open, blood spraying. Gave him a little satisfaction that. Not much, but he'd take what he could right now, seeing as it was in such short supply these days. He tossed the two pieces on to a steadily growing pile in his backyard, then picked up another log, placing it upright and tapping the axe blade into the grain before bringing it down hard on the ground.

Thack!

It didn't matter that Creech had been right all along; Shanklin had messed up his part in the coach robbery, plain and simple. There wasn't any getting round it. And now what little trust there had been between them was nothing but dust.

Thack!

Then there was Eliza Torne to think of. If Creech had plans for milling Rousingham House then he had plans for killing her. Unlike splitting logs, the man did nothing by halves. She might have a guard with her at all times after the

62

incident on the road. She might even have two. Servants and a lady's maid and whoever else watching her every damn move. But this was all part of the challenge to a man like Bob Creech. A game to him, nothing more.

Shanklin hefted the axe in both hands once another log was propped upright.

Thack!

He had to warn Eliza. The ball at Vauxhall was just around the corner and he'd find her there, whatever it took. As crazy as it sounded, he had to tell her that her life was in danger. If he could use that idiot Skim to return the necklace at the same time, then all the better.

Turning to his unsteady pile of chopped wood, he noticed that the log on the very top looked about ready to slip and bring the whole lot tumbling down with it. With a dirt-streaked forearm Shanklin wiped at the sweat under his nose. It didn't matter how Randall dressed it up or played the situation down, he'd seen the look in Creech's eye outside *The Lion* and he suspected things weren't staying 'friendly' for too long. There was dark business between 'em needed finishing, it was just a matter of when and where.

Preparing another log, he breathed in, long and deep, trying to find that place in his mind where things felt a little straighter. He was stuck on the side of a cliff with no footholds left, fifty feet above a raging river and jumping in seemed the only option. 'Cause damn-well staying where he was meant only death.

Thack!

'You building a bloody gallows?' asked Sarah. 'Winter's a way off; how much wood you think we're gonna need?'

Before Shanklin had time to toss the two halves onto the pile, the whole lot collapsed, scattering logs across the grass.

If I was building a gallows you'd be the first to try it out, he thought as he started re-stacking them against the yard wall. 'Can't be too prepared,' he said.

'Well, supper ain't gonna *prepare* itself, so if you're passing by the butcher's later ...?'

'Lost your legs? You can see I'm busy.'

'Busy?' Sarah scoffed. 'Aye, I can see that. Busy building a bloody wall between us.'

'Not now, Sarah,' Shanklin said, wiping his grubby hands on his shirt and heading back into the house.

'So when then?' she asked, following him through the kitchen and into the cluttered sitting room. 'When's a good time, Samuel? I need to schedule appointments now, do I? When can you fit me in to your *busy* day?'

He was searching for his coat but it wasn't over the chair where he'd left it. The necklace was still in the pocket and he was getting the ache now, pacing around the room as a mild panic set in. 'Where is it?' he asked. 'You moved it?'

His wife's arms were folded, clearly taking some delight in his frustration. 'Your coat? Well, hang me for wanting to keep the place tidy, eh?'

'Where *is* it?' he asked, again, his search becoming frantic.

'Why don't you try looking by the front door where it's supposed to be?'

Stomping into the hall, Shanklin found his coat, hanging on a hook, just where she'd said it'd be. Plunging a hand into the pocket he fished for the necklace and his heart leapt into his throat when his clumsy fingers couldn't locate it.

'Missing something else?' asked Sarah, hovering in the hallway like his shadow.

'What have you done with it?'

'Done with what, Samuel?' she replied, looking perplexed. 'Something wrong? Can't find your precious neck—'

He lunged at his wife so fast she had no time to move, pinning her to the wall with one hand clamped round her throat. 'Where the *fuck* is it?' Shanklin snarled, lips stretched back over his teeth as both Sarah's hands wrestled with his wrist, her eyes wide while she fought to breathe.

'Pa!' Harry cried, appearing from nowhere.

Instantly, Shanklin let her go and Sarah shoved him away, massaging her neck, coughing, leaning against the hallway wall. 'Bastard!' she gasped.

Panting, Shanklin couldn't bring himself to look at Harry, still standing there, sobbing.

'Go and play, son,' he said, grabbing his coat. But Harry didn't move.

Sarah's coughing became a mocking laugh as she rubbed at the red hand marks on her neck. 'Aye, go and play Harry, like me and your father were doing. Just pretending, weren't we, Sam? Pretending everything's all right?'

Shanklin found the necklace in the pocket he hadn't previously checked and a concoction of relief and guilt tore through him simultaneously.

'Found it, have ya?' Sarah said, as she watched his telling expression. 'I'm so pleased for you, Samuel. So pleased it didn't cause another war between us.'

A sharp knock came at the front door and she pushed her way past him. 'I'll see who it is, shall I?' she said. 'Though I'm sure they'll be disappointed they just missed the show.'

Opening the door, they were met by Randall, his eye darting between the three of them and clearly noticing the marks on her neck.

'Oh, here he is!' Sarah exclaimed. 'My knight in shining armour! But if you're gonna come to my rescue, try not to be late next time, eh?'

Randall was frowning. 'Bad time?'

'When's a fucking good time?' Shanklin said, snatching his hat from the bust of Caesar and leaving the house.

'Your share's all there,' Randall said, slapping a bulging leather purse on the tavern table. He was sitting on a stool opposite Shanklin and stroking at his beard like something was bothering him. 'I'll give Bob his cut when I see him.'

Shanklin picked up the pouch and weighed it in his hand. Not a bad day's catch considering he had so little to do with it, and the one item he *had* stolen was still in his pocket. Just.

'I told ya, I don't want paying,' he said, tossing the purse down and picking up his ale instead.

Randall sniffed, glancing about the *The Lion* like he didn't know these walls better than the ones at home. 'Take it, will ya? You were there too ...'

'No, I'm done!' snapped Shanklin. 'How many times I gotta say it?'

Silence, and it didn't take a genius to tell something was haunting his old friend.

'Say your piece or let's just call it a day.'

Randall sighed. 'So, what of that necklace then?' he said. 'I ain't meaning to be picky, Shank, but it wasn't in the pouch with the rest.'

Shanklin might've known the question was coming but his head had been stuck too far up his own arse to pay it any real consideration. He set his beer down. 'Didn't Kremer mention it? It's a tooth. A child's tooth. It's worthless.'

'A tooth? You sure?'

'As sure as your Jewish friend is anyway. We can go there now and ask him if you like?'

'No, no, I ain't disputing it,' Randall said. 'If Kremer says it's a tooth then it's a fucking tooth.'

More silence.

'Then what?' asked Shanklin, taking a sip of ale.

Randall leaned forward. 'Well, if it's a *tooth* then maybe it has some very real sentimental value for our Lady Torne?'

Shanklin could see where this was going, he'd been here before. And he wasn't budging. 'It's ... worth ... *nothing*.'

And then he saw something shift in Randall's one remaining eye. Like a long burning candle suddenly snuffed itself out. He straightened up on his stool and he drank, wiping froth from his beard when he'd finished, a strange quiet setting in, cold as a church altar. His tongue began making that clicking sound it always did when he had something else to say. Shanklin knew it. It was hidden in plain sight. A seed of doubt had taken root in that balding skull of his.

'Now would be a good time to get whatever it is off your chest,' Shanklin said.

Randall puffed out his cheeks and fumbled with the handle of his tankard, gazing into his ale. 'Just wondered what was going on with you and Sarah, that's all.'

Shanklin should've seen that one coming too, being as the pair of them had known her as long as they'd known each other.

'Going on? There's nothing going on. It's Sarah. She's no different to any other whinging wife. Show me a married man that ain't listening to shit like that on a daily basis and I'll show you a deaf one.'

Randall looked up. 'That's not what I meant, Shank. She had marks on her throat.'

Placing his ale down, Shanklin asked a question of his own: 'You ever heard of Judge Thumb? I've got every legal right to hit her. Besides which, you're not one to preach at me.'

'Aye, I've hit women, Shank, and I'm none too proud of it neither. But ... it's *Sarah*. And I'm just saying ...'

'Well you've got a habit of saying it lately, ain't ya? And it's starting to give me the wrong impression, truth be told. Is there more to this? Something else I should know?'

'More to what?' Randall's face was red to his eyebrows, top lip twitching. 'So I'm not supposed to care about the pair of ya now? I see your marriage crumbling but I've got no right to ask what's going on? You've got a good woman there, Shank, and they ain't easy to come by.' He finished his beer in one swoop and slammed the tankard down on the table. 'Fuck it here!' he said, standing to leave.

It dawned on Shanklin that he was fast running out of friends.

'Sit down, will ya?' he said.

Randall didn't. He remained right where he stood, glaring around *The Lion*.

'I've never hit her,' Shanklin went on. 'I've not touched her till today. I don't know what came over me but it was a madness I haven't felt till now.'

'Aye, well, seems there's a lot of that going about,' Randall said. 'You ask me and I'd say that beau monde tart you robbed put a spell on ya. Ask me again and I'd say that fucking necklace is cursed. I'd sooner get rid of it but ... well, I ain't you, thankfully.'

Randall strolled for the door, pausing halfway. 'Oh, and from what I hear,' he said, 'Creech *is* going after your lovely Lady Eliza's fancy fucking mansion. He knows you're not keen, but ... well, you know what Bob's like. He's in no rush about it though. Seems to think it's better to wait a while. Give her time to get over the robbery before he goes upsetting the apple cart again. Teach her a lesson, like.'

Making a fist, Shanklin fought hard to stop himself from leaping up and smashing the stool he was sitting on straight into Randall's face. 'And what *lesson's* that?'

There was a blank look in Randall's eye, while the patch with the diamond in the centre twinkled. 'To never let your guard down, Shank,' he said, and he left, slamming the door behind him.

Suddenly, Shanklin's little fight with his wife didn't seem too big a deal anymore. He pulled the necklace from his coat pocket and held it tightly. He had to warn Eliza that she was in danger. Had to give her time to step up her security. And he had to finish Bob Creech for good.

9

PARADISE

A firework popped in the pink and purple evening sky, sprinkling a shower of glittering gold above the ball. The Vauxhall pleasure gardens consisted of a grid of elm, sycamore and lime trees grouped in perfect rectangles and separated by long, straight, tree-lined avenues that ran the length of the park. To the west was Spring Gardens House, its shuttered windows overlooking the Grove – a large open area inside the entrance to the grounds. In the middle of this perfectly manicured green space was an octagonal bandstand from which the soothing scrape of violins floated on the warm evening breeze. The fashionable rococo crowds wandered around in their masquerade masks and silk dresses, the women wearing tall wigs and the men looking no less flamboyant.

'Pardon me, Mr Shanklin,' said Skim, 'but how the hell are we gonna find him in here when everyone's dressed up like twats.'

Shanklin glanced sideways at his recruit who wore a Venetian-style masquerade mask with a long curved beak, his curly hair sprouting from the back and those sharp ears only adding to his impish appearance.

'Aye, so they are,' Shanklin said, adjusting his own mask which, compared to Skim's, was very much on the sombre side; plain black, covering the top part of his face and leaving his clean-shaven jaw exposed. He hadn't failed to spot the irony in this, being as he'd worn a scarf over the lower half at the time he'd robbed Lady Torne. And now he was scrubbed up like a Spruce Prig, having put on a fine summer suit; well-fitted, dark green, with a patterned silk coat which bore some fine embroidery along the edges, the curved tails cut low. His waistcoat was a little more understated and his breeches were fastened below the knee where they met white stockings. His shirt was frilled at the cuffs and around his neck was tied a knotted muslin cravat. He'd had the sense to leave his tricorn at home, instead having donned a powdered wig, the ponytail tied with a black bow. Shanklin's buckled shoes were polished to the point of being mirrors and, for once, he resembled quite the dashing gentleman. Yet he felt more like a prize tit.

Being as this was mainly an event for the fashionable and those floating at the higher end of society, he'd left his pistols at home, instead opting to carry a small-sword on his hip, with the sole aim of blending in. And there were so many here to blend in with. The ball was crawling with the middling sort; aristocratic Londoners, the beau monde, thousands of 'em sweating under their fancy wigs and facepowder. Men parading like peacocks while the women daintily shuffled alongside, stifled by the weight of their richly-brocaded sack-back gowns and stiff corsets, fanning themselves and laughing at the terrible jokes told by their male counterparts.

Give me the wild wood over this so-called paradise any day, Shanklin thought, loosening his cravat.

But it wasn't only the quality here tonight. Every shade of

status was welcome and everyone *did* come. Every sort of sharper, rogue, whore and knuckler having paid their shilling (or not) to rub shoulders with those better off and see what was on offer. Like fleas on a well-groomed cat they lurked here in the shadows of this magically manicured Eden. A rot, festering beneath the veneer of a fantastical escape from the stench and monotony of their everyday lives.

But that wasn't Shanklin. Not today. He'd raised his own game a little higher for this occasion. Tonight, he was in a different class, here to honour Lord Torne and the splendid charity work he so honourably undertook. He was on the other side of the wall this evening, a Bow Street Runner, should anyone ask, under the employ of Sir Henry Fielding and keeping a watchful eye out for—

Skim was bouncing up and down like he had a frog in his breeches, his mask on top of his head, while he pushed a finger so far up his nose it looked like he might lose it.

'You're here to pick pockets, not your fucking nose,' Shanklin said. 'So, when you've quite finished searching for the brain you haven't got, d'ya think you might keep still for a minute? If I wanted someone jumping around like a puppy I'd have brought my boy along.'

'Sorry, Samuel. Need a piss.'

'Jesus. My Harry's got more self control. Find a shrub to leak behind, there's plenty of 'em about. And put your mask back on properly.'

'Aye, 'course,' said Skim doing as he was told.

Yet Shanklin couldn't knock the fool for having some jitters. He was feeling a little anticipation of his own, being as the woman he hadn't stopped thinking about for a week was most likely here somewhere. So he hoped. Or didn't. Christ, it was all a bit much. Second thoughts about this grand scheme of his were creeping in and his fingers toyed with the necklace in his coat pocket, thinking how he had a good idea of getting Eliza Torne's attention but none, as yet, on how he'd return what he'd stolen. Skim had a reputation for being a very decent diver, but putting things *back* in pockets seemed like a task too tall.

Shanklin curled his lip as he watched his accomplice wipe something he'd removed from his nose on to his shirt. What was needed right now was a drink.

Beyond the ebb and flow of the colourful crowd, he caught a glimpse of an arched wooden arbour set amongst a cluster of trees. Revellers were hovering around what appeared to be a makeshift tavern, above which was a crudely painted sign that read: *The Bejewelled Goblet.*

'Go drain your bladder then and be quick about it,' Shanklin said. ''Cause I'm about ready to fill mine.'

The chatter all around him made his skin crawl. The shack that served as a temporary alehouse bubbled with it; the 'civilised' tip of society, flaunting their self-indulgence. With a flagon of small-beer in his hand he watched Skim attempt to navigate drinking from his tankard, the beak of his mask dipping into his ale each time he brought it near his mouth.

A ball of flame burst up into the evening air, causing Shanklin to flinch as he felt the hot blast on his cheek. The culprit responsible was a semi-naked dwarf in nothing but a loincloth, skin painted with blue spirals, prancing around whilst spitting more flames skyward, to the obvious delight of gleeful onlookers. Instinct told Shanklin to take the torch from him and shove it so far up his cracker he'd be farting fireballs for a week, but it wouldn't do to cause a disturbance this early on. That was planned for later, not that Skim had any idea yet as to what his real role consisted of. They each sunk another ale as darkness descended on the gardens, seeping into every nook and corner. Lit oil lamps threw strange shadows around what was increasingly becoming a freakshow. Ghoulish masks blurred past Shanklin, men and women dressed as demons, drunken grins twisted in devious delight, blood-red lips and eyes sparkling with devilish intent. A woman swept past in a huge gown and a pair of stag antlers clasped to her oversized bright red wig. Her face was powdered as white as snow and she shot Shanklin a glance from beneath her feathered mask that said she'd have him right there if he desired. She was soon gone though, disappearing into the masses and leaving him with a fluttering in his gut that made him wonder if he'd walked past Eliza Torne a hundred times already and not known it. But no, disguised or not, he was certain he'd be able to tell if he was within ten feet of her.

A jester flitted past, closely followed by several people wearing masks like the plague doctors of old, except that these were brightly-coloured and glittering with sequins. *The Bejewelled Goblet* was starting to feel like a safe-haven; a calm little oasis in the centre of this strange circus. And for all the idle talk swirling around, Shanklin was beginning to think he'd be better off just staying here and getting top-heavy on ale.

'I thought I'd seen some things in my time,' said Skim, as they watched some mutton-head dressed as Pan merrily prance along, playing a tune on his pipes.

'Your *time*?' Shanklin scoffed. 'You ain't lived, lad. How old are you? Eighteen?'

'Twenty.'

'Right. Well, your *time* starts now. Get it right tonight and there might be some more work for ya.' Shanklin wiped froth from his lip and made sure he had Skim's attention. 'You heard of Lord Jasper Torne?'

'Can't say I have.'

'Nor I, till recently. He's involved in a children's charity which is running a collection stall here. Taking donations. Raising awareness about poverty. It attracts a lot of attention every year and Torne is their main speaker. I've got no idea what he looks like but it'll be obvious once he opens his mouth. We just have to make sure we're there when he does. That's where you come in. When I say, you slip up close to him and get what ya can. I'll do the rest from there. Whatever happens from that point on, you just follow my lead, that clear?'

'Aye,' said Skim, frowning like it wasn't.

'Good,' Shanklin said, taking another swig of beer and looking around. 'Now all we need to do is find that stall.' But he wasn't so sure of his chances. The number of people attending was steadily growing and it was starting to look as likely as finding a smile in *The Lion.*

'A charity?' asked Skim.

Shanklin looked sideways at his new apprentice thief. 'That mask covering your ears as well? Yes, a fucking charity. They help people. They give society's poor and under-privileged a foot up the ladder, a lot like I'm doing with you today, so—'

Shanklin followed Skim's finger, pointing to a woman weaving through the crowd and holding a placard high, upon which was written: *The Childrens' Charity Movement for The Poor*

'Like that one?' said Skim.

The sign bobbed above the crowds, gradually getting further away.

Quickly finishing his beer Shanklin tossed his flagon aside and adjusted his mask. 'Aye, just like that one,' he said, heading off after it. 'Keep up.'

. . .

They kept their distance from the stall and the temporary stage that had been set up, lit by flaming torches wedged in the ground. More fireworks snapped in the indigo sky and the smell of sulphur and sizzling meat wafted towards Shanklin. But, despite his stomach grumbling, food was far from his mind as he scanned the small crowd already gathered there, smiling politely and talking with a sobriety that the rest of this arcane event seemed to lack.

'You see him?' whispered Skim from under his disguise.

But it wasn't Lord Torne that Shanklin was hoping to spot first, his eyes darting across the gathering. Most of the women in attendance appeared to hold masks of some description, covering their eyes in a mysterious manner. And *all* were dressed for an occasion such as this, ball gowns trailing, feathered fans fluttering at their faces.

'I'll tell ya when,' he replied. 'Until then, keep quiet.'

A gentle round of applause rippled through those clustered near the stage as a man in a military uniform ascended the three little wooden steps. Shanklin guessed that he was in his late fifties. He was of medium build and the ponytail of his grey wig was tied with black ribbon. He walked tall, straight and proud, his red army coat embroidered with gold trim. A sword hung from his belt while the chain of a pocket-watch concealed in his waistcoat glinted in the firelight.

'That him?' hissed Skim as the clapping died.

'How should I know?' Shanklin's eyes moved to a woman who'd appeared at the edge of the stage. She was wearing a black domino cloak with the hood pulled up over her head and she held a half-mask to her eyes, while black silk gloves stretched the length of her arms. Yet, despite her concealment, even from where he stood, Shanklin knew it was her. Eliza Torne. He felt her. He sensed her. Her very *essence* calling him. And it cut his heart in two to see her gazing up at her husband on that stage as though he was a god to be worshipped. Closely behind her loomed a bodyguard, easy to spot. Broad-shouldered with small, pig-like eyes and wearing a tricorn above a face made for fairy tales. The ones with trolls in 'em.

Lord Torne cleared his throat. 'Thank you, thank you!' he boomed with all the pomp of a commanding officer. 'I am honoured once again to be here and I am truly humbled to be a part of the inspirational work that this charity continues to undertake.' He gestured then to the woman at his feet. 'My beautiful wife Eliza joins me in our appreciation of your attendance and we ask that you give generously tonight.'

Straining his neck, Shanklin noticed that Eliza was smiling shyly beneath her mask as the crowd clapped their approval.

'You know what to do,' he said to Skim though his eyes remained fixated on her. 'Just watch for the big bastard guarding 'em.'

Like a fox-hound released from its leash, the young thief sprang away, skirting the crowd and doing a decent job of not taking anyone's eye out with the pointy mask he was wearing. Shanklin watched him edge as close to the stage as he could without drawing disapproval from those already stood around. He took in a deep breath when his eyes found Eliza again, his fingers once more tinkering with the necklace in his pocket. Her husband's speech had become nothing but background noise to Shanklin now, his senses overwhelmed by her outrageous beauty. Like a moth to a flame, every fibre of him was drawn towards her. And then, quite suddenly, she turned her head in his direction, as if something had snagged her attention. On instinct, Shanklin lowered his face from her line of sight.

'And I only hope that this movement will continue to grow ...' Torne's overblown rhetoric went on for another few minutes before reaching its conclusion and, to rapturous applause, he descended from the stage before being mobbed by arse-kissing well-wishers.

From behind his own disguise, Shanklin saw the false smiles and the fake exchange of pleasantries before his Lordship and his loving wife were to be escorted from the area by their bodyguard. A small man in spectacles shadowed Torne, talking at him incessantly, much to the obvious annoyance of his Lordship. Shanklin's eyes skated across the congregation, thinning out now that the bragging was over and done with.

And Skim was nowhere to be seen.

Where the hell ...? Shanklin's teeth clenched. If the little prick didn't strike now the moment might be lost. Anyone around could tell that the ego-inflated Torne was looking to make a hasty exit.

Skim, you little ...

There. Weaving his way towards Torne like a snake stalking a field mouse. Shanklin observed. He watched Skim swerve the guard's scrutinous glare with dexterity. Saw him slip past the spectacle-wearing advisor who seemed ignorant of anything but Torne's busy schedule. And he prayed as Skim slid behind Eliza before brushing past her husband so smoothly that the reason for his moniker became clear. The brightly polished watch chain was no longer hanging from Torne's waistcoat pocket. Now it was Shanklin's moment to take centre-stage.

Skim was circling back around as Shanklin moved in to cut him off, grabbing the young thief's arm as he passed. 'You have something that doesn't belong to you, lad!' he cried, so that all around him could hear.

The shock on the onlookers' faces was plain in spite of their masks. Yet none were more shocked than Skim. 'What the—?'

'Play along,' hissed Shanklin, leaning close. 'Trust me.'

Gripping his coat, he yanked the terrified pickpocket towards him like he were a rag doll. 'I saw you take something, boy!' Shanklin shouted as the curious crowd looked on. 'Hand it over, you cutpurse!' He tore the mask from his apprentice's terrified face and with a trembling hand, Skim offered up the stolen watch.

'Shit, Mr Shanklin!' he whispered. 'What's gotten into ya? Let me go!'

Shanklin had every intention of doing so, but not until he was satisfied they'd put on a genuine performance. To gasps from the onlookers, he headbutted Skim causing blood to spurt from his nose. Uncalled for, certainly, but something he'd intended on doing for some time and now seemed like the opportunity to kill two birds with one stone.

'The stomach,' hissed Shanklin, as a stunned Skim wiped away blood with a sleeve. 'Hit me.'

It was a half-hearted blow but what sort of punch did Shanklin expect from a confused young man confronted by an experienced fighter? Despite the feeble strike, Shanklin groaned, bent double, releasing Skim and allowing him to make his escape, which he did, without hesitation; staggering away from the horrified gathering, fluttering their fans with added zeal.

Feigning injury from the pathetic punch to his gut, Shanklin stooped to collect Torne's discarded pocket-watch from the grass just as he and his bodyguard approached.

'What the hell was the meaning of that?' Torne demanded. 'Causing a bloody scene at *my* event, sir!'

Shanklin held up the stolen watch whilst checking his mask was still in place. 'I believe this is yours, my lord?' he asked, catching his breath and displaying a performance that would make Shakespeare proud. His eyes flicked across to

Eliza who now hovered close by, silently watching him from beneath her own glittering mask and hood.

'How the devil ...?' Torne exclaimed, swiping the watch back faster than Skim had stolen it.

'Taken by that rogue, your Lordship,' Shanklin said. 'I saw him make his move on you. I had my eye on him from the moment you gave your speech. I can spot a cutpurse from a mile.' He placed a hand to his ribs. 'I'm only sorry I couldn't keep hold of the wretch.'

Frowning, Torne asked, 'And you are?'

Shanklin was beginning to think that he should follow in Skim's footsteps and escape while he still had the chance. But instead he straightened himself up, squaring his shoulders before he spoke. 'Sir, I am—'

'A hero, my lord!' puffed a fat woman, waddling towards them. She was somewhat under-dressed for the event, her powdered grey hair in stark contrast to her flushed, saggy jowls. 'I saw everything! He attempted to apprehend the scoundrel but was assaulted for his bravery. If only there were more men like him!'

Shanklin exhaled. It had been a risky plan but, so far, it was paying off.

Torne turned to his champion. 'Then I must thank you, sir,' he said, a little reluctantly for Shanklin's taste. 'Indeed, I am grateful.' He then addressed the bodyguard who was looking somewhat redder in the cheeks himself. 'Scour the gardens, man! Find the thieving bastard so that I might consider you keeping your job!'

'No!' Shanklin interjected, a little hastily. 'If you'll pardon me, my lord, as a constable, I have experience in dealing with the likes of this particular breed of vermin. By now, he'll be long gone into—'

'A constable?' asked Torne. 'One of Fielding's men?'

'Correct, sir. A Bow Street Runner.'

'Are you alone? Are there not more of you here catching these scum?'

'It is a rare night off for me,' Shanklin said. 'And I am afraid that, with an event such as this and with so many dark nooks to hide in, our efforts to seek him out would be wasted. I wouldn't be surprised if he had another disguise at the ready.' Shanklin held Torne's eye. 'A criminal's career is short, sir. He will have his day at Tyburn, of that I'm certain.'

With his jaw clenching, Torne studied his so-called hero, glancing him up and down. 'Very well,' he said. 'My feeling is the same.' He checked that his watch was returned undamaged and slipped it back into his waistcoat as his spectacled advisor flustered around him again like an annoying fly. 'I have pressing matters to attend,' Torne added. 'Forgive me, but I must take my leave. Good evening, sir. I thank you again. What's your name? I'll be personally putting in a good word to Fielding.'

'My name's Knight,' said Shanklin. 'Robert Knight.'

'Ah, my knight in shining armour, eh?' said Torne, and those around him laughed nervously. All except Eliza, who hadn't taken her eyes from this gallant stranger in their midst.

Bidding farewell, Torne spun on his heel and made off, motioning for his wife to follow. 'Come, dear! We have people to see.'

However, Lady Torne did not follow. She remained precisely where she stood, removing the mask from her eyes so that her full and exquisite beauty was now revealed to Shanklin.

'Shortly, husband,' she said.

Torne paused, bewilderment on his face. 'We are done here, Eliza. There is much to see and do. Now follow, immediately, if you please.'

'I shall, my love. Though I wish to briefly speak with the constable.'

He approached her, his voice dropping to a hush. 'Do not embarrass me in front of our guests, dear. We have appointments.'

Eliza's silk-gloved hand rested gently upon her husband's chest. 'Allow me a moment, Jasper, please. I will follow shortly, you have my word.'

The advisor was close to popping a blood vessel. 'Sir, we really should be going …'

Torne frowned at Shanklin before conceding to her request. 'Five minutes,' he said and gestured to the bodyguard. 'George will accompany you.'

'No!' Eliza said, her frustration becoming obvious to those still gossiping. 'Must I have a guard with me every second of the day?'

'Have you taken leave of your mind, woman?' Torne asked. 'You were robbed on the road just days ago! Even now, here amongst friends, I've had my pocket picked by some cowardly scoundrel!'

Eliza brushed her fingers over the watch now safely tucked back inside her husband's waistcoat. 'I am in good company, Jasper. Allow me a moment where I am not fearing for my life!'

Torne's dithering associate cleared his throat. 'Sir, really, we must—'

'I'm coming, you persistent fool!' Torne snapped, almost blowing the wig from the man's head. 'You have five minutes,' he hissed at Eliza. 'I'll see you *back here*.' With that, he strode off, followed by his advisor, the fat maid and George, the pig-eyed bodyguard.

Alone finally with the woman he'd so longed to see, only then did Shanklin speak. 'I wished not to cause you any problems, my lady. I apologise. Perhaps it's best I go.'

'No,' Eliza said. 'It is *you* who deserves an apology, sir. I feel that my husband's thanks have fallen short. I bought him that watch as a gift and I too am indebted to you. Please, will you walk with me?'

Shanklin tried to swallow what little spit there was left in his mouth. 'But you only have five minutes ...'

Eliza smiled. 'A caged bird does not make for a proper companion. My husband does not rule me, sir.' She turned and began walking away, followed only by the sheltered stares of those still lingering around the charity stall.

'Where are we going, ma'am?' called out Shanklin.

Lady Torne glanced back over her shoulder, the half-mask having returned to her face. 'These are the pleasure gardens. Why, to paradise, sir!'

Once more, Shanklin adjusted his own disguise. 'Then it's a fucking pleasure indeed,' he muttered under his breath and strode after her, unaware that he was being watched by Eliza's fat maid.

The pair strolled along a narrow lane while nightingales sang a lament to the dying of the day. Glass oil lamps softly illuminated the long path adorned with brightly-coloured ribbons which hung from the trees and manicured hedgerows. Now that he was finally with her, the wonderment of this place struck Shanklin. It was like a re-creation of Eden itself. The closest he'd get to heaven and an angel to accompany him.

Others in masquerade dress were promenading, exchanging tender words or stealing kisses in dark corners of this secret lovers' lane. They were some distance from the bustle of the main square but the orchestra could still be heard; the sublime drone of melancholy cellos floating on the air and soothing Shanklin's soul. As they strolled, he chanced a brief glance at her. The glow of the lamps accentuated the redness of her lips, and her eyes, though half-hidden by the mask she held, sparkled beneath her hood. Her expensive jasmine perfume teased his spiralling mind. He was yearning for her, as though his very spirit was being manipulated and bent towards hers so that they might entwine. And in that tiny moment he wished that he could stop time.

He realised then that her lips were moving.

'I asked if you have been a constable for long, sir?' Eliza's voice came flooding back to his ears as though he'd just surfaced for air after swimming deep underwater.

'I, er … no, not long.'

Lady Torne chuckled. 'Well, I am officially pleased to make your acquaintance, Mr Knight,' she said, gazing straight ahead as they walked. 'My name is Eliza, but I expect you know that by now.'

He knew of nothing else.

'Have you come to the ball alone?' she asked. 'Are there no other heroic lawmen here with you?' She was teasing but he didn't care.

'Lost,' Shanklin said. 'That's to say, I took leave of them somewhere near one of those makeshift taverns erected about the place. I wished to hear your husband speak rather than listen to the dribble of drunks.'

'Touching,' Eliza replied, 'but I fear you do not know my husband. Believe me when I say that he too can dribble. And you must forgive his rudeness earlier. I was robbed whilst travelling last week and his concern for my welfare is … overcompensating.'

'Robbed?' Shanklin asked, feigning outrage. 'Were you hurt?'

'Only my pride, thank goodness. Though an item dear to me was taken. A necklace.'

That tiny tooth weighed as heavy as a rock in his pocket. 'I'm sorry, my lady.'

She stopped in her tracks. 'Sorry? Why sorry, Mr Knight? Did *you* take it?'

An ice-cold panic chilled Shanklin's blood. 'No, of course not, but I—'

'Then do not be sorry, sir. I have servants spending half their day bowing and scraping and apologising to me for one thing or another. I have come here to escape all that for one evening.' Her smile had vanished and she appeared troubled. 'I only wish to walk and to talk.' She sighed. 'And sometimes I wish to never stop walking.'

They continued on down the path, the soft, melting music like butter on warm toast. If she never stopped talking Shanklin wouldn't care. He'd be happy to listen to her all day.

'Was there no guard with you at the time of this robbery?' he asked, knowing the answer well enough.

Eliza laughed, far too loudly. 'Only if my sister-in-law can be considered as such. Extremely protective of me like her brother is, yes, but no match for armed villains. She remains indoors, too terrified to step outside of the house – the incident has shaken her to a great degree.'

Her sister-*in-law*, Shanklin realised.

'I spend my life surrounded by those who claim to wish only the best for me,' Eliza continued. 'Their intentions are virtuous, Mr Knight, but often all that I feel is suffocation.'

What Shanklin lacked in servants he made up for with frustrations and so he understood, as best he could.

Lady Torne stopped walking and gazed up at the stars prickling the inky sky above. 'The truth is, Mr Knight, I married not for love but for security,' she said, though Shanklin wondered if she'd meant to do so aloud. 'And now I am ... trapped.'

Standing there in that dimly-lit, leafy lane, Shanklin felt his desire for this woman beside him border on overwhelming. He sensed something in her that ran deeper than the suffocation she spoke of. Perhaps the pain of losing a child? A child whose tooth was attached to the very necklace he carried in his coat pocket. A necklace that was in need of being returned to its rightful owner. But more than that, he felt *magic* between them; as vibrant and as real as anything he'd experienced in his wretched life. Sorcery of the blackest yet most wonderful kind, tearing through his soul and twisting him in knots. He felt a *connection* with her. A oneness. He finally felt alive.

'Forgive me, my lady, but why are you telling me this?' Shanklin asked.

A tear slid from beneath Eliza's mask. 'Because I feel that I *can*,' she said, her voice stretched with raw emotion. 'It seems like madness but ... It is as though I already *know* you.' She laughed, embarrassed. 'It's crazy to speak as such, I know it is, I just ...'

Removing the mask from her face, she wiped away another tear and, once more, her beauty stunned him to his very core.

'But would you change your life if you could?' he asked, his pulse racing. 'Would you swap all that you have?' Christ, how he wished the answer could be 'yes'.

Lady Torne looked at him, her green eyes sparkling, even under the shadow of her cloak's hood. 'To be happy?' she said. 'In a heartbeat, sir.'

Shanklin had hardly noticed quite how dark the lane had become while they'd walked. The lamps in the trees were less frequent here and the dark corners and nooks were ideal places for robbers to lie in wait. Of all people, he should know how the mind of a thief operates. Yet he wondered if they might become lost here, just the two of them. Stolen away from the madness of the world into their own personal, uncaring insanity. And he wouldn't have worried if that were the case. He had a sword at his side and, having once been the man who'd frightened the wits from her, he was now her protector, a position he would gladly hold till his dying breath.

Except that Shanklin knew only too well the real trouble which awaited her. Trouble by the name of Bob Creech.

'I must warn you of something,' he said. 'You're in danger.'

Eliza laughed again but this time it was more out of surprise than embarrassment. 'Are you an angel sent to watch over us, Mr Knight? First you stop a thief in his tracks and now you warn me of further trouble?'

But his eyes must have conveyed the gravity of the situation as her surprise turned into concern. 'What kind of danger?'

'The kind that kills,' said Shanklin.

Eliza looked frightened. Of him? Perhaps. 'And how would you know this?' she asked.

'I work for Henry Fielding, ma'am. We are few in number but we're intent on ridding the streets of the filth who prey on Londoners.' The lies spilled forth but he couldn't stop now. 'One such rogue slipped through my fingers tonight but there are others. We have sources in the criminal underworld. Intelligence. Thief-takers from whom we acquire information in exchange for a reward. We've been informed by a reliable source that Rousingham House is to be milled and—'

'*Milled?*'

'A violent robbery.'

Eliza's expression of concern became one of horror. 'By whom? Who would do such a thing?'

'I'm not obliged to say, my lady, but please, trust me when—'

'Is this why you came to the stall, sir? To warn me? Or was it that you could you actually no longer endure the *'dribble of drunks'*?'

Shanklin steeled himself. 'I came because I care.'

A heavy silence settled upon the lane and all was quiet save for the distant flutter of violins. Eliza was gazing at his mouth, studying his lips. 'There are many people in my life who claim to *care*, Mr Knight. What makes you so special?'

'I only ask that you trust me when I say you should listen to your husband,' he said. 'Make sure that you have guards around you, always. At least for now. At least until the ... the *problem* goes away.'

'Goes away?' asked Eliza. 'And when will that be? What guarantee of security can you give me? How will I know when I am safe?'

'Please,' said Shanklin, 'it's against protocol for me to discuss it further. Just be vigilant. When the threat has passed I'll inform you.'

The nightingales had stopped chirping. The world around him had faded into obscurity. All that was real to him now were her lips; red as rubies and pulling him in. He was more frightened and more thrilled than he'd been before any robbery. Shanklin had tried to conceive of how he might discreetly slip the necklace upon her person but she had no reticule or bag to speak of. His impossible task now seemed insane. The only choice he had left was to hand it over. As a man of the law it wouldn't stretch the imagination so far as to assume that he'd come by her stolen item in his quest for those who operated outside of it. And yet none of that seemed to matter right now. All that mattered was that he kissed her.

'Your eyes are familiar to me,' Eliza said as though reading his thoughts. 'Can you be certain we haven't met before?'

'If we had then I'd not have forgotten it,' Shanklin replied.

She smiled, a little shyly, but the expression in her eyes remained the same. 'If there is a woman in your life, Mr Knight, then she is blessed to have you watch over her.'

He paused. 'There is no woman. None that compares to you.'

Eliza's smile widened. 'It's lucky for me that it is dark, sir,' she said, 'for it conceals my blushes.'

Slowly, Shanklin brought his hand to her face and brushed his fingers upon her cheek. 'And yet you'd appear even more like a rose.'

Eliza flinched.

'I'm sorry,' he said, pulling his hand away, but she took hold of it in hers, the silk of her glove soft on his skin. She brought his hand back to rest against her face and Shanklin prayed that she wouldn't spot the **T** branded into his thumb but it had escaped her attention and she pressed his palm to her cheek.

'You returned my husband's watch, Mr Knight,' Eliza whispered, her lips moving towards his. 'Now is there something you have for *me*?'

His other hand was now on the necklace in his coat pocket, carefully pulling it free when a rocket exploded in the sky above them, illuminating the lane and casting long shadows.

'Eliza?' A man's voice. An *angry* man.

Shanklin and Lady Torne came apart like a log being split in half, both of them turning to find her husband was standing twenty feet from them, an eerie shape under the glow of the firework. The huge bodyguard was at his side as they came striding forward, moonlight glinting on the small-sword at his waist. Eliza's fat maid was present too, lurking in the darkness.

'What's the devil is the meaning of this?' Torne growled and the peaceful tranquility was shattered.

'You had me followed?' Eliza accused her flustered maid.

Inside, Shanklin groaned. He should've seen this situation coming. Jasper Torne may have once been a soldier but his best days were behind him, and so it was the bodyguard with whom he now locked eyes.

Eliza took three strides towards her husband. 'Jasper, I—'

'Cheap whore!' Torne exclaimed, stopping her in her tracks like a bolt from a crossbow.

With nothing but idiotic pride in his skull, Shanklin moved towards Lord Torne and the bodyguard mirrored his action, a hand clasped on the hilt of his sword.

'Are you forgetting that I'm a constable, sir?' Shanklin said. 'Think about drawing that blade and I'll see you hanged, if I don't first run you through myself.'

Pig Eyes scowled.

'It isn't what you think, Jasper,' protested Eliza.

'Then just what the hell is it, my *dear*?' Torne asked. 'Why don't you enlighten me as to what you're doing in this place with a man who was a complete stranger until half an hour ago. My old ears may fail me at times, Eliza, but my eyes are as keen as ever.'

A cornered cat often has the sharpest claws and now Shanklin saw a flicker of that same fury he'd witnessed the day he'd robbed her.

'Mr Knight has come to warn us,' she said. 'We are in danger and he only wishes to help.'

Torne laughed. 'By tickling your throat with his tongue? Do not take me for a fool, woman!'

Eliza closed the gap between her and her husband. 'We have no done no wrong! But perhaps if you didn't have me on quite so tight a leash then I may not pull so often.'

The inch or so of air between them shimmered with hatred.

Shanklin was bored of being a bystander. 'I'm aware of how this appeared, Lord Torne,' he said, 'but I can assure you that I only have your interests at heart.'

Torne's glare slid past his wife. '*Assure* me?' he said. 'You may have saved my watch, sir, but you have stolen my trust. Just what did you say your name was?'

'Robert Knight.'

'Then I'll be enquiring with Mr Fielding in the morning. I assume he'll vouch for your position as one of his Runners?'

'Of course,' said Shanklin. 'I have nothing to hide.' *Yet only my life to lose.*

'Then remove your mask,' ordered Torne, 'and let us all see the face of our *hero*.'

But Shanklin's worry remained beneath his disguise. 'You may command your staff, sir,' he said, 'but I take instruction only from Mr Fielding.' He bowed gracefully to Eliza. 'I apologise for any inconvenience I have caused. Farewell.'

Her chin was high, her shoulders squared. 'Until we meet again, Mr Knight.'

Shanklin left the party behind him, heading his way towards the main square. He didn't look back at them as he walked, his hand still gripping the necklace in his pocket. Though not as tightly as he'd liked to have gripped Torne by his throat.

A DARK DISCOVERY

The weeds reached Jack's waist. Like everywhere else in and around the house, Mother had allowed their garden to fall into ruin since she'd become ill and stopped paying Mr Jenkins to keep it mown. But Jack didn't mind. It meant that he had more places to hide behind and duck into and crawl through when he was pretending to be a brave redcoat soldier. Just as he was that unusual morning, his imagination burning as brightly as the sun was on that clear warm day. An unusual morning, not because he was playing alone, as this he did more and more often. Even when he'd knocked on Charlotte's door earlier, only wishing for some company, she'd told him to go away, saying she was getting too old for stupid games. No, it was unusual because, while he was kneeling in the undergrowth killing pirates with a perfectly pistol-shaped branch that he'd found, his attention had been snagged by a cluster of frantically buzzing flies gathered near the broken fence at the far end of the garden.

Jack rose from out of the weeds he'd been using as cover, one hand shielding his eyes from the sun's glare and he began walking, or wading, given the length of the coarse grass which scraped at his bare shins. It had been far too warm for stockings and now he was paying the price, but he was a soldier and soldiers didn't gripe over scratches.

As he walked, he watched a butterfly bounce on the still air, swiftly joined by another before they both spiralled off into the sky like whirligigs. But Jack's gaze was still fixated on the swarming flies, the disturbing din of their incessant buzzing growing louder as he approached.

They scattered when he finally reached the spot that had piqued their interest and he discovered the source of their frenzy: a tuft of ginger fur poking through blood-stained hay. Fur that he recognised. Kneeling down to take a closer look, Jack gently pushed the yellowing grass aside and recoiled when he saw an eye gazing back up at him. A cat's eye, frozen wide with fright. His stomach churned and he clamped a hand to his mouth, thinking he might be sick. Still the flies buzzed around him and his first thought was to leave them to their feast. To go back to his game of soldiers and pirates and forget that he'd stumbled upon the poor animal at all. But his morbid fascination with the unfortunate creature found him rooted to the spot and keen to know more. He glanced behind him, back towards the house, standing black and bleak against the cloudless sky, its windows like scornful, prying eyes.

With his pretend pistol, Jack prodded at the soft carcass. *Not long dead*, he thought, and he bent the grass back with his hand, revealing a paw. Then a leg, the matted fur caked with dried blood. And the cold realisation dawned upon him, making him gasp when his fears were confirmed; it was Acorn, Tilly's cat! His body was misshapen and broken, mangled limbs bent at strange angles as though savaged by a wild beast.

Taking a deep breath, Jack composed himself before getting closer still. Despite the cat's clearly violent death, there were no bite marks that he could see. Nothing to suggest that a dog, a fox or a badger had sunk its teeth into the poor animal. He'd witnessed sheep that had been torn to shreds by dogs, stomachs ripped open and intestines strewn for many yards. But if a crazed dog had done this to Acorn then there'd be virtually nothing left of him! It was more as if he'd been ... *beaten* rather than savagely mauled.

Standing up, Jack's heart raced. He was dizzy and a lump had formed in his throat. He'd liked Acorn. He'd been a friend to him on lonely days, always popping over to say hello in the hope of being fussed. And now ... to find him like this, brutally killed! By what? By *whom*? And what of Tilly when she heard the news? Who would break it to her? Jack couldn't even look her in the eye after what had happened before, insulting her in front of the others the way he had. He couldn't be the one to add further injury. No, Charlotte would make it all right, she always knew what to do in a situation such as this. Charlotte would ... Jack's blood turned to ice. She hadn't been herself lately. Far from it. She'd been acting odd since the last hanging day. Since she'd had her seizure when the man who'd beaten his children to death had been the last to die on the gallows, his defiant spirit fighting to stay in this world. No. Jack wouldn't give in to wild notions. Charlotte was sick, certainly, and she needed help. Professional care. Her mind was not at ease, but was she capable of something like this? And why would she do such a thing? Charlotte was never keen on Tilly, not one bit, but to kill her cat? He couldn't conceive of it.

He scratched at his scalp, itchy from the heat and the sensation of the flies around him. Perhaps he could just bury Acorn and never mention it to anyone? Surely it would be the best thing for Tilly not to know of the violent end he'd met? To spare her such pain. Maybe that would be his good deed, his way of settling his debt to her after calling her such awful names. But how would that help her? She'd forever be wondering what had happened to her cat and was the uncertainty worse than knowing he was dead?

Jack scrunched his mop of blonde hair in frustration. 'I don't know, I don't know ...,' he muttered. He was too young for decisions like this. He only wanted to play and he wished he'd never bothered to come down here and ...

He could tell Mother. She'd know what to do! But after their last conversation he wasn't holding out much hope for a sympathetic ear. Mother hated Acorn. She said that his fur made her sneeze and tickled her throat and made her eyes sting. Jack swallowed. Could *she* have killed him? It appeared as though the cat was slaughtered on this very spot, as there was no visible blood trail leading down here. And Acorn had bled, that was certain, his tiny skull smashed. But would Mother have come all the way to the end of the garden to kill a cat? She barely had the strength to get out of bed let alone beat a defenceless animal to death. No, she could not have done this. This *had* to be the work of another animal. But not a wild animal or a crazed dog that would waste no time in ripping him to shreds. Perhaps Acorn had got into a fight with another cat from the village?

For now then, he'd do nothing. He'd tell no one. He'd keep quiet until he figured out what the best thing was. He needed time to think. He couldn't very well just go charging back to the house announcing what he'd discovered. Mother was too sick to worry about anything other than her own health, and his sister was shutting him out more and more each day. So he'd leave Acorn where he was, just until he worked out what to do. Just until he found an ounce of courage to speak up.

Jack's shoulders slumped as he gazed down at the ruined animal. He was no soldier. Not even close. He wasn't brave and he wasn't a warrior, despite how much he pretended. He was frightened of his own shadow most days. He couldn't even face telling his family about Acorn and he felt a burning shame at that. Shame that he was letting the creature down.

Acorn's eye was still staring up at him, wide with shock, as though the terror of his final moments was frozen in time. That eye had seen the killer and now it was pleading with Jack to uncover the truth. Maybe then, when he *did* discover what vicious animal was responsible, perhaps only then Acorn's soul could be at peace. But Jack remembered what his sister had told him, that animals don't have souls and that was one thing they'd agreed on. No, he was dead, it was that simple. His suffering had ended and he was at rest now. Acorn would get the burial he deserved, he'd just have to wait a little while. Just until this soldier decided the best course of action to take.

Jack turned to make his way back to the house, the sun on the back of his neck and flashing on Charlotte's bedroom window, where he briefly saw the shape of her, standing, staring down at him before she vanished from sight.

11

NO CHOICE

The lonely moor stretched off for miles under creeping clouds that bled like spilled ink on parchment. Sarah was standing with her back to Shanklin, dressed all in black muslin and a hooded cloak covering her head while a shawl draped her shoulders. Her arms were wrapped tightly around herself as though she had no one else to hold her. No one to offer comfort. To keep her safe. He couldn't see her face but he could tell that she was sobbing as she gazed down into a small, freshly dug grave. Small enough for a child.

'Sarah?' His voice was dead on the air, as empty as this barren, bleak place he found himself in. Slowly, he approached her, his linen shirt fluttering in the icy breeze, his legs heavy as though he was pushing against the current of a strong river. The ragged hem of Sarah's black cloak flowed like the tendrils of a deep-sea creature. Her whimpers whispered to him on the wind, the only sound out here aside from the cawing of jackdaws.

'Sarah, it's me,' Shanklin said, as he edged closer to her, his hand outstretched in front of him. 'It's Samuel.' She needed him now more than ever and well he knew it. And yet, he was a ghost to her. Always missing. Never around. Too busy drowning in his despair to truly feel hers. Her anguish of having buried two children.

'Sarah?' His fingers were now only an inch from her shuddering shoulders, her painful sobs raking at his heart. 'Please, let's talk ...'

He noticed it then: a silver necklace curled around her pale fingers, from which hung a tiny white stone. Eliza Torne turned towards him and he saw that her red-rimmed eyes were black to their corners. With a gasp, Shanklin pulled away but her hand darted out towards him, a scarred hand, as though having once been badly burned, and it gripped his shirt, her talon-like fingers scratching the skin beneath. His own hands sprang to Eliza's face and he pushed both thumbs into those blackest of eyes, yet she did not flinch as he drove them into the sockets.

And then, glancing down, Shanklin saw a red blotch forming on his shirt and a blood-wet blade retreating from his stomach. His surprise was even greater when he looked back up and discovered that it was Creech who had killed him, smiling, gold tooth glinting ...

Shanklin opened his eyes. A shard of moonlight sliced the ceiling above like a polished dagger in the dark. Sarah was snoring softly beside him, her back pressed up against his body. The bed they shared felt smaller every night. He pulled the sheets back and slowly swung his legs over the side, sitting with his clammy forehead resting on his palms for a moment. Then, quietly, he got up and crept downstairs, careful not to wake her or Harry.

Striking a match, Shanklin touched the flame to a candle on the mantelpiece. The study swelled under its glow, the clutter of more stolen artefacts throwing long shadows across the walls. He crouched to gather kindling from a bucket and stacked it neatly upon a length of twisted paper he'd lit, placing it in the fire grate. He watched the little amber tongues of flame take hold, caressing the thin slivers of wood. He blew gently on his creation, breathing life into the growing fire and his hatred for Bob Creech grew with it. They'd been bumping heads from the moment they'd met. A mutual disrespect, and now, like two old enemy warships, they were set on a collision course.

Shanklin placed a log on the fire and stood up, putting the candle back on the mantelpiece, its warm light catching the duelling pistol mounted on the wall above. He removed the gun from the spot in which it had lived for some time, unloved and abandoned, then he slumped into an armchair and watched the embers sailing up the chimney breast, disappearing into the void along with any hopes of quitting this life of criminality.

The filigree etched into the pistol's lock-plate felt fine to the touch. He stroked it like a father might stroke a sleeping infant's brow. He noticed the tiny grooves indented in the frizzen where the hammer had repeatedly struck. He felt the smoothness of the curved wooden stock in his hand. He wondered how often it had been fired in a duel, if at all. Perhaps it had only ever been used for practice. But though a ship can sit safely in a harbour, ships are not built for being idle. And as pretty as a pistol can be, that's not why pistols are made.

Harry was standing in the doorway wearing his long nightshirt and yawning.

'What you doing up, son?' asked Shanklin when he noticed him.

'Couldn't sleep,' Harry said, rubbing his eyes.

'Me neither. Push the door over and come here. I don't want to wake your mother.'

Shanklin wrapped an arm round his son's waist, pulling him close as they both stared into the snapping fire.

'You in trouble, Pa?' Harry asked, still gazing at the flames.

'What makes you think that?'

The boy shrugged. 'That gun's in your lap.'

The fire spat. 'Only with your mother,' Shanklin muttered. 'And I ain't about to waste any shots on her. She'll only duck 'em.'

Harry said nothing. Something gnawed at Shanklin. Guilt maybe. The boy was nine years old but he'd seen enough to stain his spirit for a lifetime. Too much. He'd seen his father stagger indoors drunk more times than he could count. Once, bleeding quite badly from a club-wound to the head. He'd watched him beat a man half to death in the very room they were in now. He'd often overheard him and Randall and a few of the others talk of how they'd hurt folks, laughing as they drank whisky into the early hours. Too many times Harry had listened to stories of broken bones and slashed faces, his young ears spared no detail. The kid was a sponge and he'd soaked up enough blood to fill a well. So Shanklin did the one thing he believed was long overdue. He handed Harry the pistol. 'Here, take it,' he said.

Harry's eyes sparkled as he held it in both hands. 'Whoa! Heavy, ain't it?'

''Course it's heavy, it's a real gun,' Shanklin said. 'Not one of those wooden toys you run around with.'

The boy peered along the length of the muzzle, one eye shut and his tongue poking out the side of his mouth. 'Is it loaded?'

'Son, I might be stupid at times, but handing you a loaded pistol while your mother's upstairs isn't on my list of things to do before I die. I reckon I'd be looking at an early death if I did.'

Wrapping his own hands around Harry's Shanklin helped his son cock the hammer back to full-position.

'You gonna kill someone with it, Pa?' Harry asked, in the same manner he might enquire as to what was for supper.

The fire popped. Shanklin's jaw was clenched tight, every muscle a coiled spring. 'Sometimes there's no choice.'

'Bet you've killed plenty of men,' Harry said, aiming at the flames, his tongue poking out the side of his mouth.

Just the one, thought Shanklin, and he'd always hoped that would be the last. 'Killing ain't a thing to be proud of,' he said. 'It's murder and if you're caught for it, you hang, no question. Killing's a last resort when there's no other choice open to ya.'

Harry squeezed the trigger. *Click.*

'You gonna kill Randall then, Pa?'

Spinning his son towards him, Shanklin saw the scared look of surprise in Harry's eyes. 'Now why would you say that, boy?'

Harry swallowed. ''Cause ... 'cause of how he is with Ma,' he said. ''Cause of how he talks to her at times.'

Shanklin's frown didn't budge. Harry was young but he wasn't daft, and unlike Randall he had two eyes in his head. Shanklin knew what the boy was getting at, yet he'd always brushed it aside: his best friend would fuck Sarah given the chance. It was as clear as the bells of St Sepulchre's Church on gallows day.

'Randall and your mother ...', Shanklin said, 'there's nothing meant by it. He's ... he's like family to us, y'understand? Like a brother to me. What's said between your ma and him, it means nothin'.'

Harry nodded but Shanklin could see that he did not in fact understand and why the hell would he? He was finding it hard to fathom himself.

The door squeaked open and Sarah appeared, arms folded

as she leaned against the frame. 'Teaching your son how to kill now, are ya?' she asked. 'You know how much I hate weapons.'

Shanklin took the pistol back from Harry. 'He needs to learn how to defend himself,' he said. 'One day he'll grow into a man.'

'Like his father has?' Sarah said, sniggering. 'Go back to bed, son. I'll be up in a minute to tuck you in.'

Harry looked at Shanklin as though it was *him* who gave the orders, but Sarah wasn't in the mood for antics. 'I said get to bed, now!' she snapped.

'Go,' said Shanklin and the boy did, past his mother and up the stairs.

Taking the pistol with him, Shanklin moved back over to the fire and crouched in front, slinging another log on, sparks spiralling upwards.

'If you don't start telling me what's going on,' Sarah said, 'then how the hell can I help fix it?'

'Nothing to fix,' Shanklin replied, prodding at the logs with the poker.

'Don't lie to me, Sam.' She came further into the room. 'What are you into this time? I have a right to know! Is it something to do with that necklace?'

'It's just business, Sarah, that's all.'

'*Business?* That's all I deserve in the way of an explanation? And does this *business* mean that me or your son are in danger? 'Cause if we are—'

Putting the poker down, Shanklin stood and turned to face his wife. Her bottom lip was trembling, her chin quivering like a jelly. She looked so lost, standing there. So utterly alone even though he was in the same room as her.

He moved towards her and put one hand on her arm. Sarah's wet eyes were locked on his and, as she blinked up at him, the tears ran.

'You're not in danger, Sarah, I swear,' Shanklin whispered. 'You're safe. Harry's safe! Nothing's changed. Just let me deal with this one thing and … and we can get on with our lives. Together. You and me and Harry.' His voice cracked then, catching him off-guard. Gently, Shanklin pulled her close to him and Sarah rested her head on his chest. She sobbed as they embraced, holding each other like they hadn't done for as long as he could remember.

But though his heart may have been beating alongside Sarah's, Shanklin's head was all clogged up with thoughts of Eliza Torne and the shadowy figure of Bob Creech slipping into her house during the night and slitting her throat while she slept. And while he hugged his wife for the first time in what seemed like forever, he was still gripping the gun in one hand and making a vow; an oath, to himself. That it wasn't going back on the damn wall until it had put a hole in Creech's head.

ALL TO ASH

'Have you seen Acorn?' Tilly Jones asked. She was standing five feet from Jack's front door, sunlight shimmering on her curly blonde hair. She looked angry and upset too. A little like she'd looked the day he embarrassed her in front of the others.

Jack blinked. 'Er...'

'My cat!' she scowled.

'Yes, I ... er, no, I haven't,' Jack said. He hadn't expected her to ever knock at his house after how he'd insulted her before. But then her cat was missing and people do unusual things in difficult circumstances.

Tilly's face was grey and slack with worry. 'Right. Fine. Well, if you do see him, then let me know.' It was more of an order than a request. 'He's been missing for two days.'

'I will,' Jack said.

Her eyes moved to a spot just past his shoulder and Jack turned to find Charlotte behind him.

'Hello, Tilly,' she said, smiling. 'Is something wrong?'

Tilly Jones was quite short for her age but she seemed to shrink even smaller then.

'Acorn hasn't come home for some time,' she said.

Charlotte raised her hands to her mouth as though shocked. 'Oh, I am sorry! When did you last see him?'

'The other day. Anyway, I must be going. Please let me know if you see him.'

She turned and Jack was close to calling out after her. He wanted to tell her that he *had* seen Acorn and that he was dead in their back garden, beaten to pulp and that he was so sorry and he wished he hadn't called her a whore that day. But she was halfway down the lane before he could open his mouth and Charlotte had already shoved her way past him.

'Tilly!' his sister called and the girl stopped, looking back, wiping at her eyes with the back of her hand. 'If I find him lying around somewhere, I'll be sure to let you know!'

Charlotte was still smiling and Jack didn't like it, not one bit. He watched Tilly run off down the lane and vanish from sight.

When she turned to him, Charlotte's smile was gone.

'What?' Jack asked.

'You know very well what! You shouldn't have answered the door.'

'Why not?'

'Because Mother doesn't like visitors!'

'She wasn't visiting. She wanted to know where her cat was.'

'Well, in future let me decide who we speak to.' Charlotte pushed past him, back into the house and down the hall. Jack closed the front door. He was angry. He sensed that she was keeping something to herself.

'You weren't here,' he said, following her into the study, still draped in darkness as the curtains hanging over the tall French windows overlooking the garden hadn't yet been opened. It was a musty room located at the back of the house and away from the sunlight, leaving it chilly even on a warm day. Mother's rocking chair sat in the corner swathed in tatty blankets.

'What was I to do, leave it unanswered?' Jack asked.

'If you must.' Charlotte knelt near the fire grate, gathering tinder and kindling from an old bucket.

Jack was staring. 'What are you doing?'

'What does it look like?'

'You're lighting a fire.'

'Well done, Jack,' Charlotte said. 'They do teach you something at school then.' Striking a match, his sister lit the tinder. 'If Mother wishes to spend the afternoon in here then I'd rather the room was warm. It's not good for her being stuck upstairs in bed all day.' She looked round at him. 'Besides, why must you always be so nosey? Go and play with your toys like a good little boy.'

'I'm not nosey!'

'You are too! You're a nosey little pig.' She began making a grunting noise that enraged him further.

'Stop it, Charlotte! You can be such a—'

His sister rose up so fast that it took him by surprise. 'Such a what?' she snapped, and her face was twisted with a scorn the likes of which he hadn't seen in her for some time. Her voice became deep like that of a man's. 'Why don't you tell me, *brother?*'

Terrified, Jack took two steps backwards as Charlotte came towards him, grunting. 'Nosey pig!'

'Stop it! Stop it or I'll—'

'Tell Mother?' she asked, grinning, her voice having returned to normal. 'You think she'd listen to you over me?'

Jack ran from the study, stumbling into the hall and upstairs, crashing into his bedroom and closing the door shut behind him, leaning his full weight against it. Yet he could still hear Charlotte, laughing hard, entertained by her own mocking of him. This was not *her*, he thought. Not the sister he loved and whom loved him.

'Boooy!' Mother's voice came hurtling from the other end of the landing. 'What's going on?' She was cut short by a bout of violent coughing and Jack covered his ears with his hands. He was breathing fast, his heart thumping. He wished everyone would just go away and leave him alone. Just let him be. But more than anything he wished he had the courage to tell Charlotte what he thought was going on. To confront her about Acorn and about the fact that she needed help. To speak his mind instead of running and hiding whenever things became difficult.

Throwing himself face-first onto his bed, he began to cry. He was ashamed of himself. Sickened by his own mildness. He was meek and pathetic, pressing muffled sobs into his pillow. He'd had no father to show him what it was to be a boy, let alone how to one day become a man. And Jack was furious then. His hurt became a rage which he poured into the pillow, screaming his frustration. He was so angry with himself. With Charlotte. With Mother. He had a duty to help Tilly.

Jack sprang for his bedroom door, yanking it open and striding along the landing before bounding back down the stairs, two at a time.

'Booooy!' cried Mother, still wheezing and coughing and gasping for breath. But he ignored her as he made his way through the hall and crashed into the study.

'Charlotte, I—'

But she wasn't there anymore. The room was empty and still dark and the fire she'd tried to start had already extinguished itself. There were no logs and there was no heat. Just a few smouldering leaves of paper. This wasn't a room prepared for a sick person.

Thump! Thump! Thump!

Mother's stick hammered on her bedroom floor located above the sitting room next door, but Jack could still hear it from here, reverberating through the house and shaking the walls.

'Booooooyyy!'

He was about to go and see her when he spotted what appeared to be an envelope in the fire-grate. Jack approached and knelt down. It was charred and the wax seal had melted, and beside it, the remains of a letter, still gently burning, the rest reduced to ash. Jack blew out the flame that clung to one corner and examined what was written.

The front door slammed and he almost jumped from his skin. He dropped the letter and made for the hallway in haste, opening the door in time to see Charlotte striding through the garden gate, hinges squeaking behind her.

'Where are you going? We need to talk!'

She turned. 'No, what we *need* is supper and it won't fetch itself. Mother's hungry and I'm going into the village to fetch some food, being that I'm the only one of us who does anything for her.'

Jack was disappointed. He'd finally summoned the strength inside of him to confront her on matters and now she was disappearing again. Who knew how he'd feel later when she returned?

'What are we having?' he asked, if only to keep her hanging on for a few more moments, hoping and yet not hoping that she might stay.

'Cat!' his sister said, smiling, before skipping away.

Despite his anger, Jack felt a kind of calm was restored to the world now that she was gone. But it wasn't a peace he welcomed and he teased his tooth with his tongue.

Tyburn gallows stood in the distance, a grey smudge on the landscape. He shuddered. Death practically loomed on his doorstep, greeting him every day when he left the house.

Even when there were no bodies hanging from its beams he'd see them in his mind, kicking as they hopelessly clung to life like the flame had to the letter he'd found.

The letter! He'd almost forgotten. He went back into the study and took a closer look. The handwriting was elegant, not hastily scrawled and only two words had survived the flames. Jack's heart almost stopped when he read them:

sincerely,
  Ruth

13

A MEETING

S hanklin had been doing a lot of thinking since he and Sarah had talked. So he'd asked Randall to arrange a meeting with Creech. To try and straighten things out. To call a truce, of sorts. Better for all if things were settled between them. Both men knew it'd been building to something ugly and both were getting a little old for long-running disputes. Grudges were like graves; big holes that consumed you and Shanklin was done with looking over his shoulder every time the tavern door swung open. Done with wondering when he was going to get something sharp in his gut. Done with the drama and the worry. It was time to end it. Now.

So he was stood round the corner from the front door of *The Lion*, his back to the wall as another shower pissed down on London. It didn't bother him, though, as long as the powder in his gun stayed dry – the duelling pistol he'd taken from above the mantelpiece, now tucked inside his coat, primed and cocked. Because the fact was that Bob Creech wasn't one for talking. Men like him simply didn't have it in 'em. And as much as Shanklin might've seen the benefit in a conversation to calm the situation, his many years of experience had taught him that certain people will only listen to violence. So today's topic would be a demonstration of just that.

Eliza's necklace was buried deep in the lining of his coat pocket. It had found a hole to sneak into and he was happy enough knowing it was there, safe. What he was about to do was for her as much as anything. Shanklin shut his eyes and took a long breath. Someone had once told him it was good for steadying the nerves, getting some air into the lungs. It wasn't working now, though.

Randall wasn't aware of what was planned, of course. As far as he was concerned it was just a meet to discuss certain differences and to see if they could find some middle ground. Shanklin chose *The Lion* because it was 'out in the open', so to speak. He might've killed Creech somewhere quiet; an alley or a backstreet, having followed him staggering home from somewhere, drunk. He might've shoved him into the Thames with a blade in his ribs and no bastard would ever have known he'd done it. But where was the message in that? Folks would be scratching their heads, left wondering what could've happened, leaving some no-name, low-life rat to claim the credit. No. If the robbing of a stagecoach wasn't to be Shanklin's last job then *this* surely was. And it wouldn't be quiet or out of the way. It'd be loud and messy and in front of an audience and Fat Fucking Landlord Tom would be mopping up Creech's blood after pouring Shanklin a pint and telling him he was sorry for letting the place ever sink so low. Apologising for allowing the likes of Skim and all the other shit to stroll in from the street as and when they felt like it. It was time to reclaim his rightful throne. Time to show 'em who was still the Upright Man in these parts.

Shanklin clicked his neck to the side, rolled his shoulders a few times and stepped round the corner. It sounded a little livelier than usual in there, laughter seeping out into the wet evening air. He unbuttoned his coat and pushed the door open.

Faces turned towards him as it banged shut again; familiar, most of 'em, ugly, all of 'em. Tankards hovered, half-raised to toothless mouths. A couple of respectful nods came his way, but most eyes were downturned and the volume in the tavern went down with it. Shanklin moved forward, punters parting as he approached the bar. Randall was there, in his usual spot, standing with his back to him and nursing a drink as he spoke with Tom, cheeks already white as bird shit.

'Shank,' said Randall with a nod. He looked worried. He had every right to be.

'Where is he?'

Randall pointed to a far corner but there were bodies blocking the view. The waxy shine of a freshly-shaved head belonging to someone sat at a table could be seen between the drinkers standing around, and everything else seemed to fade from sight as though Shanklin was in a tunnel, the edges of his vision blurry while only that polished scalp remained sharply in focus. He wiped a little rain from his chin and, on wobbly legs, he began walking towards it, faceless folk shuffling from his path. His panter was pounding hard and fast, nothing but the sound of his own breath was in his ears.

The full, brazen, ugly image of Bob Creech gradually appeared, sitting with both hands on the table in front of him to show he had no weapon. He looked up as Shanklin approached, that gold-toothed grin splitting his scarred face wide open. Even now, some distance from his own turf, he was grinning. Shanklin watched that very grin melt like wax on a warm fucking stove as Creech realised something wasn't right. As it dawned on him that death had just walked in the door.

Time slowed to a slug's pace then as Shanklin pulled the

pistol from inside his coat, smooth as a swan gliding across a lake. Shouts went up and chaos quickly followed, everyone jostling to get away, beer spilling, mugs bouncing on flagstones. That old barking iron that had been fixed to the wall for far too long was now aimed right at Creech, stuck frozen to his stool like a limpet on a rock.

Shanklin squeezed the trigger.

Click.

'Cause it isn't always about keeping your powder dry on a wet night such as this one. A misfire can happen for many reasons, one being if there's no spark when flint meets frizzen. A frizzen that is perhaps too soft because it hasn't been tempered to the correct degree.

No spark, no flash, no shot.

And now Shanklin had a big problem, yet it didn't come from Creech who was still sat gawping up at him no doubt wondering how he was still alive. Instead, it came from a cudgel that struck Shanklin's extended forearm so hard he yelped like a puppy being kicked and dropped the gun clattering on the floor. And then more problems came, many of them, thick and fast and in the form of a flurry of sticks beating at him from all angles. Shanklin's elbows came up high and he tried to protect his head by tucking it inside his arms as the cudgels pounded. Constables, *had* to be! He should've smelled 'em when he walked in. Should've known something was wrong when he saw the look on Fat Tom's face. Too late now. Survival was all that mattered.

He tried to spin away from the barrage bludgeoning him, attempting to flee but taking a kick to his side, propelling him back into the melee. Hands were on him, gripping and grabbing, men grunting and shoving and shouting and Shanklin couldn't see a damn thing, keeping his face low while the cudgels continued their dirty work on his shoulders and his back, sending pulses of pain jolting through him. On it went, relentless, yet somehow he remained on his feet, whirling this way and that, trying to get his bearings for the door but unsure which way was up and which was down.

Lunging forward he bounced into the bar, using it as support. A brief pause in the onslaught then, just enough time for Shanklin to glance up and see where the next attack was coming from. Enough time to place a headbutt crunching into a constable's face, popping his nose and spraying blood down his nice clean shirt. A quick left cross he stuck on another one of 'em before a stick cracked into the back of his skull and made colours ping before his eyes. He whirled round, his vision spinning like a kaleidoscope of mean-looking lawmen, hell-bent on battering the life from him and a last-ditch effort found Shanklin throwing wild punches, no match for the cudgels swinging at him again from all sides.

He buckled to the floor, on all fours now, the metallic tang of blood on his tongue as they stamped and kicked and he flopped onto his face, his cheek pressed to the cold flagstones. Curling himself into a ball, Shanklin prayed it'd soon pass, somehow clinging to consciousness until he was being lifted up and dragged over to a table upon which he was shoved face-down while his hands were cuffed behind him.

'Samuel Shanklin,' one of the breathless Bow Street Runners spat into his ear, 'I'm arresting you for highway robbery, attempted murder and anything else I can find on ya!'

As he was hauled through the suddenly half-empty tavern, a few grim faces flashed past, though not one was Creech or Randall. Tom had a sheepish smirk about him though. An ambush it had been then. A way for the thief-taking fucker to finally have his say on how things were done in *his* tavern.

And there it was, thought Shanklin, as he was bundled into a waiting carriage outside with three happy constables and one nursing a broken nose, *the end of the line, and about time.*

He'd delayed the inevitable for about as long as anyone might but there's only so far you can stretch your luck before it snaps.

The coach started to move, hooves clopping on cobbles, while through one swollen eye Shanklin watched *The Lion* roll from view for the last time.

14

ALFIE KILNE

The schoolboys spilled from the yard, screaming and running into the arms of their waiting mothers, a swarm of excited, happy children now that classes had finished for the day. Jack was among them, jostling his way through the bustle as he tried to keep sight of Alfie Kilne.

'Alfie, wait!' he called out.

Whether or not Alfie had heard him, Jack couldn't be sure, but the boy continued on, clutching his satchel to his side.

'Alfie!' Jack caught up as they left the tide of noisy pupils behind. 'I need to talk to you,' he said, trying to keep pace, though Alfie clearly wished to be left alone, his eyes fixed ahead of him as the pair made their way through the school gates and on to a winding lane that meandered down to the village.

'Your father...,' Jack said, 'he's a physician, isn't he? A man of medicine?'

'What of it?' asked Alfie, narrowly avoiding a woman coming the other way.

'I'd like him to come and visit my mother. She's very sick. She needs professional help.'

'My father is a busy man,' Alfie said as they hurried onwards. 'Though I'm sure there are plenty of other physicians in London—'

'She won't leave the house,' said Jack. 'She's stubborn. She refuses to see anyone.'

'She can't be helped if she won't help herself,' Alfie said with that same smugness Jack often found so irritating. 'That's what my father always says.'

They were clear of the school grounds now but Alfie's strides showed no sign of slacking. The lane led to his own house, a mile or so further on and in quite the opposite direction to Jack's.

'Please, Alfie, I need you to at least ask him if he would come and see us. I need you to try!'

Alfie almost laughed and he had every right to. Jack often spent a good deal of his school day poking fun at him, a nasty little habit he seemed to have acquired from Charlotte, and now here he was, pleading for his assistance.

Jack grabbed hold of the boy's arm. 'Stop!'

'Let go of me!' said Alfie, squirming.

But Jack did not. He didn't consider himself a bully. Bullies were boys like Edward Crevick who threw their fists around. But certain situations demanded certain measures.

'My mother is sick!' said Jack. 'I fear she has the White Plague.' He relaxed his hold on Alfie now that he had his attention. 'My sister is also unwell,' he added. 'There's a ... *madness* upon her. I need your help, there's no one else I can turn to.' He pulled two pennies from the pocket of his waistcoat. 'I have money! I'll pay your father whatever he wants.'

Alfie was rubbing at his arm. 'My father charges a little more than you have there,' he scoffed.

'Then I'll find it!' Jack said. 'Whatever he wants I'll make sure he gets it.' The words were coming from his mouth but he had no idea how he'd make that happen. He knew that Mother had money hidden somewhere in the house and if he looked hard enough then maybe he could locate it.

Alfie sighed. 'I'm sorry to hear your family are sick, I am. But if you're to speak with my father then it must be done in the right way. The proper channels. He has a practice in London; if you could make it there then perhaps you could arrange an appoint—'

Quite without thinking, Jack clutched at Alfie's shirt collar with both hands and pulled him close. 'Tell him to come to my house or I'll fucking kill you!' he screamed into the boy's terrified face. 'I'll make your life so bloody miserable you'll wish you were dead!'

Alfie's shock mirrored that of Jack's who took a step back. 'I'm sorry!' Jack said. 'I didn't mean to…'

But Alfie said nothing as he adjusted the satchel that had slipped from his shoulder and humbly, Jack crouched, picking up the dropped coins from the ground. When he stood, the boy was gone and with him went any hope of saving Charlotte.

15

THE SPY IN THE DARK

The gallows' struts groaned, the thick rope taut with the weight of the girl. Her back was facing him but Jack knew who she was. He'd seen her in his mind every day since Charlotte had taken him to the executions. Innocent, as his sister had claimed at the time, yet she had still died up there in front of a mob demanding entertainment. Jack hadn't forgotten her. How could he? Perhaps, in time, her milk-white face would fade from his memory, but for now she would haunt his dreams. And he knew he *was* dreaming. He knew because every single time it was the same. The girl's feet were always hovering just an inch from the barren ground, only that tiny space separating her from being alive or dead. On or off. A small gap of air between her toes and the hard earth and Jack wished so hard that he could somehow fill it with something, *anything* that would support her so that she could breathe again. So that she could *live*.

His tongue teased his wobbly tooth. As hopeless as he felt, he remained there with her, as if he was all she had in her dying moments. The last person she would ever see before she left this world and even now, he couldn't bear to part from her. So he remained there, alone, and he watched her sway and the *Deadly Nevergreen* sang its creaky song and her breath rose, tiny puffs of mist curling into the cold air ...

Breath?

The girl's body began to twist round, slowly turning towards him and Jack was filled with a terrible fear, rising from the pit of his stomach and working its way up his throat. He wanted to run but he realised that he was stuck fast, looking down to find that he'd sunk knee-deep in black, oozing mud, trapping him where he stood.

This dream was not the same.

He struggled, grunting with the effort of trying to flee but his legs were fixed firmly in the ground. He noticed a slick trickle of blood running towards him from the gallows, a glistening stream creeping closer to the spot in which he was rooted. Frightened by what he might see, Jack looked back up at the hanged girl to discover that it was Charlotte facing him, her nightdress spattered with blood and her blue lips smiling—

He screamed as he awoke, pulling the bedsheets up to his chin, shivering and blinking in the blackness of his room. He was cold and ... wet! Throwing the covers aside he groaned when he realised that he'd emptied his bladder. Clambering from his bed, Jack removed his sodden night-clothes and fished blindly through a cupboard drawer for some dry garments. He was accustomed to getting changed in the dark; candles were expensive and Mother didn't wish to waste her money just so that he could see what he was doing. Lacking one sense often meant that the others worked harder to make up for it. 'Training' as she called it. *Annoying*, was Jack's term.

Once changed, he yanked the wet sheets from his mattress and left them in a heap on the floor. Preparing to remake his bed, he froze, standing there in the dark and listening to voices coming from downstairs. Mother and Charlotte.

Padding over to his door, Jack opened it carefully so that he could better hear what was being said. Mother's voice was muffled, sounding as though she was in the study, talking above the faint snap of the fire. Sneaking out onto the dark landing, Jack edged towards the stairs and made his way down as quietly as he could, his fingers brushing along the cold bannister. Mother's voice grew steadily louder as he descended, aware that the slightest creak might give him away, but the squeak of her rocking chair covered that of his creeping and for once he didn't despise the thing.

Ambient light from the study spilled into the hallway through a gap in the door. But it was through the thin space where the door and the wall met, just above a hinge, that Jack spied his sister and his mother.

Charlotte was practically curled up like a cat at Mother's feet while the rocking chair whined and the fire crackled. Her face was buried in an old, heavy-looking book, stiff paper crackling as she carefully turned the pages. Submerged in shadow with a tatty blanket across her lap was Mother, stroking her daughter's hair with an outstretched hand.

'I haven't seen anything like this before,' Charlotte said, wonderment flashing in her eyes.

'It is a rare thing,' Mother replied. 'Rare and precious, like you, my child.'

Charlotte smiled up at her and Jack's stomach turned while his heart hammered so hard he thought they might hear it.

'When you were just a baby,' continued Mother, 'you would look up at me, staring above my head and around my shoulders whenever I would bend over you to tend to your needs. A perfectly normal thing for babies to do, of course; to gaze in awe at the world. As babies, we can all See. Each one of us. But just as a newborn soon loses the ability to hold its breath underwater, so too do we lose the gift of True Sight.'

Jack watched helplessly as his sister hung on Mother's every word.

'But not you, my dear,' she continued. 'Your Gift remained with you, for whatever reason only the Universe can know. And I gave thanks, because I knew that whatever trick this wicked world sent your way, whomever crossed your path or tried to deceive my daughter, you would See them for who or what they really were. You would use this rarest of skills to your advantage. You would slip past those who meant you harm and you would seek out those who offered you help.'

Jack clasped a hand to his mouth in frustration, suppressing the urge to burst into the room and yell at Mother for poisoning Charlotte with her twisted tales. But, as always, fear kept him paralysed.

The rocking chair whined to a stop and Mother leaned towards Charlotte so that Jack could now see her eyes, glinting sharply with purpose. Her finger uncurled like the limb of an octopus might and it came to rest beneath his sister's chin, lifting her face upwards and thus ensuring that she had her full attention.

'The veil between this world and that of the departed is thin, child,' Mother said. 'Just as a butterfly leaves the womb of its chrysalis, so when a spirit departs from the body it begins its journey to the Other Side.'

'Other Side?' asked Charlotte, her eyes wide. 'Where ghosts dwell?'

'No, my dear,' said Mother, easing back into her chair. 'A ghost is no more than a memory seen by those who were not there. An impression in time; like a fingerprint on glass or a stain on cloth, it is simply a trace of an occurrence being played out for all eternity. Residue of the moment itself.' Her narrow eyes glimmered. 'But a *spirit* … now that is something else entirely.'

Charlotte appeared as confused as Jack was angry.

'I'm not sure I understand,' his sister was saying, 'what I am to do with these … *skills*.'

Mother sighed. 'You will learn in due course. For it is true that most of us wear a blindfold. We do not See the Universe as she intended us to. Our reality is constricted by a mere five senses, such dull creatures that we are.' She aimed a finger. 'But for those Chosen … for those who retain True Sight … the world is theirs for the taking.'

Jack fought not to scream. He could hardly bear to hear it. He wanted to ask Mother if she knew of Charlotte's other 'talents'? If she was aware that his sister was utterly convinced she could absorb the energy of the dead? He was certain that she had no idea her beloved daughter attended public executions regularly! How impressed would she be then?

'And yet, sometimes it feels as though I'm cursed,' Charlotte said, gazing at the book in her lap. 'For I can't tell anyone but you and Jack of what I See and Hear, or of how I feel, and, try as I might, Jack doesn't seem to under—'

Mother's violent coughing cut her short. Pressing a blotchy-brown handkerchief to her mouth, she clutched at her chest in pain. When she took the cloth away it was spattered with fresh blood.

'You are not cursed, child,' Mother wheezed, 'you are *blessed!* And as for your brother, he is weak. He lacks courage. He's as timid as a flower and as soft as the down from a goose. He is a burden.'

Tears welled in Jack's eyes. Her words were daggers in his heart. All his life he'd wanted only her love but it never was and never would it be. Why was he even here in this house? What was the point in staying? Why was he not living with his father whom he hadn't seen or heard from in years? He could run away in the morning. He could find out where he lived and escape this forsaken place. But to leave Charlotte? Was it possible? Even now, when he wished so much to run back upstairs and hide under the sheets, Jack couldn't tear himself away from the spectacle playing out before his prying eyes. He had a front row seat at the greatest performance on earth and he hoped with all the hate he had in him that it would be Mother's last. He prayed that Consumption would kill her before the madness consumed his sister.

'I'm frightened for you, Mother,' Charlotte said.

'Do not be, child. No one lives for long. We must die so that we can allow room for our offspring to flourish. So that our lineage may grow stronger, more skilful and more advanced than we were before them.' That talon-like finger was again pointed with intent. 'And you are *very* advanced. You have a talent that you must harness in every conceivable way you can.' She pointed to the book in Charlotte's lap. 'What you have there is *my* gift to you, now that I'll soon be gone. Let it guide you when I'm no longer here to show you The Way.'

'Don't speak like this!' said Charlotte. 'Who will look after Jack and I if you leave us? I can't be responsible for us both. I don't know how!'

Relaxing back into her rocking chair, Mother sunk into shadow once more. The chair creaked and the wind moaned down the chimney. 'I am not asking you to be responsible for anyone but yourself,' she said.

Jack flinched away from the gap, blinking as silent tears ran. What did Mother mean by that?

'You hold an ancient and powerful knowledge in your hands,' continued Mother. 'That book is a *grimoire*. One of only a few that were written a long, long time ago. Tell no one of it! It must remain hidden. Most of it you won't be able to read as yet, but you will learn. In those pages you will discover that our ancestors once worshipped those who retained True Sight; extraordinary people, like you. But this was a better time. A time when those who possessed these abilities were not persecuted and punished as witches. They were celebrated and revered! Honoured and immortalised in paintings on the walls of caves and tribal dwellings. Yet the Church chose to eradicate this knowledge. To destroy any notion that to be Gifted was to have direct commune with the universe itself. To them, it was nothing less than evil. The Christian paintings that we treasure today celebrate only those who are so-called 'saints' and 'martyrs'. 'Holy' people. And how do we depict those 'saints'?'

'With halos,' muttered Charlotte.

The creases in Mother's frown were deep, the shadows dark. 'They have twisted The Truth to suit their own.' She coughed and spat a globule of blood into the hissing fire. 'Deceivers!'

Charlotte looked horrified.

But Jack had seen and heard enough of this! He quietly made to leave but Mother's next question to his sister found him unable to.

'Do you know on which day you were born, Charlotte?' she asked.

'Of course,' his sister replied. 'October 26th.'

'No, child. It was several days later; on the first day of Samhain, the sacred Feast of the Dead: October 31st, when the veil between this world and that of the spirits is at its thinnest.' Her eyes narrowed. 'When the souls of the departed return home.'

'But why was I made to believe differently?' Charlotte asked.

After a pause, Mother said, 'Fear is born from that which we do not understand, child. And fear breeds hate. If those who worship the one true God were to know of your ability *and* that you were born on Samhain, then there is no telling how they might act. Only your father was aware and if he'd been working away from home at the time of your birth, then I would have done my best to keep it secret from him too.'

'But a witch has not been burned for years,' Charlotte said.

'And you would be the first to *re-kindle* such barbarity?' Mother replied. She reached forward and took Charlotte's hand in her own. 'Something happened the night you came into this world, Charlotte. A beautiful magick. The Gift of True Sight was bestowed upon you and it has remained with you ever since.'

Another coughing fit ensued and Mother brought the bloodied handkerchief to her mouth once more. Charlotte's eyes darted towards the gap in the door. Jack recoiled, his heart hammering as he dared not breathe, certain that she'd seen him. That she had *sensed* him. Quietly, and so carefully, he slid back into the darkness of the hallway, creeping upstairs to his room to the sound of the coughing of a dying woman. And he was not in the least bit sad about it.

GENEROUS HOSPITALITY

'Welcome back to *The Stone Pitcher*, Mr Shanklin!' said one of the turnkeys, grinning. He was a big bastard, shoulders like cannonballs under his grubby tunic and a set of heavy-looking manacles in a pair of very large hands. But Shanklin didn't need reminding of where he was. It was that familiar smell of piss and shit that affirmed he was right back where many would say he belonged. And the noise, of course. The wailing and the crying and the moaning coming from the cells. The shouting. The insane laughter. That awful din that one can only associate with Newgate gaol.

Two constables pushed him further into the lodge for booking; a small, dark, stuffy room located near the Keeper's House. Lurking behind the turnkey was a skinny clinker with blotchy skin and a hunch in his back, teeth as crooked as gravestones. He had long, lank hair down to his shoulders and a blotchy, dismal complexion.

One of the Runners removed Shanklin's cuffs. They'd taken his knife when he was arrested but hadn't found the necklace hidden in the lining of his coat. A small victory in a war he wasn't winning. 'I've got chink on me,' Shanklin said as the big turnkey made to pull the coat from him. 'I can pay, so let me keep my clothes, eh?'

The skinny hunchback stepped out from the shadows and helped himself to the purse in Shanklin's pocket, taking two-and-sixpence.

'You can keep your clothes, Mr Shanklin,' Skinny said, rubbing the coins between his thin fingers. 'This'll get you into the Common Felons' Side, but I fear there ain't enough to move you to the Masters. Nor indeed is there a sum to cover easement of those chains, so it looks as though you'll be wearing the heaviest jewellery we have in this fine establishment.'

The gaol steward was he then. The one you garnished if you wanted clothes, candles and coal. An inmate who'd been here so long he was part of the fucking furniture — if you could find any in this cesspit. Some years had passed since his last stay here but Shanklin hadn't forgotten the process. You didn't upset the steward unless you enjoyed misery and there was enough of that to go around already.

Within moments of the cuffs being taken off, the irons were clapped on, nearly one hundred pounds of 'em, administered by the big warden with more than a little satisfaction. Shanklin briefly thought of offering the necklace as payment to lighten the load on his wrists but quickly decided against it.

'You'll be pleased to know that not much has changed round 'ere,' the turnkey said, bent low as he snapped the fetters on his new inmate's legs. 'It's still the same shit-hole it always was.'

Shanklin's urge to spit on the back of his head was a little overwhelming. 'So I can smell.'

The turnkey stood up, towering over him, leaning so close that the fetid air in here was preferable to that of his breath. 'We'll take good care of ya, Samuel,' he whispered. 'Real good care.'

Shanklin tried to match the grin but even that hurt. It hurt to swallow. It hurt to walk. It hurt to see. His black eye tingled. They didn't serve steak here in *Ackerman's Hotel* but even if they did he reckoned there wasn't a cow with an arse big enough to take the edge off the swelling.

'My name's Morton,' the turnkey added. 'This here is Gripe. Anything you need, be sure to tell him. He'll be more than happy to decline.'

The steward winked. With some effort Shanklin could almost get his head around a man being paid to hold the position of gaol warden, but an inmate behaving as such was more than he could chew on.

'Right, let's get you settled in, shall we?' said Morton. 'There's someone I want you to meet.'

The noise only got louder out in the dank corridors, where the rats scurried along the edges of the walls. Shanklin shuddered. He hated 'em. Hated 'em about as much as he hated dark, confined spaces so he was thrilled to be back.

Newgate, how I've missed you, he thought as he shuffled along, the chain from the fetters scraping on the flagstones. He was flanked by Morton and another turnkey, with Gripe limping behind. There were five wards on the Common Felons' Side of the gaol: three for men, two for women. A warren of damp interconnected passages and rancid cells. Bed-pans clanged against walls and heavy doors were kicked. It made Shanklin long for Harry's thumping around the house, chasing imaginary foes. *Harry*. Christ, he'd even take Sarah's nagging over this. What the hell had he done to be back here? His jaw was clenched despite the pain and the bruising. He was already so close to losing control but he had to keep it together. *Had* to. If he lost his mind in here there'd be no finding it again. Sweat trickled down his back while he walked. He'd paid to keep his coat but now that he was shackled he was starting to regret having it on for there'd be no removing it. He only hoped the cell had a window so he could get a little air as the corridors were stifling.

Before long, the men arrived outside a door on the Middle Ward. With one hand holding a posy of flowers to his nose, Morton took a set of keys from his belt and unlocked it. The door squealed open, releasing a vapour so venomous Shanklin recoiled but was given a helping shove across the threshold. He spun, shooting the turnkey a glare that said he'd tear his head off if he wasn't clamped. Morton seemed none too bothered by that though as he followed him into the room, moonlight filtering through a small, grated window and bouncing off his boulder-sized shoulders.

'Oh, I'll undo those manacles free of charge, Samuel, if that's what you're after?' the turnkey said. 'I'll finish what those Runners started, if you'll do me the honour?'

With his one working eye Shanklin glanced at the other guard hovering by the doorway, smiling like he fancied some of that fun too. He might've had the brains kicked from him but Shanklin retained enough to know when a fight wasn't to be won.

'Nah, didn't think so,' said Morton, hooking the keys back on his belt and returning the posy to his nose. 'Besides, I'm not so sure I wanna be rolling around on the floor with you in here. Bit ripe, ain't it? You never know what you might end up in.' Lumbering back to the doorway, the gaoler uttered a few parting words. 'Enjoy your stay, Samuel, short as it may be, for soon you will hang. Yet it's not all doom and gloom, you've got some company in here this time. I'm sure you two will get along like flies and ... well ... shit.'

Gripe was sniggering as the door was pulled shut and a key clattered in the lock, followed by a bolt squeaking into place.

Shanklin glanced around. There was a window, thankfully, though it seemed to be doing little to quell the stench in here. No bed was provided. The flooring was plank and not stone; of little comfort but he'd take what he could right now. Twisting the manacles on his raw wrists he strained to see into the darkest corner of the cell where two long, thin legs in ragged breeches extended outwards from the shadows, black toenails curled like rotten potato peelings. As his sight gradually became accustomed to the gloom, he could just make out the shape of the old man they belonged to, grey hair matted in long clumps draped about his bony shoulders. The moon's pasty light caught the edge of a gummy grin but Shanklin wasn't returning the gesture, especially now he'd discovered the source of the offending stink. The walls were daubed with long, black streaks of it.

'Jesus,' he muttered.

'No' quite,' said the old man in a thick Scottish accent, 'but what with my beard an' all, you'd be forgiven for the mistake.'

Shanklin narrowed his eyes at his cellmate. 'You go smearing your shit around while I'm stuck in here with ya and I'll smear your brains up the wall along with it. That understood?'

'Aye, I wouldn't blame you for that. Not sure I'd want to share a room with me either but we are where we are.'

Desperate for something resembling fresh air, Shanklin dragged his feet over to the window. 'Not for long, I'm not,' he said, looking west towards the spire of St Sepulchre's, stabbing at the inky sky amid a black jumble of sloping roofs and slanted chimneys. Its bell would toll on execution day and already he was thinking that the noose couldn't come quick enough.

'That's what I thought when they first brought me in,' the old man said. 'Been here so long now they even let me decorate ma room.'

'Well now the decorating stops,' said Shanklin. 'If you need to shit do it in the pot provided. That clear?'

'Fair 'nuff. I wasn't too keen on the colour anyway but it's all I had to work with.'

Somewhere in the opposite direction in which Shanklin was gazing, on the outskirts of the city and far from here, was home. The simmering rage he'd tried so hard to keep a lid on was now bubbling up inside him, but giving it a chance to boil over was akin to lighting a bundle of fireworks in a room with nowhere to run, and apart from the smelly cunt sat in the corner, a wall was about the only thing constituting a punchable surface. He'd learned long ago that when fist and brick meet there's only one champion. With his nose to the iron grate Shanklin took in gulps of air and wondered how many breaths he had left now that an execution was looming. Fewer than he had this morning anyway. *Savour 'em*, he thought. Every last one. How had someone who'd intended on leaving behind a life of crime managed to end up back in this hell? Twelve years it had been since his last spell in Newgate and the mark of a thief burned into his thumb hadn't been enough to keep him clear of trouble. There'd be no magistrate's pardon this time though, nor from the King. At least if he'd managed to put a hole in Bob Creech then he might've gone to the gallows for good reason, but no, he'd be remembered for failing at that too. So much for legends.

He turned to get another look at the old man. 'Seeing as we're sharing a room for a while,' Shanklin said, 'you got a name or just a stink?'

A wheezing chuckle, like the sound of broken bellows,

came from the shadows and sooner turned into a cough which became so violent that, for a brief, blissful moment, Shanklin thought the old bastard might drop dead right there and then. His delight turned to concern. It might be that he'd have another smell to worry about if that happened, being as the staff weren't too bothered about the upkeep of the place.

'Aye,' the old man finally replied when he'd regained some breath. 'Had me a name once. Had plenty of others whilst enjoying my stay here too. But you can call me whatever ye like, I'll not take offence.'

'*Stink* it is then.'

'I've been called worse.'

'I don't doubt it.' Leaving the window he shuffled over to a corner that didn't appear to be so heavily soiled, rummaging through the lining of his coat, chains rattling, fishing out the silver necklace before slumping to the floor with his back to the wall, careful not to lean in anything he shouldn't. The tiny links glittered and he gently rubbed the little tooth between his thumb and forefinger, his thoughts turning to Eliza Torne.

'Pretty,' observed Stink.

'Aye. She is.'

'Wife? Girlfriend?'

Shanklin sighed and put the necklace away, propping his head back against the wall and closing the eye that wasn't already half shut. 'You smell terrible and you talk too much,' he said.

'Well, I don't get many in here with me these days,' replied the old man, 'so you'll have to forgive me.'

'Forgiving is God's job, not mine.'

'Och, God's forgotten me, lad,' Stink said. 'It's just us here now.'

'Then make your peace with the devil, old man, 'cause he's the only one listening.'

Shanklin tried not to think about the smell. He tried not

to think about the stupidity of getting himself thrown back into Newgate. And he tried not to think about how he'd let Sarah and Harry down or the noose that he'd soon be swinging from. But the unfortunate truth was that cells were perfectly made for thinking in and if this one was hell then the devil felt a lot closer than he did before.

1 7

A VISITOR

The sweating man standing on the porch was dressed smartly in dark red breeches, matching waistcoat and jacket. His white wig tumbled from beneath his hat and he was holding a large, shabby leather case in one hand.

'Hello,' he said, smiling, kindly. 'You must be Jack?'

Jack said nothing as he gawped up at him, unsure of who this visitor was.

'I'm Francis Kilne,' the man added. 'Alfie's father.' His voice was soothing and kind.

'Oh,' Jack said, surprised. 'Come in!'

Mr Kilne stepped into the hallway, dabbing perspiration from his forehead with a handkerchief. Jack couldn't take his eyes from him. He was amazed that he was actually here! And then he worried that it had been his threat on Alfie that had forced the boy to take action.

Mother's stick thumped on the floorboards above them. 'Jack!' she called from her bedroom. 'Who's there?'

Flustered, Jack took Mr Kilne's coat and hat from him. 'Er, no one, Mother!'

'Is that the patient I hear?' Alfie's father asked, clearly sensing Jack's embarrassment.

'Yes, that's her,' he replied and at that moment Charlotte came scurrying down the stairs, stopping when she was halfway, one hand gripping the bannister.

'Hello,' Mr Kilne said. 'And you are?'

Charlotte's eyes were fixed on the large, silver crucifix hanging round the stranger's neck. 'Jack, who is this?'

Jack knew his sister wouldn't be pleased but it was too late now. Mr Kilne was here and he would stay until what was needed to be done was done.

'He's a physician and I invited him here,' he said. 'Mother needs help and—'

'Are you *mad?*' Charlotte asked, her green eyes piercing into his.

But Jack thought this a little rich coming from her. 'Charlotte, please, just give him a chance to—'

The thumping on the ceiling began again in earnest. 'What's going on down there?' Mother's outrage causing her another fit of coughing. Jack was thankful for it in some part; it put an abrupt end to her protests and only confirmed that he was right in asking Alfie for his father's help.

'May I?' asked Mr Kilne, moving towards the stairs. But Charlotte was blocking his way.

'No, you may not,' she scowled. 'Mother doesn't like visitors.'

Mr Kilne's smile remained firmly in place. 'I'm sorry, Charlotte, but if your mother is sick then I should attend...'

'You'll attend to no one.'

'Then you would rather that she suffered?'

'I'd rather you left,' Charlotte replied. '*Now.*'

'Charlotte, please!' Jack said. 'It can do no harm for Mr Kilne to see her.'

'And since when do *you* decide such matters?' his sister

snapped. 'Mother will be furious. She'll beat you fiercely and if she hasn't the strength to do so then I'll do it for her!'

Her scathing remark shocked him, rendering him speechless.

Mr Kilne intervened. 'Charlotte, I have a moral duty of care to the people of this parish. I am under obligation to help anyone in the village who may require it. Now please step aside and allow me to attend to your mother.'

Looking the doctor up and down, Charlotte reluctantly moved just enough to allow him to brush past her and proceed upstairs.

'Don't think that you're off the hook, *brother!*' she hissed at Jack. 'You should have checked with me first!' Then she turned and took off after Mr Kilne.

'And just who is this?' Mother wheezed as the physician entered the dark room with Jack close behind. She was merely a dark shape in the gloom, the curtains still drawn, keeping the sunlight at bay.

'Hello, Mrs Hunter,' Mr Kilne said. 'I am a physician. I'm here to take a look at you.'

'Then you're no use to me,' Mother said. 'So you can take your bag and your things and you can leave my house.'

Mr Kilne sighed. 'I cannot force you to be examined,' he said, 'but I should advise that it is in your best interests—'

'Quackery!' Mother said. 'I should think it is in nobody's interests but your own! What are you charging for even being here? I shan't pay it!'

'I am no quack, Mrs Hunter, I can assure you of that. My practice is in London, yet I live in the village and—'

'Ah, then I am saved!'

'*And* ...' continued Mr Kilne, 'on this occasion I shall waive my fee. I am here because your son requested it.'

'My son?' said Mother. 'The boy meddles in that which does not concern him.'

'I think you will find that his concern for you is paramount.'

Jack listened to the exchange of words from a safe distance, by the door. Of course he wished Mother to be well but his real worry was for Charlotte's condition and with nowhere else to turn he could only pray that Mr Kilne might be able to assist there also. Yet it was difficult enough in getting Mother to comply with the good doctor's wishes, so he held little hope for his sister doing as she was asked.

Mr Kilne placed his case on the floor and approached the window. 'But I can't very well see what I'm dealing with if there's no light to actually see by,' he said, yanking open the curtains.

Mother's protest was too late in coming. Sunlight swamped the room and Jack brought a hand to his mouth when he saw the full extent of the pus-filled lumps plastering her face.

The physician's brow furrowed. 'Hmmm,' he said, pulling the handkerchief from his waistcoat pocket and placing it to his mouth.

'Indeed!' said Mother, shielding her eyes and half-hiding the grotesque sores with her hand. 'So you will see that I have no need of your powders and potions, sir. I have exhausted my own supplies and am quite beyond whatever you have in that case of yours.' She stared up at a patch of damp which had spread across the ceiling. 'Like the decay that creeps through this house, so too am I rotting,' she whispered, turning her eyes then to the doctor's shiny crucifix. 'And neither God nor medicine can stop the Consumption.'

The room was silent. Jack's eyes moved between Mr Kilne and Mother.

'I am ... terribly sorry, Mrs Hunter,' the physician said. 'If we had caught the disease it in its earliest stages then perhaps—'

'Perhaps a prayer might have worked for me? Perhaps your God would have shown mercy? I have come not to rely on such notions, sir. Rather, my wits guide me. And they should guide you too; straight from this room and somewhere safe. Now, kindly leave and allow me to die in peace.'

Jack saw from Mr Kilne's eyes that there was nothing to be done.

'Good day to you then, Mrs Hunter,' he said at last before moving back around the bed to retrieve his case. 'I hope that you can find some comfort in your final days.'

He left the room and Jack followed, dismayed but still wondering how he would broach the subject of his sister's sickness.

Charlotte scoffed as Mr Kilne passed her on the landing. 'A fine physician you are then!' she said. He ignored her as he swiftly descended the staircase with Jack close behind. 'Do you leave all your patients to fend for themselves?'

Ignoring her comments, once they reached the hallway, Mr Kilne turned to Jack, stooping so that their eyes were level. He took hold of his hand in his own. 'There is no easy way to say this, Jack, but I'm afraid that your mother has very acute tuberculosis. She may not have long to live. I am *terribly* sorry.'

Jack blinked. His thoughts were all clogged up like wet leaves in a gutter. He'd known in his heart that Mother was dying. He'd seen what Consumption did on his trips into the city. But was it right that he felt more for his sister's plight than that of his own mother? Charlotte had always been kind to him. Had always loved him.

'Do you have a relative that could care for you?' asked Mr Kilne. He was squeezing Jack's hand as though to offer comfort, but to Jack it had quite the opposite effect. The physician lowered his voice to a whisper.

'You are not entirely safe here,' Mr Kilne said. 'Perhaps if Charlotte could see to it that your mother is made comfortable at home, then you could come and stay at my house with Alfie?'

'He's going nowhere,' Charlotte said, as she descended. 'But it's time that *you* did.'

Mr Kilne stood up. 'In all my time visiting the sick and infirm, I have not encountered such hostility,' he said. 'But grief can take many forms and so I wish you well on the journey ahead.' He turned to collect his coat and hat from the hooks by the front door.

'No,' said Jack, 'don't go! Not yet.'

'It's been made perfectly clear that I'm not welcome here, Jack,' Alfie's father said. 'Your sister is right, it's time I left.'

'Please, Mr Kilne! I know that Mother is dying and I wish it wasn't so, but...' He swallowed and glanced at Charlotte. 'It's my sister ... she is also unwell. She needs help too.'

'Shut up!' snapped Charlotte. 'Shut up now!'

'It's true!' Jack said. 'Though her ailments are not of the physical kind. It's her mind. She's deluded!'

'I'm warning you, Jack Hunter...'

Mr Kilne studied the pair of them, scrupulously. 'This is not for me to comment—'

'Then who can?' Jack begged.

'If she is unstable in her mind, Jack, then it is not my help she needs but—'

'I'm standing right here, you know?' Charlotte shouted. 'And it's my little brother who's taken leave of his senses, not me! Now get out!'

But the physician's attention remained on Jack, ignoring the girl as though she was a pesky wasp that would soon grow bored and disappear.

'I know a man that I could speak with,' Mr Kilne continued. 'He could take her to London. They have facilities. He could run some ... tests.'

'What sort of tests?' asked Jack.

Thump! Thump! Mother's stick hammered on the floorboards.

Mr Kilne placed a hand on Jack's shoulder. 'Have you heard of Bethlem Hospital?'

Charlotte laughed. 'Ah, good doctor,' she said as she gazed at the cross hanging from his neck. 'A man of God *and* a physician. Such hypocrisy.'

Now she had Mr Kilne's attention, his bitter smile like her own. 'And why would that be so hypocritical, child?'

'Is it not obvious? Where does your faith lie, doctor? In medicine or in prayer?'

Jack prickled with embarrassment at his sister's questioning of their visitor. Mother's influence was becoming deeply ingrained in her.

Mr Kilne chuckled. 'You are still a young girl, Charlotte. One day you will learn that it is not a choice between one or the other. This is not how the world works. We are all God's children. We are all part of His flock. His family. And I am certainly not Jesus and cannot perform miracles and so therefore—.'

'Family!' said Charlotte. 'Well, I have to confess that since our father left my mother for her very own sister, I have never really understood the meaning of the word.'

Thump! Thump! Thump!

'A shame then,' said Mr Kilne, putting on his hat and turning for the door. 'I'll see myself out. Take good care of your mother in her final hours. I'll be in touch, Jack. I will speak to my colleague at Bethlem Hospital. You have my word.'

But Jack wasn't so sure this was what he wanted now and a sharp panic rose in him.

'Yet I fear that you do not appreciate the true meaning of family either, doctor,' said Charlotte as Mr Kilne made to step outside into the sunshine.

He paused, the door open. 'My dear child, I am both lucky to be part of a very loving family and blessed to also be a member of God's.'

'And will *He* forgive your sins?' she asked. 'As cruel and wicked as they are.'

The physician's narrowed eyes fixed themselves on her, his warm smile now a thing of the distant past. 'God forgives us all, child.'

'Even those who touch their son's little cock when his mother isn't around?'

'Charlotte!' Jack cried. He noticed that the colour had very quickly drained from the doctor's cheeks.

'I'm sorry?' said Mr Kilne.

'Oh, you should be,' replied Charlotte. 'Because what you've put that boy through is nothing short of obscene!'

Thump! Thump! Thump!

'How dare—'

'And how dare *you* play innocent with me, doctor!' She came down from the stairs slowly, brushing past Jack.

'For I See like no one else,' she said. 'And I See you, *good* sir. I See you for who you truly are. Your crimes are as clear to me as that pathetic cross around your neck; a cross that I should wish swapped for a noose! And how it would please me to watch you hang! How I would delight in sharing with the world your disgusting exploitation of your own child.'

Visibly shaking, Mr Kilne took a wobbly step outside into the warm morning. He no longer had the flushed appearance of a man who'd walked some distance to get here. Rather, his complexion was ashen grey. Once he was several strides along the path, he spun. 'You won't be hearing from me again,' he said. 'I can assure you of that.'

'Correct answer,' said Charlotte, as the children watched him almost bump into a tree in his haste.

Slamming the door shut, she turned to her brother. 'Go and see what Mother wants,' she ordered. 'Then you and I are going to have a little talk.'

18

SMALL PRIVILEGES

The rattle of keys in the cell door woke Shanklin with a jolt and, gripped with the feeling that another beating was coming his way, he sat upright, blinking in the stark brightness.

'Up!' barked Morton. 'You've got a visitor.'

The other turnkey he'd seen earlier was standing at the doorway yawning as Shanklin struggled with the weight of the heavy irons.

'We ain't got all day, Samuel, come on,' said Morton and soon Shanklin was being jostled outside and along a musty passage.

A visitor? Randall, come to beg forgiveness for being such a fucking clunch and letting Fat Tom know what had been arranged in *The Lion*?

'Consider this a privilege,' Morton was saying as they walked, 'you're going to the Gigger. Not every common felon who can't pay their fees gets a chance to enter the Masters' Side. But then, money does tend to grease the old cogs around here and she did have a good purse on her.'

The wailing and the howling continued throughout the

length and breadth of the gaol. They turned a corner, narrowly avoiding a puddle of vomit before entering a spacious hall in which a small grate in the door allowed for conversation. But only for those who'd paid their 1s 6d to the Keeper for visitation.

'You don't have long,' said Morton and the turnkeys made off to a far corner, talking amongst themselves as Shanklin's bleary, bloodshot eye met those of his wife, staring back at him through the door's grate. He wasn't sure who he'd been expecting but it shouldn't have come as a surprise that Sarah was here. Yet the feeling of disappointment that it wasn't Eliza Torne standing there sobbing for his doomed soul sunk his heart into his boots. Perhaps he'd have to wait a while longer for that particular fairytale.

He made his way towards her. She looked pretty. She had on make-up and a nice dress. She'd made an effort. For *him*? He had to assume it was the case though who knew why. It wasn't like he deserved a damn thing from her.

'What have they done to you?' Sarah asked as Shanklin approached the window, the words catching in her throat, her worried, wet eyes scanning his face.

'Seems a man can't go for a drink these days without bumping into a cunt-stable,' he said.

Silence. His jokes had worn a little thin with her down the years and he guessed that now wasn't really the time. He could see that she was fighting not to scream at him or not to bribe her way in just to murder him herself.

'You're a fine mess,' she said.

'Where's Harry?'

'Randall's keeping an eye on him. I couldn't bring him here. Not today. I couldn't face it. Not without seeing you first.'

'Well, he's only got the one, ain't he?' Shanklin said.

'One what?'

'Eye. Randall.'

'Oh.'

Definitely not the time for jokes then.

'He says he'll come visit you,' Sarah added. 'Randall, that is. Says he's ... he's sorry for not helping out when they arrested you.'

Aye, Shanklin would have a few questions for his friend when he did decide to pay a visit. 'There was nothing he could've done. They were all over me in a flash. They knew about that meeting. *Had* to. It was an ambush.' He was back in his own thoughts again. 'Tom, the landlord. The fat, thief-taking...'

Sarah wiped her nose with the back of her hand, tears spilling down her cheeks. 'So, what now? What are we gonna do?'

It was hard to look at her. 'The trial's in a few days. The Old Bailey, next door.'

'And you'll plead innocence, yes? You'll tell them that they've got the wrong man?'

Shanklin swallowed. Christ, it even hurt to do that. 'They know who I am, Sarah. There's no way round it.'

She was shaking her head. 'No. There's always a way. Don't give up, Sam. Don't you dare—'

'Sarah ...' Lifting his arms against the weight of the heavy shackles, Shanklin gripped the iron grate. If he'd had the strength he would have pulled it free of the door and squeezed through that tiny space just to hold her. Just for a moment.

'Listen to me,' he whispered. 'You need to be strong. For Harry.'

'Strong?' Sarah wiped away more tears. 'Oh, you've taught me how to be just that, Samuel Shanklin. I've found a strength I never knew I had.'

'Then find some more. It's me who's facing the noose!'

His wife's glare burned so hot it might've melted the door from its hinges. 'No, we *all* are in one way or another, so don't you dare damn-well preach to me! We're all paying the price for your stupidity!'

For a moment, Shanklin saw just what she meant. It was he who'd committed the crimes but his family were suffering too. 'I'm sorry,' he said, finally, and it didn't seem quite so hard to say once he had. 'Sorry I ever got you into this.'

Sarah dabbed at her cheeks. 'Aye, so am I.'

He watched her for a moment, trying to compose herself. Brushing a hand down her dress and trying to hide the tears. 'We don't have long,' he said. 'Tell Harry that I love him. Tell him I'll make him proud when ... when I'm up there, on the gallows tree.'

Gazing at him through the grated window it seemed that all her tears had at last dried up. That perhaps, after a lifetime of loving him, she had no more to shed. Then Sarah's line of sight flickered past Shanklin's shoulder, over to where the turnkeys were talking. 'You can tell Harry yourself when you see him,' she whispered and her hand slipped inside her dress.

He wondered what she was doing when suddenly a pocket-sized saw appeared through the grate. 'Take it, quickly,' Sarah hissed and without sparing a second thought, he did, swiftly hiding the chive in the waistband of his breeches.

Her voice remained low as Morton and his colleague approached.

'Use it however you can,' she said, 'but get out of here, Sam! You hear *me* this time? Get ... out.'

'Time's up,' Morton said, wearily, like he'd seen too many of these visits already. His big hand clamped itself on Shanklin's arm. 'Let's go,' he ordered, giving his prisoner a helping shove towards the exit. 'I'm sure she'll be back here to see ya before your big day.'

As he was being bundled from the hall. Shanklin could think of a few uses for a blade right now and they didn't solely involve escape. He glanced over his shoulder but Sarah was gone from view and he was once more walking the dim passages back towards his cell, the cold, friendly steel of the little serrated knife pressing at his stomach.

19

DOWN AND OUT

I t was dark outside, rain pinging on the bars of the cell
window and plipping in a puddle that had formed on
the floorboards. Shanklin sat huddled in a corner,
chains lying coiled around him like an iron snake, his arms
draped over his knees. He was thinking about the chive Sarah
had smuggled in, now hidden in his coat pocket away from
the attention of Stink. It was a thoughtful act on her part but
it'd take more than a poxy little saw to get him out of here.
It'd take a miracle and miracles didn't happen to men like
Samuel Shanklin. Granted, there'd been masterful escapes
from Newgate before; Jack Sheppard had managed it twice.
But they'd still caught him and he'd still hanged. Death can't
be cheated when he knows every trick in the book. He's the
most cunning sharper at the gaming table and when he's
marked your card you pay your debts.

Plip. Plip. Plip. That puddle ticked like the hand on a
clock, marking time Shanklin no longer had. Even the trial
had been faster than he'd expected. A quick, confusing
affair, most of it rattled off in Latin. Despite Sarah's request,
he'd made no attempt to defend himself. What was the

point? The judge had made up his mind the moment he'd laid eyes on the infamous outlaw standing in the dock. *Highway robbery! Attempted murder! To be hanged by the neck until dead!* That being in ten days. The courtroom had smelled of herbs, hung up all around the place to cover the scent of the unwashed prisoners streaming through the door, and now he was wishing he'd tried stealing a bunch just to mask the stench that clung to the air in here. The culprit was awake, Shanklin sensed those pale eyes on him again, gazing out from his corner as a candle flickered nearby. And that stare was starting to irritate more than the damn shackles.

'Something on your mind there, Stink?'

The faintest outline of a grin. 'When you're here as long as me, laddie, there's always something on yer mind.'

'Well, I don't have time for secrets,' replied Shanklin, 'so spit it out or turn away.'

Plip. Plip. Plip.

'Hmmm, time,' mused the old man. 'I got me some o' that, but *you* ...'

Shanklin shifted, trying to get a little more comfortable. 'Tell me something I don't already know, o' wise sage. Master of the somewhat obvious, ain't ya?'

'Well, I'm no intellect,' said Stink, 'but it seems to me like you've lost your spark.'

Closing his eyes, Shanklin leaned his head back against the damp wall. 'And what makes you sure there was a spark to start with?'

'Och, there isn't so much that separates us, lad. I've been where you are.'

'That so? Well, when I'm swinging from the gallows I'll spare a thought for you still being alive while I'm slowly becoming dead. I'd say there's a big difference.'

Stink's chest crackled like sizzling pork whenever he

laughed. It was a sound Shanklin wouldn't miss when they finally took him from here.

'But there's a chasm between living and simply breathing, d'ye not think?' the old man asked.

'Oh, and you breathe so beautifully.' Shanklin said. 'I'll tell you what I think when you give me a minute to do so without staring or speaking. It's a little distracting, so fuck off.'

'Ah! Looks like there's still some fight left in you.'

Shanklin glowered. 'Aye, and you might get to see it if you keep on, old man.'

Stink raised a callused palm. 'Och, I'm not meaning to hurt your feelings, laddie. I'm just talking about choices. But, well, it sounds like you've already made yours.'

'Choices? Aye, I've made some good ones. Might be why I'm stuck in here listening to you and lacking the luxury of making any more.' Shanklin sighed, staring up at the ceiling, thinking of Harry. 'The only choice I've got now is whether to die like a man or not, and I've made my mind up on that. If Tyburn wants a hero, I'll give 'em one.'

'A *hero*? Well, I've seen plenty of men come through here but I've not met many of those.'

'Me neither,' Shanklin replied, pondering on 'Gentleman' James McCabe. 'All mine are gone.'

'Which brings me back to choices!' said Stink. 'Because, when you think about it, when you *really* look at a situation, there's always a choice to be found.'

'And I suppose you're going to enlighten me?'

'Aye,' said the old man. 'I am.' He leaned out from the shadows, wild eyes gleaming in the candlelight. 'For I know this gaol better than any man or woman or beast that's ever been here. And there's a beast, that's for certain. A black dog prowls this place, eyes as red as hot coals, teeth sharp as blades. Roamed here for centuries it has, since the monks were imprisoned here, starved and forced to eat each other.'

Shanklin frowned. 'A dog?'

'Aye, or the ghost of one. A demon. They say it belonged to a scholar who was brought here many years ago under charges of witchcraft. A sorcerer, he was; killed and eaten by the inmates not long after arriving. *Good meat,* they said. So the sorcerer's dog hunted down every one of those cannibalistic bastards and tore their limbs off, feeding on their flesh till they were nought but sticky bones. Still haunts the gaol, it does. A hellish spirit, it comes through the veil that separates this world from its own, taking on its real form only when it smells fresh blood. Yet it only appears when it's pitch dark and there's not a trace of light to be found.'

Shanklin noticed the candle waver. You can say one thing for sharing a cell with a madman: it was cheap entertainment. 'And who doesn't like a good tale, eh?' he said. 'Don't believe all you hear, old man. Stories like that'll drive you crazy.'

But all trace of a grin was gone from Stink's gaunt face. 'It's no myth, lad. 'I've seen it; when they had me stuck in Limbo for a long spell. I've seen those red eyes in the darkness.'

'Limbo?' asked Shanklin. He'd heard it mentioned somewhere.

'Aye. A condemned hold in the depths of this place. A dungeon reserved only for those prisoners of a particularly rebellious nature. Below ground, beneath the Keeper's House. No window. No air. Blacker and more stinkin' than any cell you've seen. You think this is bad? Limbo's the closest to hell I've come.'

A shudder ran down Shanklin's spine but he wasn't for showing it. 'And there was me thinking I'd already arrived. Sounds pleasant. I think I'm getting used to your smell. Think I'll stay right here, thanks all the same.'

'Och, I'm touched,' said Stink, 'but they'll put you in one

of the holds anyway on the eve of your execution so, if you want my advice, I'd get down there just as soon as you can.'

Shanklin stared into those mad un-blinking eyes and he wagged a finger. 'I was right about you from the start.'

The old man shrugged, easing back into his black corner. 'Take it or leave it,' he said, 'but sometimes you've got to go down to go up.'

'Save your riddles for the next unfortunate soul who comes this way,' said Shanklin.

'Suit yerself. But there's only one dungeon I know of in here that has a loose stone in front of a wee bench which leads to a funnel which then drops to a sewer that in turn gets you out of this fucking place. But then again how would I know that? It's not like I spent any considerable amount of time down there.'

He had Shanklin's attention now. 'A sewer?'

'That's what I said. Choose death if you will, laddie but I suggest you choose *down* … then *out*.'

Then Shanklin said something he thought he never would. 'Keep talking.'

Stink was silent though. Thoughtful. Then he said: 'You've got a wee chive on you.'

Shanklin's eyes lingered on those yellow peepers peering right back at him. 'And just what makes you think that?'

Stink leaned forward. 'And just what makes you think I'm stupid?'

'I asked the question.'

'And I gave you the answer. I see it all here, laddie. More'n anyone ever should. I see things clearer in the dark.'

'Is that right?'

'Aye, it is.'

Shanklin lifted up the chain between his manacles. 'Yet it seems to have escaped your notice that I'm wearing an awful lot of heavy jewellery to be going very far. Sewers included.'

'You call that heavy?' asked Stink. 'I've shit heavier.'

'I'm sure you have. But riddle me this you mad old bastard: if your so-called *Limbo* is the one way out of this hole then I don't see you rushing to go back down there.'

Stink grinned. 'I said that *you* could leave, not me. My legs are too buckled for doing anything more than just about standing up and that's pushing my luck. Might be why they took my fetters away a long time ago; better off on some other bastard who can actually get around.' He aimed a bony finger. 'If you keep a dog roped to a tree for long enough there'll come a time when all you need is a thin piece of string and he'll stay exactly where he is.'

'That you then?' asked Shanklin. 'Aside from the big four-legged black one roaming this gaol, are you their little mascot in here?'

'Aye, seems that way. The other dog doesn't play quite so nicely.' Stink winked. 'The turnkeys prefer my tricks.'

Shanklin glanced around at the walls. 'Like smearing your own shit? Is this some new form of torture they've adopted here? Put me in with a lunatic and hope I'll crack before I make it to Tyburn? I'd sooner go the Press Room than listen to this. The authorities have got all they need on me, Stink, you can stop now. You practice this speech often, do ya? Tell it to all the doomed souls that come this way? I get the feeling that after a day or so with you most of 'em were glad to be carted off to their deaths.'

The old man chuckled, a sound like gravel being shaken in a bucket. 'I've been alone a wee while but not everyone gets to partake in my wisdom. There's something special about you, though.'

Shanklin sniggered. 'Flattering, but if this is your way of making a move on me then I regret to inform you that I'm married.'

Married. As soon as he'd said it, he felt like that noose was already squeezing his neck, cutting into his windpipe, like a large, bitter-tasting almond lodged in his throat. It took him by surprise that did; to really feel something for Sarah again.

'Ah, your wee visitor?' asked Stink. 'The one who slipped you that little saw?'

Shanklin closed his eyes again and let his head lean back against the cold wall. 'That's all for now,' he said but he felt the old man's eyes still on him.

'Aye, perhaps it is,' said Stink.

20

THE INTRUDER

The breeze coming through Jack's bedroom window stirred the pages of the book balanced on his lap. He was sitting cross-legged on his bed with his back pressed to the wall whilst reading his favourite story: *Jack The Giant Killer*. But he wasn't really absorbing the words. There were far too many things on his mind. Charlotte, for one. She had become more distant from him, and even from Mother. She had retreated into a world of her own making and it was one that he wasn't welcome in. Perhaps, he mused, it was her way of dealing with the pain of Mother being so ill. Of feeling so helpless. The bond between them was strong but at least *he* had tried to help! He hadn't sat idly watching while she'd grown worse. Poor Mr Kilne; to be spoken to like that! A man of his professionalism. The thought made Jack feel sick. Charlotte had behaved awfully.

The house was quiet. Mother was having a nap, as she did so often these days. Charlotte was out somewhere, he knew not where and he didn't care for all that. His tongue teased his wobbly back tooth, hanging on now by a thread of skin. He considered if he should pull it out himself but Mother had instilled in them that nature is patient and therefore we should be too. So he would allow it to fall freely and in its own time like he had done for all the others.

Yet something else bothered Jack. What if Charlotte had been right about Mr Kilne? He'd acted strangely when she'd accused him of such ... *indecency* towards Alfie, and he couldn't leave their house fast enough when challenged. No! He wouldn't allow his sister's warped mind to confuse his own.

He was startled by a thud which came from her room next door. He strained his ears to listen if Charlotte had returned home without him having noticed, but no further sound came. She was out, he was sure of it. He'd heard her leave just an hour earlier. Though *something* had dropped in there. Was Mother up and creeping around? Surely she'd have called for him if she'd taken a fall?

Jack laid his book down on the bed and padded softly to the door, a floorboard creaking despite his careful tiptoeing. He winced. If Mother was still sleeping then she needed her rest and her wrath would be fierce if she was woken by his clumsy movements. He wondered if he should just abandon the investigation, but the thump had been rather loud and his curiosity was piqued. So, as quietly as he could, Jack peered from his room out into the long landing to find that Mother's door, located at the far end, was still closed. She couldn't have stirred or heard the noise at all. Charlotte's door was ajar. Not unusual; he often left his own open when it was warm, but the breeze from his sister's room felt ice cold and goosebumps prickled his forearms.

'Charlotte?' he whispered.

No reply.

Quiet as a mouse, Jack approached the door and very gently opened it further. But, as he suspected, she wasn't there. His sister's room was out of bounds to him, *always*.

She'd made that perfectly clear on several occasions. But it was freezing in there and she wouldn't appreciate coming home to a cold bedroom, so, carefully he made his way inside.

The thin, threadbare curtains moved as if they were alive. It wasn't *this* cold in his own room and something didn't feel right. He shuddered. The atmosphere was strange in here. Arcane. Alien. He approached the far window and pulled it closed, noticing a large heavy-looking book on the floor next to Charlotte's bed. It was lying open, its ochre pages scrawled with a strange script. It must have been the book he'd seen her reading when she was speaking with Mother! It had clearly fallen from somewhere. A shelf? Or from the bed itself? Perhaps, but Mother had told her to keep it secret so he couldn't imagine that Charlotte would have left it sitting around. Jack looked towards the open door, knowing that he should leave the book precisely where it lay and quickly return to his own room.

Stooping, he picked the book up. It was heavy and old. *Very* old. Upon its black leather cover was a symbol, gilded in silver: a five-pointed star inside a circle. A pentangle, he realised. He'd seen an etching of one somewhere. And then he remembered; this was a symbol of witchcraft. He opened the book and began to turn the pages which were stiff and crinkled like skin. The leaves were made from vellum and the words upon them appeared to be a mixture of Latin and what may have been a very early form of Anglo Saxon. Jack was educated in reading English, even a little French, and he could decipher some of it but most of it was nonsense to him. He turned the pages and discovered more symbols drawn throughout: runes and ornate letters, none of which he understood. There were diagrams of star constellations and sketches of snakes and trees and mutated animals missing limbs or possessing two heads. Some had the appearance of monsters; obscene creatures with protruding tongues and wild eyes. Why was Mother even allowing Charlotte to see this? *Encouraging* her to do so! This was no book of fairy tales. This was a *grimoire* of nightmares! Of spells and … summoning demons! One particular chapter seemed to depict crudely drawn stick-people with discs around their shoulders and heads. Arcs similar to the halos he'd seen in Christian paintings. Except that these were very simplistic drawings, as though they were replications of an older, more ancient art, and underneath them were captions which he couldn't understand. Overleaf was a drawing of someone lying on the floor; an old man with long hair. His eyes were closed as though he were dead and a long line extended from the top of his head, linking him to another figure standing nearby. A girl.

'Find something interesting?'

Clapping the book shut, Jack spun to find his sister standing in the doorway. 'Charlotte, I—'

'Why are you in my room?'

'Your window … er, it was wide open and—'

'Why do you have my book?'

'I heard a thud. It must have fallen from somewhere.'

'How could it fall when it was hidden under my bed?' Charlotte asked, striding towards him and snatching it from his hands. 'Your lies will be the death of you, Jack Hunter!'

'I'm not lying! I heard a noise and I came in because I was unsure if you were here and I thought that perhaps you might have had another seizure and hurt yourself. I found your window open and the book was on the floor and—'

'You're not to touch my things, do you understand?' she snapped. 'How many times have I told you?'

He watched his sister crouch and slide the book back under her bed.

'There was a time when we shared things, Charlotte, do you remember?' Jack said.

His sister glanced up at him, still wearing that dark frown, looking him up and down like she didn't even know who he was.

'There was a time when we'd play,' he went on. 'Do you remember how good it felt to run? To be free of this house. Free of the decay and the rot. Free of Mother.'

For a moment, Jack thought he saw a glimmer of recognition in her. That perhaps she remembered the young girl she once was. *Still* was.

'Times change,' Charlotte said, standing up. 'But I have a question for you. Why do you insist on watching me? Prying and sneaking and following me around like a lost puppy?' Her eyes became narrow. 'Is there something you hope to see, is that it? Something you'd like to ... catch me doing?'

Jack was blinking. 'What do you mean?'

Her smile made him very uncomfortable as she took a step towards him and he was forced to retreat. 'I think you do,' Charlotte said. 'I think you're just a little boy growing up far too fast and would like someone to show him what he's supposed to do when he finally comes of age.' She snatched hold of his hand and yanked it towards her crotch.

'No!' Jack cried, pulling himself free and edging back towards the window.

But his sister stalked him, her wide eyes studying the air around his shoulders. 'If only you could see what I See, Jack,' she whispered. 'Your halo; how it has changed! How *you* have changed.'

He was shaking his head as he backed away. 'No, I haven't! And there's no such thing as halos. You've been listening to Mother for too long!'

'No longer is it bright and golden,' Charlotte continued. 'No longer pure. It's red and it's black and it's stained by such dark thoughts—'

'Stop this!' Jack begged, keeping his voice low so as not to wake Mother. 'You have to stop believing what she tells you!'

'Come here, little brother,' his sister hissed, licking her lips and reaching for his hand again. 'Why don't you feel what—'

His punch knocked her back onto the bed where she lay propped on one elbow, holding her mouth in stunned horror. Save for Jack's rapid breathing, a silence swallowed the room.

'Why did you do that?' Charlotte asked, dabbing blood with a shaking hand. 'You cut my lip!'

'You deserved it!' Jack said, tears in his eyes, his chin quivering. 'You deserved it for what you did to Acorn! You killed him, I know you did!'

His sister sat upright. 'So fucking what if I did?' she snarled and her voice was deep, like a man's. 'I battered that little cunt of a cat till it didn't move.'

Jack was stunned. Shocked. Scared. 'How could you? Why would you?'

Charlotte seemed vacant then, her glazed eyes were blank. Like she'd just woken and didn't know where she was. 'I ... I don't know.'

He stepped towards her. 'You need help, Charlotte, don't you see?'

Regaining herself, she focused back on him. 'And you would have me sent to London to be experimented upon? Is this the help you suggest?'

'No. No, I ... I don't know what to do but this cannot carry on.' As he spoke though, Jack felt something he hadn't felt before: hopelessness. That actually there was nothing to be done for his sister. He'd failed her. And he'd failed himself. And yet, strangely, he also felt a sense of relief. A calm. Because now he knew that he didn't have to try anymore. Now he could just simply ... stop.

But Charlotte's glare had become darker. Her expression so bitter it chilled him. It was malignant. It was evil.

'You're right,' she said, rising slowly from the bed. 'This cannot carry on.'

'Boooyyyy!' Mother was calling from her room and for once in his life Jack was thankful to be summoned. As he left one bedroom for another, he sensed Charlotte's stare follow him and he knew in his broken heart that he'd helped unleash a terrible thing within her.

21

LIES AND DECEIT

Shanklin was dreaming of trickling water, cool and refreshing, tapping and splashing on slick, mountain rocks and slipping down into a stream...

He opened his eyes, both of 'em, now that he could. Beyond the iron grate of the window was an iron sky and that sinking sensation punched him in the stomach when he remembered where he was.

Yet that trickling sound continued ...

He rolled over. The cell door was open. Stink was asleep and Gripe was standing above him, pissing into the jug of water the prisoners shared. The steward twisted his hunched body, allowing the steady flow to wet the old man's face.

'Gah!' Stink woke up with a jolt and Shanklin had never seen the old fool move so fast, scuttling into a corner, hunched up in a ball and wiping at his eyes and beard.

'Rise and shine!' said Gripe.

Sitting upright now with his back to the wall, Shanklin's first thought was to kill this worm except that it'd be the single most stupid thing he ever did, save for attempting to assassinate Bob Creech in the middle of a crowded tavern.

'Get a thrill out of that, do ya?' he asked as Gripe was tucking his prick away.

'What's that?' replied the steward, limping over. 'Got something to say, have we, Shanklin? 'Cause I'd suggest you keep your mouth shut unless you want it filled! Thirsty too, are ya?' He shoved a hand back inside his breeches. 'I reckon I could squeeze another drop out. All you gotta do is open up wide and—'

'You've had your fun, Gripe,' said Morton from the doorway. 'Now leave.'

The steward's smirk slid from his blotchy face and he lumbered towards the exit. 'Not long now till the big day, eh, Mr Shanklin?' he remarked before disappearing as the incessant sounds of banging and screaming came from somewhere down the corridor.

Whilst Stink flicked piss from lengths of matted hair, Morton's slitted eyes were on his other prisoner. 'He's got a point, Samuel,' the turnkey said. 'A man with a reputation like yours should be keeping his mouth shut and his head low. Very low.'

Shanklin reckoned he couldn't get much lower, truth be told. But then he wasn't the one sat dripping wet with some other bastard's bladder water. The old man was breathing fast; fast for someone who could hardly breathe at the best of times anyway. Seemed he couldn't bring his eyes from the ground as he drained more drops from his beard and, for a moment, Shanklin reckoned he saw a little pride behind 'em still. Apparently it was acceptable to smear your own shit up the walls but there was a line to be drawn at having someone piss on you.

'Anyway, I'm not here to save you from getting wet,' Morton said. 'You've got another visitor, Samuel. My, my, ain't you popular?'

From the grey sky beyond the window came the sound of

thunder.

Shanklin was surprised to find that Eliza Torne was standing in the hall, her glowering, pig-eyed bodyguard behind her and the Gigger door at their back.

Morton was smiling. 'Let's just say that some visitors pay better then others,' he said. 'But you're still on the clock, so make it quick.' He ambled off with the other turnkey and left the three of them alone.

She was wearing the same black domino cloak that she'd worn the night they'd met in Vauxhall and her emerald-green eyes were half-hidden beneath the hood. Shanklin's stomach was in his boots but his heart was leaping despite being unsure if it was sheer disappointment or utter euphoria he was feeling. A small part of him had hoped it would be Sarah standing there again.

He pulled back his aching shoulders, straightening up as best he could before shuffling towards her.

'Well, it isn't quite the pleasure gardens is it, Mr ... *Knight?*' Eliza said.

Although partly obscured by the grate, her lips reminded him of why he'd risked everything for her safety.

'I feel a change of scenery works wonders for the soul, my lady,' said Shanklin, attempting a smile that was as painful as it was false.

'Well, I must say, you looked better wearing a mask, sir,' replied Eliza. 'But, I'm curious, how does a Bow Street Runner find himself on the wrong side of a gaol door?'

She was lacking a little of the sentiment she'd shown him when they walked together at the ball.

'A simple misunderstanding.'

'A rather serious one by the look of it.'

Her jasmine perfume was a welcome respite from the

stench of this place and it reminded him of their time together. But that was all that was familiar. There was no emotion in her voice. None of the affection and warmth she'd shown him in Vauxhall. A warmth that Shanklin found he now craved from her, yet she was as cold as a corpse.

'A scuffle, that's all,' he said. 'Once these fools realise they have the wrong man, I'll be freed.'

Eliza frowned, cocking her head slightly. 'Is that so? Then I assume that Mr Fielding is on his way here right now to correct the situation?'

Before Shanklin had time to produce another lie, Lady Torne's silk-gloved hands were on his, holding them tightly. There was a glint in her eye that he'd not seen before; sharp and deadly. She gripped Shanklin's thumb and turned it towards her so that she could now plainly see the letter **T** branded into his skin.

'A liar *and* a thief, Mr Shanklin,' she said. 'How very skilled you are.'

He pulled his hands from hers. 'My name is—'

'I am not here to play games, sir!' Eliza hissed, removing her hood. 'I don't have the time for them. *You* don't have time, so I'll spare us both further trauma. You have something that belongs to me: a necklace. I want it back.'

Shanklin feigned confusion, trying his luck despite the fact he'd had none whatsoever of late. 'A what? I don't know what you're talking about.'

She sighed, softly, as though gathering her patience from a well that had long since run dry. After a time, she spoke. 'Do you know, Mr Shanklin, people do fascinate me. They are never happy with what they have. Forever moaning. Always scheming. Turning upon each other on a whim. If it's not the Catholics it's the Protestants. If it's not the Jews it's the Irish, or the silk weavers of Spitalfields or the gin-crazed drunks, eager for uproar. Why must there always be a murmur of unrest on the horizon? Someone looking to trick or deceive. To turn on you for the sake of their own greed or pathetic cause.'

'What's your point?'

Eliza smiled, wickedly. 'That it pays to truly *know* people, sir. For there are so many in number. Approximately three-quarters of a million souls inhabit this fine city of ours. You must trust me when I tell you that I am very good at reading those I meet. Twice now have you disguised yourself from me: once on the road and again at the gardens. But I *know* you, Mr Shanklin. I always have.'

His teeth were clenched. 'You were playing me like a cello that evening at the ball.'

Lady Torne's smile widened. 'Did you honestly think that wearing a mask could hide your true identity from me? I knew who you were the moment I saw you in the crowd. It was a somewhat admirable and ... *unique* approach: to arrange a robbery on my husband just so you could get close to me. But why come at all? To warn me of 'impending danger'? Why even care?'

Lessons in life can often come hard and in that moment it felt to Shanklin like someone was teaching him a harsh one. He'd been so utterly bewitched by Eliza's beauty that he'd failed to see what lay beneath the surface.

'It was because you'd fallen in love with me, wasn't it?' she continued when he found that he could not.

Her innocence had been a pretence. She'd been playing a game but it was a game no longer. For neither of them. And now she was here, yet she did not sob or offer devoted words and assure him that she'd beg for a reprieve from the magistrate. No. She delighted in his torment.

The weight of lifting his eyes from the floor seemed heavier than the chains he had to carry, but Shanklin did manage to look up at her; at this woman to whom he may as well have handed his heart on a plate for all the use it was to him now. Yet, though it was torn from him, he wasn't for letting her eat it. He'd be swinging soon enough and, like him, she could swing for her damn necklace.

'It's lost,' he said.

Eliza's face went slack. 'You're lying.'

'Am I, my lady? You tell me, if you're so good at *reading* people.'

'Where ... is ... it?'

Shanklin leaned closer to her, whispering: 'Get me out of here and I'll show you.'

'And how do you suppose I do that?' replied Eliza.

'You have connections.'

Lady Torne laughed though she appeared unamused. 'I'm married to a lord not a magistrate.'

'Then go fast and find one to marry or the location of your precious necklace goes with me to the grave.' He watched the rage rise in her again. He knew how that felt – to have something slip from your grasp when you thought you were so close.

Eliza's eyes studied his battered face, her gaze inching its way over every scar and crease. 'It is a pity that we did not get to know each other a little better,' she said. 'It is a rare thing is it to feel such a ... *connection* with another.'

Slowly, Shanklin shook his head. 'Yes, I have deceived you, my lady,' he said, 'but the truth is that I came to the ball not only to warn you of the danger you were in but to somehow return what I'd stolen.' He sneered at Pig-Eyes who hadn't removed his glare from him. 'Only, I was chased away before I had the chance.'

There finally seemed to be a hint of something other than hatred hiding behind Lady Torne's emerald eyes. Something similar to what he'd seen on the evening they'd walked together. 'And yet it is too late now,' she said.

But something else troubled Shanklin. 'If you knew it was me who'd robbed you that morning, why not have me arrested at the ball?'

'And disappoint those who believed you to be a hero?' Eliza scoffed. 'No, it wouldn't have done to cause another scene, sir. Besides, I was having too much fun.'

Shanklin wasn't convinced. 'No. You meant every word you said as we walked together. You're trapped in a loveless marriage and I offered you a glimpse of—'

'You offered me nothing!' she hissed. 'Yet the one thing you *can* give me you now use as a bargaining tool for your life.'

'I'm not sure if you've noticed but my life is over.'

'*Yours*, yes,' replied Eliza. 'But now you have a chance to save the lives of others.'

'Others? What do you mean?'

Lady Torne paused. 'Have you ever seen the sun rise over Tyburn gallows, sir? It is a sight to behold, made even more splendid when there are still bodies hanging there, silhouetted against the blood-red sky.'

Morton and the other turnkey approached. 'Time to go.'

Eliza was smiling, sadly. 'Goodbye, Mr Shanklin,' she said. 'I shall see you soon enough as I watch from Mother Proctor's Pews while you hang. In the meantime, I will give my personal condolences to your wife and son. This must be a most terrible time for them.'

'Stay away from my family,' snarled Shanklin.

Eliza appeared ponderous. 'Ah, family. Yes. How precious they are to us.'

Placing a hand on Shanklin's arm, Morton attempted to move him. 'I said it's time to go.'

Shanklin shrugged him off and lunged for Eliza, gripping her by the hand. 'Stay away from them!' he shouted. Pig-Eyes sprang forward to defend his Ladyship but the turnkeys were already pulling their prisoner away. Her glove had come off in the scuffle, dropping to the floor and Shanklin noticed that the skin on her hand was scarred as though having once been burned. In her shock, Eliza quickly hid it with the other.

'Who did that tooth belong to?' Shanklin cried out as he was being bundled from the hall.

Her expression turned from one of surprise to horror. 'What did you say?' Lady Torne asked as her guard stood scowling in front of her.

Shanklin struggled with Morton and the other turnkey. 'Your daughter? Your son?' he cried from across the hall, dragged nearer to the door he'd entered through. Then she was gone from view and he was being bundled back down the mouldy passages while outside could be heard the distant growl of thunder.

22

BUTTERFLIES AND RAINBOWS

'Does that often, does he?' asked Shanklin, sat propped against a wall.

'My morning wash?' replied Stink. 'Och, s'pose I should be used to it by now.' The old man was huddled in his corner, still damp with the steward's piss. 'Another visitor then, eh?' he said after a while. 'Who was she this time?'

'What makes you think it was a she?'

'I was a young man once, believe it or not.'

Shanklin laughed. 'So your eyes *and* your mind are failing you; I ain't so young and I certainly won't grow to be old like you, thank God.'

Stink was deep in thought. 'Well, my guess is that it wasn't the wifey this time. No, I reckon—'

'And I reckon that it's none of your damn business,' said Shanklin. His mind was whirling with Eliza's parting words: *I will give my personal condolences to your wife and son.*

The old man shrugged. 'Fair 'nuff,' he said. 'It's just that, what with the lack of visitors I get these days, it's always nice to know there's still a world out there. Beyond that window.' He was watching Shanklin, probing, looking for another reaction. 'Aye, a lover, I'd say she was. Had me a few of those down the years too. Yer can see how though, right?'

Shanklin hardly had the will to argue anymore. 'I can just picture you curled up with one of the rats in here.'

'Heh, heh. Aye, I see that look in yer.' Stink was wagging his finger. 'That's a look that comes with a lost love. The kind of love yer can never have.' The old man stroked at his long beard. 'They come and go, don't they; lovers? Flitting into your life like bright little butterflies. Like rainbows during summer rain, they are. But there's no pot of gold at the end of 'em, is there? Only trouble. And like a spell here in *The Stone Pitcher* they'll leave a mark on yer all right.' He showed his thumb, the letter **T** branded into yellow skin. 'Rainbows fade, lad, but a wife ... a wife's for life, eh?'

'Then you ain't met mine,' Shanklin said. 'More of a thunderstorm in your *summer rain*.'

Stink chuckled. Then coughed. Then coughed some more. 'I had me one o' those too,' he said when he'd settled down. 'Sweet as a rose but a tongue as sharp as thorns. Owned a small dairy farm just outside of Aberdeen, we did. Kept us going, but it wasn't enough. Never is, is it? She didn't know what I did to earn us a few extra coins. Had her suspicions, I don't doubt it; she wasn't an ignorant woman.' He was gazing at the wall like the memories of his former life were painted there. But all Shanklin saw was shit.

'What happened?' he asked. 'She kick you out after growing tired of cleaning the walls? Or did some pretty little butterfly flap her wings in front of ya?'

'Heh, heh, och, no, not that time, lad,' replied the old man. 'I walked outta my house one morning to go to 'work' and ended up walking straight in here instead.' His bony shoulders seemed to slump a little further. 'That was eight years ago.'

Shanklin was frowning. 'You've been in here for eight

years, is that what you're telling me? You really are crazy. No one survives Newgate that long.'

Stink's wild eyes stared out. 'No, lad, they don't. Not unless they make a choice and I made mine soon after they dragged me in here. When they proposed an offer: a pardon from execution in exchange for my silence – I was to speak my name to no man or woman. To keep my identity secret.' He leaned forwards. 'I chose to live rather than face the hangman's noose. I chose so that my wife and child wouldn't see me leaping like a lamb on the end of a bloody leash as I slowly died in front o' them. And I'd call that the choice of a coward, wouldn't you?'

Shanklin gazed long and hard at the mad fool then burst out laughing. 'Eight years in this rat infested hole? You've been talking to yourself so long you're starting to believe it.' It was bad enough that there was no respite from the shackles, let alone having to listen to the ramblings of someone who belonged in Bedlam instead of here. 'So where's your wife now, eh? Does 'Lady Stink' ever come to visit, 'cause I'd like to look my best if she does?'

The old man relaxed back into his corner. 'She's out there somewhere, I imagine. Might even still be wondering where I got to that day, but, well, I pray she's forgotten all about me by now.'

'You're saying that she doesn't know you're in here rotting?'

A pause. Quiet, save for some clanging coming from somewhere. 'I'm just a ghost, lad. Nothing more than a memory to some.'

Staring at that craggy, shambolic shape sat hunched in the darkness, Shanklin began to wonder just who they'd slung him in with. 'What *is* your name?'

Stink tutted. 'Och, now I swore an oath ...'

Shanklin stared a while longer, in silence. 'Then take it to the grave with you if that's your choice,' he said.

It felt as though it had been raining for hours. Like it would never stop. It was coming through the window and plopping in the puddle and it was somehow soothing, mildly distracting from the noise of the surrounding cells. But after a while the clanging and the crying becomes normal to an inmate's ears. Shanklin thought that the clamour might've all been for him when he'd first arrived. Now he was starting to doubt his popularity in this place. No matter. The crowds would flock come his big day, spurring him on, buying him a final drink when he got off the wagon at *The Bowl Inn* or *The Mason's Arms*. He'd no doubt see some friendly faces. Randall. 'Tall' Saul. Ned. And some not so friendly, itching to get a glimpse of the so-called 'legend' before he was turned off.

He closed his eyes. Maybe Sarah would be there. Harry too, gazing up, proud of his pa as the mob cheered.

There was that tightness in his throat again.

'Got children?' asked Stink.

Shanklin swallowed. 'Aye.'

'Many?'

'A son.'

'How old?'

Sighing, Shanklin tipped his head back and tried to focus on the dripping of the rain. 'It ain't your business.'

The old man was examining something he'd just picked from his nose. 'You're right, it's not. Just another kid soon to be without a father, though. A shame that.'

Despite the cool, evening air sweeping in through the window, Shanklin's blood was warming up. 'This conversation's over.'

But the old fool either didn't seem to notice the warning given or simply didn't care. He looked like he had some grit of his own. Might be that's what happens when someone pisses on you frequently, wearing you down to nothing till you've got nothing left to lose.

'I'll say this though,' Stink went on regardless, 'if yer wanna give up on yerself, then that's one thing, but giving up on your son ... that's another.'

Shanklin was prickly hot. 'I ain't given up on anyone.'

Stink sniffed, rolled up his ragged shirt sleeves and pulled another sticky lump from his nose. 'Well, from where I'm sitting—'

'And where I'm sitting is five fucking feet from you,' said Shanklin, 'and if you've got any sense left in that shrivelled skull, you'll keep quiet.' His lips were stretched back over his teeth. Prowling demon dog or not, he was for ripping this old bastard's throat out himself if he didn't shut up.

Now it shouldn't take a particularly wise man to recognise a real threat from an empty one and, though Stink may have been shy of brain matter, he surely knew what he was getting into. This did not seem to stop him though, as he wiped a snotty finger on his leg and sat up straighter, as if preparing for something.

'Och, not to worry then,' he said, fixing his insane eyes on Shanklin. 'I'm sure you'll be a hero to your boy as he watches you twitching up there on the Triple Tree, taking fifteen minutes to die with a patch o' piss on yer kicks and shit running dow—'

Despite the leg irons Shanklin moved lightning fast, wrapping his hands around the old man's scrawny neck before either of them knew what was happening.

'Aaaakkkkkaakkkk!' Stink gasped as powerful fingers squeezed his throat, his own skeletal hands feebly gripping the highwayman's wrists, no match for his strength.

'I ... said ... shut ... up!' snarled Shanklin, pressing his thumbs into Stink's flaccid flesh. It wouldn't be long before the life was drained from him and those wild yellow eyes would dim like two distant torches on a carriage bound for someplace better than this. Not that the old fucker put up a fight, his withered fingers slackening, thin, frail arms flopping ...

Shanklin sprang backwards, sliding across the wet floorboards on his arse, letting the old man slump to one side, coughing and spluttering. He'd seen a tattoo engraved into the pale skin of one particular skinny forearm: two crossed pistols and a dagger. How had he not noticed it before? Because Stink had never rolled his sleeves up till now.

Heaving great gulps of air, the old man rubbed at his neck, chest rattling. Shanklin sat and watched, numb. Watched as he fought for a breath he probably didn't want. There was no other reason for pushing his luck as far as he did. It was a way out of here. The only way he knew. An escape of his own making, not some notion of funnels and sewers.

Stink was sick, all down his front and on the floor. Shanklin's back was pressed to the far wall, his head spinning. He knew that tattoo! He'd seen it before, when he was young, just a lad, in fact, out with one of the Butler Brothers, doing the rounds. Billy Butler, that's who he'd been with that day. They were meeting someone ... in a marketplace. It was hot and glorious. Money was exchanged with another man. A true gent, freshly shaven and looking like a proper rogue. As handsome a man as any that a young Samuel Shanklin had seen. 'Gentleman' James; that's who they'd met that day! He'd given Shanklin a wink and tussled his hair, standing as straight as a broomstick with his shirt sleeves rolled up and a fresh tattoo on show ...

'Christ,' Shanklin whispered.

The old man wiped vomit from the corner of his mouth,

panting hard. 'I already ... told yer, lad ... it's just ... the ... beard that ... gives yer ... that impression.' He was wheezing and coughing. 'But why'd ... yer ... stop, y'bastard? You should ... have turned me off!'

'You're James McCabe.'

Slowly, painfully straightening up, Stink peered out from his corner. 'McCabe died ... the day ... that I made ... my choice ... to *live*. And you just ... threw away the last ... chance you had ... to do something decent before ... joining our highwaymen friends ... in hell.'

Climbing to his feet, Shanklin crossed the cell over to the window, the black shape of St Sepulchre's leering before him. McCabe must've known the view well enough to guess what was going through Shanklin's mind.

'I've heard ... that bell ring,' McCabe said, 'more times than I care ... to count. But not fucking once ... has it chimed for me.' There were tears brimming in his eyes.

'It's not too late,' Shanklin said. 'Shout your name loud enough in here and we might even hang together.'

'Heh, wouldn't that ... be something, eh?' replied McCabe, wincing as he rubbed his throat. 'Two legends ... dying on the same day. Wouldn't ... the people roar?' He was quiet then, for a moment. 'No. I'll not give *them* the satisfaction ... of killing me.' His wet eyes stared hard up at Shanklin. 'But *you* ...'

It was a sorry sight: once the finest rogue of an era reduced to a *nothing*. A rat had more status in this place.

'You almost did a job of finishing me there, laddie,' McCabe went on, still massaging the angry red marks across his neck. 'D'yer think you can do it properly ... next time?'

Cells were for thinking in all right. It was all there ever was to do. Think and piss and eat, if you were lucky. And go mad, of course; slowly, before spreading your shit up the walls.

Shanklin was done thinking. 'Aye,' he said. 'I think I can.'

23

AN UNEXPECTED ARRIVAL

M other's cough had grown much worse. Her veiny, shaking hand took the glass of water from Jack and she gulped at it, dribbling some down her chin which was encrusted with sores. When she'd finished, she gave it back and the blood-speckled handkerchief returned to her mouth for another bout of coughing.

He watched her from where he was sitting, on a stool in her dark bedroom, a sliver of daylight peeping through the curtains, barely highlighting the pus-filled, bulbous sores which were now thick and numerous. He'd seen how frail she'd become these last few days; bed-ridden and barely able to walk without assistance which, lately, had been provided by him alone.

'Where's your sister?' Mother asked, once she'd regained her breath. 'Has she forgotten I lay here dying?'

'I think she's in town buying food for supper,' Jack replied.

'Pah, food! Just the thought of it makes me ill.'

'You should try and eat.'

Her hand swatted the warm air like he was a fly. 'And

why's that? To prolong my suffering? Your father was the same; always giving out orders.'

Jack couldn't imagine Mother taking orders from anyone, but he was in no mind to argue. All he wished for now was to see that she was as comfortable as she could be. Her tongue was often cruel but she still remained his mother, and he would do all he could to ease her pain.

'I wonder which shall claim me first,' she muttered, staring towards the window, 'starvation or consumption?'

A question still plagued Jack. 'Who ... who will look after us ... if you should...?'

She turned her ruined face towards his. '*Die,* boy, is that the word you seek?'

He remained silent.

'Your sister is fast becoming a young woman,' Mother said. 'She is skilled in the kitchen. And she has talents she doesn't yet fully understand.' Her next words were said almost with contempt. 'You'll be safe with her.'

No, Mother, Jack thought, *it's* you *who doesn't understand what she's capable of!*

'What if we were to stay with Aunt Ruth?' he said, and the moment that he did, he knew it was a mistake.

Mother's face became contorted with malice, making her appear more hideous than ever. 'Do not mention that woman's name in my company again, do you hear?' she said, pointing. 'I'd sooner your sister took lodgings with the devil than live with her!'

Standing, Jack picked up the near-empty glass from the bedside table. 'I'll fetch you some more water.'

Mother ignored him.

Pausing at the door, he turned. 'And what of me?'

'What *of* you?'

'Do I have talents? Have I ever made you proud?'

Silence. 'You make a half-decent cup of tea,' Mother said. 'Many can't.'

They looked at each other for just a very short moment, but it was long enough for Jack to notice something other than disappointment in her eyes. Something that might have passed for a mild appreciation of him.

'While you're standing, open the window, boy,' Mother ordered. 'It's stuffy in here. We need a storm to clear the air.'

Placing the glass back down on the table, Jack went over and pulled the curtains apart, flooding the room with light. He unhooked the window latch just as a carriage drawn by two horses came clattering to a halt in the lane below. A very pretty woman wearing a cream dress stepped out, paying the driver before turning to look up at Jack. She smiled when their eyes met and her sincerity was something he had not seen or felt for so long.

'I think that storm is coming,' he said.

'What's that?' asked Mother. 'Speak up. Who's that pulled up outside?'

Jack hurried past her bed, making for the door.

'Wait! Close the curtains, boy!'

But he didn't answer for he was too busy concentrating on not falling down the stairs he found he was so quickly descending, his knees shaking, the door-knocker banging. Jack raced along the hall, reaching for the door handle, slippery in his sweaty palm. He opened it, creaking ...

She was even prettier up close. Her smile even warmer.

'Hello,' Aunt Ruth said. 'I came as soon as I could.'

She was sitting very upright on the sofa, her hands placed neatly in her lap. She was a little younger than Mother, her auburn hair pinned up high in a bun at the back of her head, just a few loose strands hanging down, framing her soft face. Her eyes were of a brown colour. They were the kindest eyes Jack had ever seen.

'Is she in bed?' Aunt Ruth asked.

He nodded.

'Booooy!' came Mother's cry from upstairs.

Aunt Ruth did not move her gaze from his. 'Would you like me to wait until your sister comes home before I go up there?'

Jack swallowed. He wasn't sure what was for the best. All he knew was that he wasn't alone now. Not anymore.

She adjusted her position slightly, flattening the creases on her dress with her hand and she cleared her throat. 'Jack, now I know this must be difficult for you; meeting me, I mean. I'm sure it's the last thing you expected or even wanted, for that matter.'

No, it was all he'd wanted.

'But, I couldn't *not* come,' Aunt Ruth continued. 'When she—, when your mother did not acknowledge my letters, I became worried...'

Jack remembered how he'd interrupted Charlotte in the study, burning papers. The letter! He remained silent though, for now, not wishing to get his sister in trouble.

'I wrote to her, several times,' Aunt Ruth went on. 'When I heard that she was ill. I don't expect she would have mentioned it though, as I'm not exactly her favourite person in the whole world.' She tried another smile on for him but Jack saw through the pretence.

'The last letter I sent was two weeks ago. I did not wish to arrive unannounced but I couldn't postpone the visit any longer. I had to see if you and Charlotte were—'

Boom! Boom!

Mother's stick shook the floorboards above them, making Aunt Ruth flinch and gaze up at the ceiling.

'I should go and see her,' Jack said, getting to his feet. 'She'll be wondering who was at the door.'

Aunt Ruth also rose. 'Then I'll come with you.'

'What if she doesn't want to talk to you?'

Taking a deep breath, his aunt appeared even taller than when she'd arrived. 'I'm afraid she has no choice.'

On the landing, outside Mother's bedroom, they could hear her raspy breaths. Aunt Ruth's warm eyes willed him on though he saw the fear in them.

'Mother?' Jack said through the door. 'There's someone here to see you.'

'Ah, finally decided to answer me, have you?' came the response. 'Who is it? No more quack doctors I hope? I thought I made it perfectly clear I wanted no visitors!'

After a deep breath, Aunt Ruth entered the bedroom and Jack followed, safely tucked behind her but still able to witness Mother's face twist in horror when she saw who their visitor was. She squirmed under the sheets whilst attempting to sit up, coughing and fighting for breath as she pressed the blood-spattered handkerchief to her cracked lips.

'Please, be still, Catherine!' Aunt Ruth begged. 'Do not be alarmed!'

Jack lunged for the glass on the bedside table, offering up what was left of the water but Mother knocked it from his hand and it smashed upon the floor.

'What ... in the name of...?' she gasped.

Aunt Ruth's shock at seeing her sister so disfigured was plain. 'Catherine, please—'

'You have a nerve!'

'I received news that you were ill. I had to come!'

'News?' hissed Mother. 'From whom?'

'Someone in the village. It matters not. You're sick, Catherine. You need help!'

'I need *nothing* from *you!*'

Aunt Ruth's expression became fierce. 'Then what of the children? Who is caring for them?'

Mother coughed more, phlegm bubbling in her chest . 'They're quite … capable of caring … for themselves. '

'No! They are children!'

Jack's eyes flashed back and forth between the squabbling sisters. He felt dizzy. He just wanted all this to end. To go back to how things were, no matter how difficult.

'I know why you're here,' said Mother. 'You're here to lay claim to my estate.'

'How dare you?' Aunt Ruth replied.

'*Dare?* That's rich coming from the woman who stole my husband!'

Aunt Ruth closed her eyes, bowing her head as though trying to summon strength from somewhere deep inside. 'I stole *no-one*. He left you before he came to me.'

'And that makes it all right, does it, sister?' asked Mother. 'I am to be perfectly fine with that, am I?' She aimed a finger at her. 'Get out of my house! Out!'

'Catherine, please—'

'Out!' Mother screamed, so loudly that Jack nearly jumped from his skin. 'You charlatan! You deceiver!' But the cough cut short her shouting, giving time for Aunt Ruth to regroup. She squared her shoulders.

'If I am to leave,' she said, 'then I'll do so with the children. They cannot live like this!'

Mother's head was resting against the board of her bed, each scraping breath sounding as though it might be her last.

'Not content with stealing my husband, you've come to take my children too,' she said.

'I did not come for the children, Catherine! I came to help *you*.'

'I have all the help I need, thank you, *dear* sister. Charlotte is the rock beneath me.' She waved a lazy finger in Jack's direction. 'I can't speak for the boy.'

'*The boy* has a name!' said Aunt Ruth.

Jack's throat throbbed, but he would not cry here. He'd suffer no more shame in front of Mother.

Her scabbed face turned towards him. 'Was it you that summoned her here?'

'I came of my own accord,' said Aunt Ruth, before Jack had time to answer. 'I wrote several letters and I thought it likely you wouldn't respond but I had—'

'What letters?' asked Mother. 'I received none.'

Aunt Ruth blinked, her face turning pale as snow. 'Then you don't know?' she whispered.

'Know of what?'

Placing a hand softly on Jack's shoulder, Aunt Ruth turned to him, her eyes glistening wet. 'Your father ... there was an accident ... whilst he was at work. He fell. He died suddenly, Jack. I'm so sorry.'

Jack was frowning up at her. He didn't understand. He felt the room sway. His vision became blurry, just for a moment. His first reaction was to spring to his mother's side but it was as though there was a wall between them. And then his aunt pulled him close to her and held him, tightly.

'I'm so sorry,' she was saying as Jack forced his eyes towards Mother's. But there was no emotion in what was left of her face. No sympathy for him.

'Sorry, are you, Ruth?' Mother said. 'For what? For taking his father from him or the fact that he's now dead?'

Aunt Ruth turned to her. 'The hate you harbour saddens me deeply, Catherine. Even now, when this child needs you.'

Mother's eyes narrowed. 'I'm sorry too,' she said. 'Sorry that you're not dead along with him.'

Jack felt his aunt's body stiffen as she clutched him to her. A trembling hand reached down for his and with a gentle squeeze, she led him towards the door.

'That's it, sister!' Mother cried as they began walking back downstairs. 'Take him with you away from this doomed house! Take him as far as you can! But Charlotte will stay, of that you can be certain! Take the boy! Do as you damn well please! He isn't mine anyway!'

As they slowly descended the stairs hand-in-hand, Mother's coughing continued once more.

24

COURAGE

'W hat did she mean?' Jack asked. He was standing on a large, tired-looking rug in the middle of the sitting room. 'By saying I'm not hers?'

His aunt was sitting on the sofa, wringing her hands. She closed her eyes and turned her face to the ceiling, a tear running the length of her cheek. She sighed before opening them again. 'Your mother...' she said, 'your *real* mother, Jack ... she disappeared just after you were born. The ... *woman* ... upstairs in bed; she raised you as her own. Or so she had me believe!' She stared off towards the bay window and wiped at her cheeks with a shaking hand.

'I ... I don't understand,' Jack said. 'Mother is not really my mother?'

Aunt Ruth placed a hand to her mouth to cover her sobs. 'You are so young, child. So innocent. But I shall try my best to explain, because you are owed that at the very least.'

Slowly, Jack sat down on the large rug, crossing his legs and peering up at his aunt while she appeared to gather herself.

'A few years after Charlotte was born,' she said, finally,

'your father briefly lay with another woman. She was your mother, Jack. Your *real* mother. She was very young and — so he tells me — very beautiful, and he was ... overtaken by temptation.' Aunt Ruth appeared to choose her words carefully. 'She ... was a woman who ... who slept with men for money. He lay with her one drunken night and she fell pregnant.'

Jack was gawping up at her. 'My mother was ... a common tart?'

'She did what she had to do to survive, Jack. London can be a cruel place, child.'

'And where is she now?'

Aunt Ruth wiped away another tear. 'Your father never knew what became of her after you were born. She gave you to him before vanishing somewhere. She knew she could never care for you the way your father could. He loved you and he loved Charlotte more than anything, so he persuaded your ... my sister, that they should try and work things out between them, for the sake of their children and ... Catherine finally agreed. She agreed that it would be good for Charlotte to have a brother. Someone to play with.'

'So Charlotte isn't my real sister?' asked Jack.

'Yes, of course she is! You share the same father.'

'But, I was ... a *mistake?* That's what you're saying, isn't it?'

'No! No, it's not like that at all...'

'Then what am I? An *accident*, is all. An unhappy accident.'

'Please, Jack, let me finish,' Aunt Ruth begged. 'You should know everything.' She swallowed, steeling herself. 'However hard they tried, your father and my sister could not make it work between them.'

'Is that where you came in?' Jack asked, with a spiteful tone. 'Taking him from her?'

'Please, it was not like that,' Aunt Ruth replied. 'They married not for love but for convenience, as so many people do. Love is a rare thing, Jack. My sister treated him terribly, she always had. More so after what happened. She never forgave him for what he did; for lying with another woman and conceiving a child with her. She continued to punish him for it and, unable to suffer her violent episodes any longer, he turned to me for ... for support.'

'Support?' Jack said. 'Is that what's it's called?'

'I shan't make excuses for our actions, Jack. Your father only wished to be happy.'

Jack knew how that felt. Like a dog chasing its tail.

With her elbows resting on her knees, Aunt Ruth placed her head in her hands and began to weep once more. 'Your father's shame consumed him,' she said. 'He didn't love my sister but the love for his children was strong, both for you and Charlotte in equal measure. He told me so often...' She trailed off as Jack watched her struggling with the memories of the man she'd lost.

'So why didn't he take us with him?' he asked, his own anger like a hot stone in his stomach. 'Why did he let *her* keep us?'

Wiping away her tears, Aunt Ruth continued her story. 'As much as he wanted you and Charlotte close to him, he knew that he had to tread softly. Catherine's pain was such that he did not wish to heap more coals upon her. And so he let her have her way. He didn't want to split you both apart and my sister wanted to hurt him for what he did. So he backed down. They had many differences, but the one thing they agreed upon was that Charlotte should have a sibling for company as she grew older. It was the single wish they shared. So your father swallowed his pride and he came to live with me, just until he could work something out. He believed he was doing the right thing, Jack, you have to understand that. Please don't blame him.'

Jack's head swam. He couldn't hold back the tears any

longer and he too began to sob. His aunt sprang from the sofa and joined his side, kneeling on the floor, holding him close.

'What was her name?' he asked. 'My real mother?'

'I don't know,' replied Aunt Ruth. 'I never even asked your father.'

'And does Charlotte know any of this? Does she know that I'm only her half-brother?'

His aunt pressed her lips to the top of his head as she hugged him. 'It depends what has been said between her and my sister.'

Jack's world was now stranger than it had ever been. Pulled further apart in the blink of an eye. His tongue teased his loose back tooth, pressing on it in the hope that a bolt of pain might wake him from this nightmare.

Aunt Ruth seemed to notice. 'What's the matter?' she asked.

'It's my tooth. It's almost ready to come out. It's the last one to go.'

She smiled at him, her eyes still wet. 'Is that so? Well, let's hope that when it does, the Tooth Fairy will come and leave a penny for you under your pillow.'

Jack gazed up at her. 'Will she? She's never left money before, though the teeth have always been gone the following morning.'

'Have they now?' Aunt Ruth asked. 'Well, I'm certain that next time she visits there will be a surprise in store.' She composed herself. 'But our very first visitor must be a physician to attend to my sister.'

'I've tried that,' said Jack. 'She won't be seen by anyone.'

'Fine,' his aunt said with a sigh, as though understood immediately her own sister's stubbornness. 'Then you will just come and stay with me in the country. Charlotte too. If only for a while. Until things ... settle down.'

Jack was gazing at the opposite wall. 'Until Mother dies, you mean?'

Aunt Ruth cleared her throat and, firmly holding his shoulders, she turned him towards her. 'Do you think you can do something incredibly brave? Before we leave for my house, do you think that you can tell your mother how you feel?'

Jack shook his head. 'No,' he said. 'No, I can't ... I—'

'But you *must*,' said Aunt Ruth. 'If you don't then you'll always wish you had. You have to be strong, Jack. You have to find the courage to speak your mind. I'll be right here. You're not alone. Not anymore.'

But he had no idea how he would find the strength inside him to do so. Having spent so long under Mother's rule, the very thought made him feel sick.

His aunt stood up sharply and pressed her dress flat before conjuring up another smile. 'Come, we must get you packed for our adventure!' she said. 'When Charlotte arrives home we will tell her all about—'

They both turned their heads as the front door slammed. Every muscle in Jack's body tensed and he suddenly then wanted to become as still as he possibly could, as if pretending to be a statue might mean his sister wouldn't notice him.

She appeared at the sitting room doorway carrying two large cloth bags stuffed with vegetables. Her eyes were fixed on the strange woman in their midst.

'Hello, Charlotte. My name is Ruth. I am—'

Dropping the bags, Charlotte hurried upstairs. 'Moootheeerrr!'

Standing, Jack listened to the raised voices coming from the bedroom above. He cast a worried glance at his aunt, but her jaw was set hard and she was looking as though she would allow no more setbacks to her plan.

And then, after just a brief moment, his sister was hurtling back down the stairs.

'Get out!' Charlotte screamed from the doorway. 'Get out now!'

Aunt Ruth's palms were raised. 'Charlotte, please, listen to me—'

'No, I shan't! I want you out of this house!'

Jack stepped forward. 'Charlotte—'

'Shut up! Why did you let her in here?'

'She's here to help us!' said Jack. 'We need her and so does Mother!'

'We need no help from her or anyone. What did I tell you?' Her cheeks were scarlet with fury as she pointed to the front door. 'Leave, this instant!'

The banging on the ceiling began again. *Boom! Boom! Boom!* Mother's stick beating on the floorboards like a battle drum.

'Go see to her,' ordered Charlotte. 'Seeing as it was *you* who caused this mess.'

But Jack didn't move. He'd had enough. Enough of his sister. Enough of Mother. Enough of being told what to do. 'No, I won't,' he said.

'Excuse me?'

'I won't. I won't be told what to do anymore. I'm tired of it!'

His sister strode towards him as though she was about to deliver a firm slap to his face but Aunt Ruth stepped between them. 'Stay just where you are, young lady!'

'Oh, so you're his protector now, is that it?' Charlotte asked, half-smiling.

Boom! Boom! Boom!

'Your brother is upset,' said Aunt Ruth.

'And why is that, I wonder? It wouldn't have anything to

do with the fact that the woman who stole our father from us has arrived from out of nowhere?'

'I think it's more to do with his sister behaving like a lunatic!' Aunt Ruth said, edging forward, forcing Charlotte to retreat, a flash of fear in her young eyes. 'Now I suggest that you calm yourself before I give you something to scream about!'

Jack saw a different side to his aunt just then, in that single moment. And it scared him. But he seized his opportunity while his sister was still vulnerable.

'You knew that Father was dead, didn't you?' he said. 'You knew and you said nothing. You burned the letters that Aunt Ruth wrote. That's what I caught you doing the other day in the study.'

Charlotte glowered but her tongue was tied.

'And what else did you know?' Jack added. 'That we don't share the same mother? Thought you'd keep that secret too, did you?'

'I did it to protect you!' cried Charlotte.

'From *what*? The only thing I need protecting from is that *woman* upstairs! Even while she lays dying she's spiteful and cruel.'

'She isn't dying! Don't speak like that!'

Jack moved past his aunt and came as close to Charlotte as he dared to get. 'It's true! She's dying and there's nothing you can do!'

BOOM! BOOM! BOOM!

His sister was pale and breathing fast. Jack had cut the hand from the giant, now he was ready to take off the head, and he would do it with help from no one. He would climb the long winding staircase like it was his very own beanstalk. And he'd climb it alone.

Pushing past his sister, he made for the stairs, pausing only to look back at Aunt Ruth who offered him a reassuring nod. And with wobbly legs, Jack placed a foot on the first step and began his ascent.

The curtains in Mother's room were drawn shut once again. She was sitting upright in bed, her stick grasped in her veiny hand as though she might lean across and hit Jack with it, such was the hatred burning in her eyes. So he kept a safe distance, near the door.

'Where's your sister?' Mother asked. 'I wanted Charlotte but instead I get *you*.' She pointed the stick at him as though he were simply dog droppings to be flicked from her path. 'I should beat you, boy,' she hissed between shallow breaths. 'You *dare* to allow that woman into my house?'

'Aunt Ruth is—'

'Aunt Ruth is a *cunt*, do you hear me?' said Mother, wheezing, her long, black nails digging into the bed sheets as though she were tearing at flesh.

Jack swallowed. Mother's mouth could be foul but this shocked him beyond measure. The hate that boiled in her disturbed him to the core. He thought he was ready for this but he'd not seen such anger from her.

'She's here to lay claim to this house and all there is in it,' continued Mother. 'No good will come from her.'

'Why do you hate so much?' asked Jack. 'You cannot change the past. Accepting what is will help you to—'

'*Hate*, boy? What would you know of *hate?* You're a child; you have many years to learn how to hate. And you *will* learn.'

Jack already was learning. 'Why did you take me in as your own if you could not love me?' he asked.

Mother gazed at him through the gloom. 'Your sister wanted someone to play with,' she said.

'So, I was nothing more than a toy for Charlotte?'

'No,' answered Mother. 'Toys don't talk back. You'd be

wise to do the same from now on. I may be dying but I'll find the strength to teach you a final lesson.' She coughed and blood trickled from her mouth down onto her chin. 'Now leave me alone.'

But Jack moved not an inch. 'You think you know everything about Charlotte, don't you?' he whispered. 'Yet you know only the half of it.'

Wearily, Mother wiped away the blood with her hand. 'Meaning what, exactly?'

He took a step nearer to the bed. 'Meaning that your *gifted* daughter steals the souls from the dead,' he said. 'Meaning that I have witnessed her doing so because she has dragged me to Tyburn and she has shown me the true nature of her *talents*.'

Mother began coughing again, clutching at her chest.

'Yes,' Jack added, only wishing now to worsen her suffering. 'I've seen it, *Mother!* I've watched what she does and I have learned. I didn't believe it at first, thinking that she was close to madness and nothing more, but no! I've seen with my own eyes the spirits of those hanged upon the gallows tree enter her body at the precise moment of death and I've seen Charlotte fall and have a seizure, twitching like a rag doll as she is overcome by their soul. Controlled by the very darkest part of them! The part responsible for seeing them hanged in the first place!'

Mother dropped the stick, writhing in her bed, wracked by the violence of her coughing, a hand outstretched towards him, fingers clawing for his shirt.

But Jack stood his ground. 'And Charlotte is becoming just like those she has seen hanged,' he said. 'Bitter and foul and murderous. And in the same way that there is nothing anyone can do for you, now there is *nothing* anyone can do to save *her*.'

Mother was desperate for breath, grasping at the sweat-soaked bedsheets. But, even as his eyes brimmed with tears, Jack could not end his torment of her. 'Every day Charlotte becomes darker because of the souls she claims. Every day she crawls nearer to damnation. You think that her Gift keeps her close to God...' He leaned in towards Mother's face so that his mouth was close to her ear. '... but it is the devil with whom she dances.'

Snatching at his shirt, Mother pulled him to her. 'I'm sorry, Jack,' she whispered, 'that I was not rid of you sooner.'

He pulled himself free of her clutches and staggered backwards to the door, tears streaking his face.

'It hasn't taken me years to learn how to hate, *Catherine*,' he said, and turned to flee from the room, almost bumping into Charlotte, who was stood silently on the landing. Startled, Jack gasped, looking up into his sister's glazed eyes as she stared back, blankly, empty of emotion. He brushed past her and quickly went back downstairs.

25

FOUL DEEDS

'Tomorrow you hang,' said McCabe.

Meagre candlelight caught Shanklin's frown. 'Like I'm not aware of that.'

'Except that you won't.'

The old man was smiling. Again. Shanklin wondered why he seemed to have so much to grin about. 'So you say,' he replied. He was sitting in a corner inspecting the bruising on his thighs. They'd come up good; blue and purple and ochre. Painful, but it wouldn't slow him down none – not while he still had two legs attached. His ribs twinged, tender to the touch, yet the swelling around his eye had eased. Unlike Randall, he could now see out of both peepers and he'd be needing 'em for what was planned. His breeches were a little looser as he pulled them back up after inspecting the bruises. A week of nothing but gruel and water had worked wonders for his waistline.

Shanklin shuffled over to the window, chains rattling, staring out through the grate like he'd been doing for most of the day. Another evening drawing in, the sky turning near enough the same colour as his bruised legs. A warden strolled through the yard below and beyond the high walls of the gaol people were settling into their homes for the night, thin columns of smoke crawling upwards from their chimneys. There seemed nothing that unusual about it, except for what appeared to be several thicker, blacker pillars of smoke rising above a distant orange glow.

'What do you see, lad?' asked McCabe, sitting on the floor in his corner. 'Not sure I can bring myself to look out there for the last time.'

'I don't know,' Shanklin replied. 'But I think the city's on fire.'

The old man smiled. 'Heh, that so? Well, well.'

The noise of smashing glass drifted up on the breeze. Shanklin strained his ears. Shouting too; far off but a lot of it. 'Sounds like a riot out there,' he muttered.

'Then it's a special night indeed,' McCabe said.

Shanklin wasn't so sure about that. He looked across at the old man. 'You really want to go through with this?'

McCabe looked about as grave as anyone awaiting a death sentence might. Except this one wasn't being handed down by a judge. This was of his own choosing.

'I'm not getting out of here, lad,' he said. 'Not even if a mob stormed the gaol and tore this place apart. I've not the legs for it and I've not the heart left in me, y'understand?'

More shouting came from outside but Shanklin's eyes remained on the man who was once a legend among his peers.

'You've got a chance,' McCabe continued. 'A real one. I may not be in the Hold anymore, I've been hanging between life and death for eight long years. That's a wee while to be waiting for anything.'

In all his time of pushing people around Shanklin had learned plenty from looking them in the eye. Eliza Torne wasn't the only one with a talent for reading folk. He could tell those who meant their words and those who said them for effect. McCabe might have gone half-crazy during his incarceration but there was no madness displayed now.

'And what of this Black Dog?' asked Shanklin. 'Am I to die down there in Limbo before I even make it into the sewer?'

McCabe was quiet, like he was weighing something up, gauging if this man really had the bones for what was required. 'I won't lie,' he said, 'there's prettier places you could be. The dog may come or it may not. The darkness keeps a lot of secrets and when she gets a visitor she likes to tell 'em. She may show you them and you may choose to believe what you see or you may decide she's lying. But she spoke to me often. Told me things I didn't wanna hear. Pushed me into realms I have no names for.' He tapped a finger to his temple. 'Walls are just walls. The worst dungeon we can be in is *here*. Don't stay in there longer than you have to, lad.'

Shanklin's heart was beating at a merry pace. 'But, if you've seen it,' he asked. 'This 'dog'. How is it you're still alive?'

The old man appeared as though he'd been pondering on this himself for a long time. 'There's two possibilities for that. One: I wasn't bleeding when it came and therefore it wasn't hungry. And two: it might be that it's no cannibal and it prefers human flesh to that of its own kind.' He grinned.

But Shanklin wasn't. 'There's no other way?'

'I'm not Jack bloody Sheppard, but if there is, I don't see it now and I've never seen it all my time here.'

'I meant a way that doesn't involve me killing you.'

McCabe sighed. 'Like I said, lad, I've seen enough for one lifetime. This is an exit for both of us. And besides, when you're gone who knows what other mad bastard they'll stick with me, eh?' He winked. 'Just make sure you have that damn saw with you when they take you outta here. Without that, you can forget it all.'

Shanklin looked back out across the jagged, black buildings. Was he really considering this? Shit, he hated the dark and he hated small spaces, so of course it made perfect sense to be thrown in one.

'When?' he asked.

'It's the eve of your execution, laddie. Your last night upon this wicked earth if they have their way. Morton will bring you a final meal later, if you're lucky.' McCabe puffed out his cheeks. 'No time like the fucking present, eh? That's what my mother used to say. God, she did swear like a cunt.'

Beyond the sloping roofs and chimneys, that faint orange glow was growing, and the noisy disturbance right along with it. More glass breaking. Angry voices on the wind.

'What *is* that?' Shanklin asked, looking out.

'That's the people finally speaking, lad,' the old man said. 'And I can sleep easy now knowing that they did.'

McCabe was sitting in the middle of the cell with Shanklin close behind him, awkwardly angled – the fetters on his ankles didn't allow for the most comfortable of positions when it came to strangling a man to death. But then Shanklin didn't suppose that his gaolers took that into account when they'd clamped them on him. The old man didn't smell any better the nearer you got either and now the both of them were looking to get this over and done with.

'Remember,' McCabe said over his shoulder, a quiver in his voice, 'whatever happens, whatever I do to fight you off, don't stop, y'hear me? Not this time. Not for nothing.'

From where he'd placed himself, Shanklin wouldn't be able to see the life leave those mad eyes and he was glad of that. 'I may be the most dishonest man I've ever known,' he said, 'but you've got my word.'

McCabe smiled, just a glimmer in the poor light of the moon and the candle. He turned his face back towards the window he'd spent so many years staring out of. 'And they say there's no honour among thieves, eh? Seems like you're doing me the biggest honour any bastard ever has.'

'And I'll take you on *your* word for that,' said Shanklin.

'I'll be sleeping easier tonight even if you're not,' McCabe said, still gazing ahead of him and he placed a withered hand on Shanklin's arm. 'Good luck, son, and I'll see you in hell. I hear the beer's a wee bit warm but if ma mother's down there waiting for me, then she cooks a fine breakfast.' He drew in a long, deep, rattling breath. 'Now, c'mon, yer cunt, let's get this done wit'.'

Carefully, Shanklin wound the long chain that hung between his manacles around the old man's narrow neck. He felt McCabe's body stiffen and his breathing speed up. Taking one last gulp of air, he said, 'Och, you've a woman's touch, lad! Don't fucking tease me with it, just get—'

Shanklin pulled hard on the chain, teeth clenched as the iron snake tightened its hold. McCabe's fingers grasped and clawed and scraped at the links digging into his skin, his frail body writhing and squirming, long legs kicking, heels bouncing on the floorboards. Even after willingly subjecting himself to this manner of death, it seemed that his body had other ideas, fighting for its survival. It felt like an age to Shanklin, stinging sweat in his eyes, but it was more a matter of seconds until the old man was unconscious and his arms finally dropped limp to his sides. Yet Shanklin knew this wasn't the end of him and he kept on pulling, harder, tighter, till the shackles were grinding into his own wrists. McCabe finally jolted for the last time, one foot twitching, till at last it stopped. Only then did Shanklin allow the chain to slacken off and a dead James McCabe sloped into his killer's embrace.

'Goodnight, old man,' Shanklin whispered, softly brushing

a clump of matted, grey hair from his face. 'Have that ale waiting for me, will ya?'

He lay the body down on the floor and made sure that his little saw was still safely hidden inside his coat alongside Eliza Torne's necklace. Then he took himself over to a corner, staring at the corpse while outside London was descending into chaos.

And Shanklin waited.

The cell door squealed open, unleashing a calamity of excitement from the corridors. News of whatever was happening in the outside world was spreading.

'Managed to get you fixed up a bit of beef on your last night with us, Samuel,' said Morton as he hooked the set of keys back on his belt. 'Gripe's bringing it along—'

The turnkey froze, almost as stiff as the corpse lying on the floor in front of him, its face about as blue as anyone might be if they'd had the life squeezed from their lungs.

'Oh my. What in His Good Name has happened here?'

Shanklin was wedged in a corner, knees to his chest and suddenly feeling like a naughty schoolboy. 'Couldn't stand the smell any longer,' he said. 'Shit happens, excuse the pun.'

Morton was tutting, eyelids narrow, a hand moving to his cudgel. 'Oh deary me, Samuel. Deary, deary me. Gripe shan't be happy. Damaged his little toy, you have. Beyond repair, I'd say.'

Shanklin's gaze was fixed on the turnkey, waiting for him to pull that stick from his belt. 'Aye, I'd say that too.'

Morton moved towards the body of McCabe, nudging it hard in the ribs with one big boot. 'Well, well, what a mess. It'll be Limbo for you, Samuel. A shame that. And I was starting to feel sorry for ya. Things just got a lot worse for you, they did. A lot worse.'

That so?

'Griiiipe!' Morton didn't turn, just kept on looking down at the deceased prisoner. 'You might wanna get in 'ere! Sharp!'

Puffing, the steward limped into the cell, lank hair swaying over the plate in his hands, a small, black lump of beef on it. 'Sorry Mr Morton, I was—'

A pause. 'Oh yes, Mr Gripe. Seems we've got a problem, doesn't it?'

Gripe looked across at Shanklin who was looking at the beef. He may have just killed a man he once admired and respected but that didn't stop his stomach from grumbling.

'Someone care to tell me what's going on out there?' he asked by way of breaking the ice that had formed in the cell.

'Oh, I wouldn't worry about *out there*,' Gripe answered, still gazing at the body of his once prized possession. 'It's what's happened *in 'ere* that is of concern to us right now.' He let the lump of beef slide from the plate onto the filthy floor and pressed it underfoot. 'Let's get our friend down to Limbo shall we, Mr Morton?'

'Aye, let's,' puffed the turnkey when he'd finished scratching his head as if working out a complicated puzzle. Then he lumbered over towards Shanklin, seizing him by the collar of his coat.

Foul didn't do the dungeon justice, but being as a sewer ran somewhere below, Shanklin thought he might've been prepared for a stench such as this. He wasn't. He was gagging as Morton and another warden bundled him into the windowless, black room, a potent blend of shit, piss, damp and vomit in his nostrils and reaching down into his throat.

But something else lingered here too; subtle, yet unmistakable.

Blood.

The light from Morton's lantern and a stubby little candle that the steward was holding pushed and pulled their shadows across the mouldy brick walls. Walls with iron staples bolted in them. And, to his dismay, Shanklin realised that he'd swapped a shit-smeared confinement for something worse.

'Aye,' said the turnkey as he watched his inmate take in the new surroundings. 'Some have dashed their heads against these walls in sheer desperation. Smashed 'em till they broke open like eggs, they did. Rather that than face another long night here alone. Night, day, it's all the same down here, Samuel. After a time I imagine you just give up. But not you, eh? I reckon you'll do all right in here till the morning. I reckon you're made of firmer stuff.'

Shanklin's line of sight settled on the stone seat McCabe had told him of before he was forced to the floor, his manacles secured to an iron ring which prevented him from standing. Once the lock was fixed the turnkeys made their way to the door, leaving Gripe holding the candle in one hand and covering his mouth and nose in the crook of his arm.

'Sweet dreams, Mr Shanklin,' said the steward and drew a breath to blow out the flame.

'Wait! Let me buy what's left of that, will ya? Don't leave me here in the pitch black.'

Gripe laughed. 'Scared of the dark, are ya? A tough rogue like you?' But he seemed to consider the offer all the same. After all, every good deed in this place had its price. Placing the candle on the floor several feet away, the steward limped over, plunging a hand into Shanklin's coat pocket and helping himself to his purse. He removed what was left of his money and discarded the empty pouch. 'Don't think you'll be needing any more chink now, Mr Shanklin,' he said. 'Not where you're going tomorrow.'

'Hurry up, Gripe,' ordered Morton and the hunchback rejoined his waiting colleagues in the passage, though he had some parting words before he left:

'*Absence is to love what wind is to fire*, Mr Shanklin,' he said, '*it extinguishes the small, yet inflames the great*. Roger de Rabutin, that is.' He nodded towards the little flame. 'Careful that *your* little fire doesn't go out, eh? It might be you've got good reason to fear the dark down here.'

The steward yanked the door closed, a rush of breeze causing the tiny flame to teeter on the brink of extinction. Yet, much to Shanklin's relief, it remained alive, just, and he watched it for a moment, burning in the stillness of the stifling air as he listened to the key being turned in the lock and bolts promptly slammed into place.

When all was quiet he wasted no time. Retrieving the chive from inside his coat's lining, Shanklin began to saw at the iron ring which had him pinned. He worked hard and fast, filing until he was forced to stop when his hands cramped, shaking them as best he could given the manacles he wore, pins and needles tingling. The sweat leaked from his brow and he wished he could lose the damn coat he'd had on since the moment he arrived, even just for a minute. As he worked the serrated blade, he thought of the necklace still hidden upon him, and of the woman it belonged to, her glinting emerald eyes in his mind as though she was watching him right now. Watching and willing him to fail. He glanced across at the faltering candle, unsure of quite how many hours of precious light he had but knowing it wouldn't be enough. And he cursed the day he ever met Bob Creech.

≈

Hacking at the iron ring was slow progress. A panic began to creep in, a voice whispering in his ear: *You'll never do this, Sam.* Shanklin tried to breathe and remain focused but, although the smell in here was thick, the air itself felt thin.

Keep it together, you fool. Don't lose your mind yet. But the task before him appeared impossible, the little file not up to the job of freeing him from the floor. *Couldn't Sarah have brought me a bigger fucking chive?*

Sarah. Harry. God, it was the reason he was in this forsaken hole, so that he could be out *there*, with *them*.

You'll go mad in here, Samuel Shanklin. Just like McCabe did. The ground is stone; you could smash your skull to pieces before that happens.

His arm burned from working the saw so fast. His fingers ached, frozen rigid with pain. But still he hacked at the staple, the rhythmic squeak of metal drowning out the voice in his ears. Yet the feeling of panic was ever present, creeping up his spine and clawing at his insides. He stopped sawing for a moment, wriggling his aching fingers again, closing his eyes while that little orange dot of flame danced behind them. Christ, it was hot. He felt like a volcano about to erupt.

'Aaaaaggghhhh!' Shanklin's screams bounced from the walls like the skulls which had done so before. He was alone now for the first time since he'd arrived. Just him and the encroaching darkness, waiting for its chance to wrap him in its cold embrace. In that moment he'd have given his legs to be back in the cell with the old man. He never thought he'd feel like that, but then he never thought he'd find himself choose *this*. His heart was hammering harder than he thought was possible. Faces flashed before him: Eliza. Randall. Creech. Shit, he'd have paid to have any one of 'em down here with him, just for the company.

Shanklin glanced across at the weak candle; such a feeble thing yet so strong in this soon-to-be-black space. His numb hand again gripped the pocket-sized saw and he filed until the blade grew hot and again he was forced to stop.

Breathe.

Stop. Start. Stop. Start. It was futile. What the hell was he thinking getting himself thrown in here? He never should have listened to that mad—

A clanging handbell sounded from a corridor somewhere outside, and a booming voice accompanied it:

'All you that are in the condemned hold do lie,
    Prepare you for tomorrow you shall die,
    Watch all and pray the hour is drawing near
    That you before the Almighty must appear.
    Examine well yourselves, in time repent
    That you may not to eternal flames be sent.
    And when St Sepulchre's bell tomorrow tolls,
    The Lord have mercy on your souls!'

The Bellman of St Sepulchre. Shanklin listened to the bell chime twelve times. *Midnight.* The melting candle dripped wax on the stone floor, a small puddle forming. He didn't have long till the light was gone and then ... ? But he wasn't about to wait to find out.

'You can ring that fucking bell all you want,' he said, 'but it ain't ringing for me. Not this time.'

Mustering what will he had left, Shanklin once more began sawing at the iron staple.

DEVILS AND DEMONS

A unt Ruth's arms were wrapped about herself as she paced in circles near the study's tall French doors. The mantel-clock ticked and the log fire snapped. Jack was on a sofa with his knees to his chest, hugging his shins, his chin tucked low as he desperately tried not to think about the awful situation he'd created. His tongue pushed at his loose tooth. He and Charlotte had never fought like that before, and the feeling of guilt at the way in which he'd spoken to Mother now clawed at his stomach.

'Your sister has been up there for some time,' said Aunt Ruth, finally standing still. 'I should go and check that she's—'

From beyond the hallway came the creak of stairs and both Jack and his aunt turned their attention towards the open door. Charlotte appeared and the first thing that Jack noticed was that her eyes were as though she'd just woken. Entering the room, she became still, as if in a trance.

Aunt Ruth moved towards her. 'Dear child, is everythi—'

A stream of vomit leapt from Charlotte's throat onto Aunt Ruth's dress. Jack's heart quickened and he jumped from the sofa, unsure of what to do but thinking he should act. He watched as his flustered aunt gasped, staring at the dripping patch of sick she now wore down her front.

Charlotte wiped her mouth and silently glided past them both before easing herself into Mother's rocking chair, her empty stare fixed straight ahead. 'She's dead,' she mumbled, the chair creaking as it began to rock.

Aunt Ruth gazed, her mouth and her eyes wide. Jack stared at Charlotte too, a feeling of dread creeping up his spine. A feeling that Mother might still be in the room with them.

'It's far too late to fetch for the coroner now,' Aunt Ruth said, as she looked out of the tall French windows, her reflection staring back from the deep blackness beyond. She turned to the children, Jack once again huddled on the sofa. He was peering up at her. The glow of the fire softened her beauty still further. She was strong. She'd know what to do.

'I'll stay here tonight, of course,' said Aunt Ruth. 'We will notify the authorities first thing in the morning.' She moved gracefully to the fire and crouched in front of it. The heat from the flames had almost completely dried out the vomit on her dress, though a dark stain remained. Jack noticed how, from her seat in Mother's rocking chair, Charlotte's eyes followed their aunt who prodded at the logs with a poker, sending a spray of embers floating up the chimney.

'It's a good job I arrived when I did,' Aunt Ruth said. 'Lord knows what you children would have done.'

'Yes, wasn't it just so very timely?' said Charlotte, now dressed in her white nightgown.

Aunt Ruth ignored the sharp remark. 'You children must pack your things in the morning,' she said, with a tone of authority. 'Once we have made arrangements for your ... my sister's funeral, you will come by coach with me and—'

'I'll do no such thing!' said Charlotte. 'And neither will he.'

Jack's fingers dug into his legs. She was pointing at him like he was a dog. *He* had a name! Even dogs had names. She'd emerged from her strange trance but seemed unchanged on the surface of it, still full of rage and throwing insults.

'But I *want* to go with Aunt Ruth!' Jack said.

'You'll go where I tell you and that's the end of it!' Charlotte snapped.

'No! You can't keep telling me what to do! You're not my mother!'

His sister's eyes blazed. 'That's right, *boy*, I am not,' she said, rising from the rocking chair and moving slowly towards him. Her voice was deep and it crackled as Mother's once had. 'But if I was, oh what lessons you would learn.'

'Enough!' said Aunt Ruth, standing up. 'I'll have no more of this from you!' She was aiming the poker at Charlotte, who in turn was smiling in defiance.

'Or *what?* You'll stab me?'

'Don't be ridiculous, child!'

'They hang you for less, you know,' Charlotte said. 'By your neck while you squirm and choke and—'

'No more!' screamed Jack, jumping from the sofa. 'Stop it, you vicious, spiteful, horrible bitch!'

'Jack!' cried Aunt Ruth.

But Charlotte's smile was wider still. 'That's it, brother; show me that you do indeed have a spine. Show me what you *really* are. What we *all* are beneath the thin veneer of respectability. Show us what is hidden under our masks of polite conversation and the lies that we tell ourselves and each other every day.'

'And what lies are they?' Aunt Ruth asked. 'What exactly

would you say we are, child? What would you have us believe?'

The logs in the fire spat and hissed and Charlotte cast a glare at them both. 'Devils,' she said. 'Demons: scratching at our insides, trying to claw their way out. There is a darkness in every last one of us.' She pointed at Jack. 'Even *you*, the innocent little boy in whose mouth butter would not melt.'

Aunt Ruth dropped the poker to the floor with a thud and came stalking forward, gripping Charlotte by the arm and hauling her towards the stairs. 'I'll have no more of this! Upstairs to your room!'

'Get off me!' Jack's sister screamed, writhing. 'Let go!' She struggled and twisted and squirmed, but her aunt was too strong. Jack followed them into the hallway, narrowly avoiding Charlotte's flailing kicks and then, quite suddenly, her eyes rolled into the back of her head and she became a dead weight.

'Help me, Jack!' said Aunt Ruth, almost dropping her. Charlotte's body had turned as rigid as a bench, her arms locked at her sides while her head violently shook, white foam leaking from the corners of her mouth. Running back into the sitting room, Jack quickly returned with a cushion which his aunt propped under Charlotte's head as it repeatedly banged against the floor.

'Ggguuurrgggguuuurrr...' The terrible noise that his sister made forced Jack to cover his ears while he looked on, horrified. After just several seconds the seizure ended as abruptly as it had begun and Charlotte quickly fell into into a deep sleep.

Exhausted, Aunt Ruth leaned back against the hallway wall, sliding down until she was seated.

'Good God,' she muttered, sweat glistening on her forehead.

Jack watched Charlotte's eyelids flicker, as though she were dreaming, and he knew this night was not over.

Aunt Ruth had managed to carry Charlotte, still sleeping, upstairs to her bed and while she recovered from the ordeal, Jack took the opportunity to look in on Mother one final time. Something told him that he needed to see her body in its lifeless form. He had to know for himself that there was nothing left inside her. No trace of the energy that had once pumped what little heart she'd had. That she was now simply an empty corpse. A shell that no longer housed a spirit. With a candlestick in his hand he waited at Mother's bedside, gazing down at her stricken face, a cluster of lumps and sores. Jack had the strange sensation that she might open her eyes at any second. He found it hard to imagine that she was truly gone. That her very essence had vanished forever. That all the hate she had harboured and what precious little love she had in her − everything that made her who she was − had simply disappeared in the one moment that it took for her body to finally fail. Was she now in heaven, seated with the angels? He suspected that she was someplace else.

When Jack had told Mother of her daughter's *soul-stealing* powers, he'd said it to hurt her because he knew she would believe it was so, even if he did not. Yet now, standing here and having experienced first-hand another of Charlotte's convulsions, he wasn't so sure of anything. Perhaps there was a slim chance that his sister *could* see halos. And that she could really tell if a person was good or bad just by looking at them. And that, if this was the case, then maybe … maybe she did possess an arcane power. He shuddered. Though what surprised him the most was how little he felt now that the woman who had raised him from birth was dead. Someone he had always believed was his mother, without question. A woman he'd loved so unconditionally, despite her lack of it for him. He was free now. Free of her spite and her sharp tongue.

Staring down as the candle flame wavered and cast strange shadows, he was transfixed by Mother's pained expression; her mouth halfway open as though there was a word frozen on her lips. And he wondered what that final word may have been. Only Charlotte could know. Only she was present at the time. At Mother's very bedside when—

The candle blew itself out and the room was swamped with darkness.

'Jack?'

He spun and saw the black shape of Aunt Ruth standing in the doorway. It struck him just how much her form resembled Mother.

'Are you all right, child?' she asked.

'No,' Jack replied, turning his face back to the corpse. 'No, I'm not.'

27

A DOG OF A DAY

I t might have been an hour or it might have been three, but Shanklin had been filing at the iron staple in the ground till his fingers bled, when, almost unexpectedly, it came apart and a feeling like no other soared through him. He closed his eyes, soaking up the surging sensation of relief. He might've sobbed if there'd not been more work needed doing.

His knees were rigid from being on the ground for so long, and, groaning, Shanklin climbed to his feet. The fetters' chain scraped along the floor as he painfully shuffled over to the stubby candle, a puddle of solidified wax having formed around it. Carefully picking it up he took it over to the stone bench in a corner of the dungeon and placed it close by, though not close enough that he might by accident extinguish it. The bloody tips of his fingers groped for a loose slab at the front of the seat and he cursed the name of James McCabe when it did not come away quite so easily as expected.

'Come on, you bastard,' Shanklin muttered as his hands tried to persuade the stone to move. Snatching up the chive again he dug the blade's tip into the cracks around the slab, prising and picking, praying it would pop out and he'd be greeted by a rush of cool air.

'Fuck you, McCabe,' he snarled as he manoeuvred the tool this way then that, losing all faith that the damn thing was ever loosened in the first place. 'You lying son of a whore. You did this to free your own soul, not mine.' How could he have trusted the word of a half-crazed, old thief? How could he have been so stupid as to think that a man like Mc—

With a satisfying crunch, the stone shifted. Then it wobbled as Shanklin pushed and pulled and now he could've kissed the dead fucker, excitement pulsing through his veins as his ruined fingers found more purchase on the edges and, with another hard tug, it came free. And with it came an overpowering stench which sent him reeling backwards. Wretching, Shanklin turned his face from the terrible smell spiralling up towards him, yet he felt a racing joy the likes of which only a dog might feel running through a muddy field. Sheer, unadulterated joy. Which very quickly turned to despair when he discovered that the hole was blocked by three thick, iron bars.

'No,' whispered Shanklin.

He scrambled for the candle, shining its meagre light into the void, his nose and mouth tucked into his arm as the unholy scent of sewage swarmed around him.

'No.' He pulled at one of the bars as if doing so might somehow magically remove it. In the blackness beyond was what appeared to be the rim of a stone funnel several feet below. A very narrow looking funnel.

'No, no, no!'

Even if there was enough bite left in his blade to saw through the bars and gain access, the funnel was barely wide enough for someone of his build, let alone wearing a coat and manacles.

'Shit, fucking, shit, shit!'

He'd always known that escaping this place was never going to be a summer's stroll in a park, but a visit from Lady Luck wouldn't have hurt right now. Yet his only visitor was a gut-wrenching terror telling him that, even if he did manage to somehow get inside that dark funnel, he would become stuck fast with no way to turn back, suspended above a sewer until the intoxicating fumes overwhelmed him and he suffocated, slower even than if he was to choke by the noose.

'Shit. Jesus, why? Why?'

Placing the candle back down on the floor, Shanklin rolled onto his haunches. His fear was swapped now for a swelling rage, building so fierce and so fast he was forced to bite down on the arm of his thick coat so that it might absorb his scream.

Breathe. Breathe.

When he'd calmed a little, he returned his eyes to the bars blocking his only way out. Then to the blunted pocket-sized saw in his hand. Then to the meek candle flame. He didn't have much light left but he had even less strength for this. He needed some time to collect his thoughts. To gather his wits. To muster an ounce of courage to get done what needed doing. McCabe's words rang in his ears: *Sometimes you've gotta go down to go up*. Well, down was the only option he had and Shanklin ran his bloodied fingers across the growth of beard on his jaw, leaving smears on his cheeks. He wondered if he'd ever get to see his own miserable face again in a mirror. Or that of Harry or Sarah. He wondered if he'd get to see them smile. Or laugh. Or cry.

Not idly sitting here he wouldn't.

Rolling his shoulders and twisting his neck, Shanklin wiggled what was left of his fingers, trying to get some life back in 'em before he began examining the stone beneath the bars and thinking that he might be able to remove that too, creating a space big enough to squeeze through. With the chive he once again started working at the cracks, the blade scraping and scratching and the sweat leaking from his pores, dripping into his eyes, tickling his nose and soaking his back, shirt clinging to him under his great coat. His arm burned with the effort and his mind burned with thoughts of his wife and son. Every so often, his eyes would flicker across to that dim candle, the soft, amber glow slowly fading and the darkness creeping in closer from all sides. His fingers throbbed, his muscles ached but on he went, digging and chipping until the stone was gradually loosened.

Taking a firm hold of its edges, Shanklin was about to pull it free when he heard the squeak of a bolt on the dungeon door. For a second he was motionless, and then he was moving, faster than ever, wedging that first slab back into place before snatching up the saw and scrambling over to the spot in which he'd been shackled. A key clattered in the lock. The door whined open. Gripe, alone it would seem, the lit candlestick in his hand making him appear even more ghoulish than he already was.

'Good evening, Mr Shanklin,' he said. 'Mr Morton requested that I pay you a visit to make sure you don't need anything.' Closing the door behind him, the steward limped a little further into the dungeon, raising the flame higher and casting his eyes over the prisoner. 'Quite comfortable down here, are we?'

Shanklin's gaze hovered on the large set of keys Gripe was holding. The ones that would unlock his fetters. 'My pillow could do with fluffing but I can't complain,' he replied, being sure to keep his bloodied hands hidden from view.

The steward smiled, scratching at a sore on his neck. 'Good, good,' he said as he wandered around the cell, keeping a safe distance from his murderous inmate. There seemed to be something on his mind and Shanklin decided to keep him talking.

'What's going on out there?' he asked. 'I heard rioting earlier.'

Gripe's pacing came to an abrupt stop. 'Going on? What's *going on* is that London has once again lost its capacity for understanding that we need a system, Mr Shanklin. Without a system nothing works. Nothing gets done. Know your place! Understand where you belong in the great scheme of things and all things shall be well. Do what is required of you and no more. We are all cogs, Mr Shanklin. Component parts that must work together for the greater good of our kind.' He wiped at his nose.

'I'm glad I asked,' said Shanklin.

'But,' continued Gripe, 'to answer your question more succinctly; a large mob have taken it upon themselves to smash and destroy everything in their path. To pillage and plunder. And *why*, we may ask? Why? Who knows, eh? Perhaps because they're unhappy with the current system that we are so fortunate to have. Perhaps 'cause they think they deserve something better. But then maybe they should try working here, eh? Maybe that'd give 'em something to riot about. Maybe it's the Catholics. Maybe it's the Protestants.' He bent forward and that hunch resembled more a hill upon his back. 'And maybe it's none of your concern what is going on *out there*, Mr Shanklin. Maybe it does not affect you one bit. For very soon you *will* be out *there;* hanging by your neck until you are turned off from this world and *their* troubles shall no longer be yours.'

The steward straightened up again, as best a man with a crooked spine could. Shanklin stared up at him. 'Well thank you for the speech,' he said. 'It seems that the wisdom leaks from the walls round here.'

Bravely, Gripe limped a little closer, stopping when he was

just a foot or so away from his prisoner. 'You're most welcome,' he said, then he carefully placed the candlestick on the floor and began pulling down his breeches.

'What you doing?' asked Shanklin as the steward pulled out his cock.

'A piss,' replied Gripe, 'for a piss is what I am in need of. Y'see, you took my toy away from me and in return—'

The chive hidden up Shanklin's coat sleeve had now slipped into his palm but Gripe's attention was suddenly turned towards the candle he'd left here earlier. The same candle that had miraculously moved nearer to the stone bench.

'How did ... ?' was all that the steward uttered before the blade was in his groin. In, out, in, out, Shanklin jabbed the little saw and, with a scream, the steward fell to the ground, knocking over his candlestick and extinguishing the flame. His horrified eyes quickly assessed the damage to his lower regions and his hand which had taken some of the impact too. Then Shanklin was on him, his own hand clamped to Gripe's scabbed mouth and the bloodied little blade pressed to his neck.

'Scream and the next one's in your throat,' he hissed. 'Now get me the key to these shackles!'

The steward groaned and whimpered, fumbling for the correct key with the hand that wasn't now mangled. When it was made perfectly clear which one would set him free, Shanklin began unlocking his manacles.

'You ... you'll die for this,' Gripe whined.

'Die I will,' replied Shanklin, 'but not for this. Not for *you*.' The shackles dropped away, soon followed by the fetters. He rubbed at his wrists, briefly bathing in the victorious moment before considering what to do: finish this bastard now or let him bleed? By the state of him he was as good as done anyway. 'Which key fits the door?' Shanklin asked, tossing the set to the steward.

'What?'

'You heard me! The key to the damn door!'

Gripe selected the right one and held it out. Shanklin snatched it, locking the cell door from the inside.

'Now, I suggest you keep your mouth shut till I'm long gone,' he ordered.

The steward nodded as he lay there bleeding.

Shanklin made for the seat, kneeling down and easily dislodging the stone. The waning candle gave him barely enough light to peek into the space. He could just see the narrow funnel and, with a deep breath, he placed both legs in. The failing light flickered.

'Be seeing ya then,' he said and finally the little flame went out, plunging the cell into a thick, oppressive blackness. Blindly, Shanklin shuffled further into the gap, his hands gripping the sides for support. It was then that there came a noise from within the dungeon. A sound the likes of which he hadn't heard before, and he'd heard some strange ones during his stay. He froze, hovering on the brink of empty space with only the thumping of his heart and the snivelling of a gaol steward to disturb the silence.

'What the hell was that?' Gripe whimpered from the dark. 'Was it you?'

Wedged to his waist in that small gap, Shanklin didn't wish to wait around and find out, but he felt compelled, straining his ears for the slightest clue. It had been a ... *primal* sound. A grunt, like that of an animal. Like that of a dog.

It only comes when it's pitch. McCabe's prophetic rambling raked at his mind.

And there it was again: a deep growl. Sniffing too, as if searching for a scent. As though seeking blood.

Shanklin's scalp prickled. Two glowing, red dots like hot coals appeared in the blackness.

'What the ...?' Gripe began to scream. 'Help me! Help me!'

The creature's musky smell dominated the darkness, an ungodly stench that put all other smells in this hole to shame. It was the stench of death, permeating every inch of the dungeon. The demonic presence edged towards the spot where Gripe lay, blade-like teeth bared, lit from the glow of its eyes.

'Aaaaggghhhh!'

The monster pounced upon the steward, biting and gnashing and scraping at his flesh with its great claws. At least that's how it sounded to Shanklin, almost grateful for the darkness in that moment. Thankful that he couldn't see the horror. He thought he'd known fear. He'd faced it all his life; hiding from his drunk father. Running from the authorities. Scrapping on the cobbles for some extra money. Watching his children slowly die of consumption. Fear was waiting around every corner. Fear was life. But now ... terror; unimaginable and all-consuming. And it consumed Gripe right in front of him.

Shanklin squeezed further into the gap, hearing bones crack and skin rip and a gurgling, juddering moan coming from the steward as the creature savaged him. Struggling to fit through the hole Shanklin knew that, at any moment, the Black Dog would come for *him* and, with his arms now high above his head, he tried to make himself as narrow as possible, wriggling and squirming his way further into the void when, quite suddenly, those hot coals that were its eyes flashed in his direction. Panicking, he gave a final, desperate thrust and he was free, falling, bouncing, sliding until he reached the funnel and again became stuck. Shanklin looked up to see those demonic eyes gazing down, Gripe's blood dripping from the dog's teeth onto his face. He was encased, held fast in what might now become his tomb, the fumes of the sewer belching up towards him. It wouldn't be long before the steward was discovered, his screams having surely drawn attention. So Shanklin pushed and fought with all his strength to fit down through the funnel, the stench from below growing stronger. Gradually, he managed to edge further in, one painful inch at a time, down towards the rot that lay beneath him. He writhed and twisted and winced while above him the Black Dog snarled and sniffed, and then … Shanklin was free of his suffocating confinement, sliding then tumbling, spinning through the air until his sleeve snagged on something sharp and he was violently jolted, suspended in black space for a second before his coat ripped and he was dropping once again …

Splash! The shallow sewage water didn't break his fall quite as well as whatever had hooked his coat and now Shanklin lay on his back, groaning amid floating lumps of unthinkable human matter. Though the drop hadn't killed him, the smell soon might and yet, despite his brain telling him to stand and run, his body had other ideas. Something stung. *Everything* stung; hot and fierce. Shanklin forced himself to move, relieved to find that he could. First, a leg. Then the other. Then his arms, both working. Scratched, torn and bloodied but unbroken.

The necklace! He was on his feet fast, swaying in the swamping darkness of the narrow tunnel and checking that it was still inside the lining of his coat, relieved to find that it was. He had no idea as to why it still meant so much to have it, just the strongest feeling that it still had a part to play and so, slipping it safely away again, he glanced around, for all the good it did him. The heavy blackness was on all sides and he wouldn't have known which way was up or down if it wasn't for the fact that he'd just fallen from *up*.

Sloshing shin-deep through turgid water, Shanklin groped for the cold, slimy wall and began to feel his way along in the hope that he was heading in the right direction. In the hope that he was finally going home, the cries of the mauled steward in his mind.

28

THE LISTENER

'I'm worried for Charlotte,' Jack said, sat on his bed with his back to the wall.

Aunt Ruth was perched on the end, her posture as upright as ever. While Jack often felt his troubles pressing down on him, it seemed that she carried hers with such strength and dignity.

'Your sister is unwell,' she replied. A candle burned brightly on his bedside table and gave a soft glow to her skin. 'And she may become worse before she's better, Jack. You have both been through so much and now ... the death of the woman who raised you.'

'She was my *mother*,' Jack said, alarming even himself with his defensive tone. He wasn't sure why it had come out that way because her dying had left him feeling nothing but numb.

Aunt Ruth smiled. 'Yes, she was, Jack. And she was my sister, despite our differences. I promise that we shall have a physician attend to Charlotte just as soon as we can. Tomorrow we will make arrangements—'

'She won't listen,' Jack said.

'Then we will *make* her listen,' said Aunt Ruth, and he saw the warmth in her eyes turn to frost. This shook him: to catch a glimpse of such coldness, as though she already had plans for Charlotte. He'd heard stories about Bedlam and what happened to those unfortunate enough to be kept there. He didn't want the same for his sister. He couldn't allow it, and he'd do whatever it took to stop it from happening.

His loose tooth was hanging on by a thread as his tongue poked and prodded. It was the only comfort he had left.

Aunt Ruth's smile had returned, although it lacked the light he had grown accustomed to in the short time he'd known her. 'Aside from your sister's ... *condition*,' she said, 'we must remember that she is a young girl going through some very real changes. Sometimes it takes a while for our minds to grow into our changing bodies. As children, our imaginations are free. We create illusions of how things are. Our realities are never quite the same. Yours. Mine. Charlotte's. We all see life a little differently. Nothing is certain except change and change is often difficult, Jack. You must be patient. She is still your sister and she loves you. I have no doubt that she'll always love you. But we must learn to let go of what once was. Like the seasons, everything alters and shifts. Things die, things grow. Yet with God's grace, you will remain friends forever. She is becoming a young woman and you will grow one day into a young man. Those playful times you shared together may be nearing an end, but the memories will never die.'

She shuffled closer to him on the bed, wrapping a gentle arm around his shoulder and pulling him towards her. 'Your ... *mother*, she was the same. Her mind was wild with ideas when we were young. She would make up stories and tell them to me. She would speak of seeing colours around people and she'd tell me that *Mr so-and-so* who lived in the village was wicked or that we should avoid talking to certain people because they had *bad energy*. But these were just games, Jack, nothing more. Granted, they were dangerous games, for we had to be careful of what was said for fear of certain folk misinterpreting her innocence for something ... sinister. But I'm relieved to say that she soon grew out of it as we aged and we became more interested in...' Aunt Ruth trailed off into her thoughts.

'Boys?' asked Jack.

She smiled, though it was tainted with sadness.

'What was my father like?'

'A wonderful man,' Aunt Ruth replied. 'In spite of everything you've heard tonight, know this: he loved you. He spoke of you and Charlotte often and he always intended on...' Her voice cracked, snapping her sentence like a twig. She stroked his cheek with her hand. 'You have his eyes.'

Jack nestled his head into his aunt's breast. For the first time in as long as he could remember he felt safe. Loved. 'I wish you had been my mother,' he whispered.

Tears ran down Aunt Ruth's cheeks. 'So do I,' she said, and she squeezed him tightly, kissing his head.

Suddenly, Jack flinched, sitting upright and cupping a hand to his mouth. He spat blood into his palm and gazed down at the red tooth while his tongue rubbed at the new stump peeking through his gum.

Aunt Ruth wiped the tears away. 'Oh Jack, at last!'

'Will I get some money from the Tooth Fairy now?' he asked. 'Will she come?'

'She will,' his aunt said. 'You shan't be forgotten this time. Leave it under your pillow tonight and in the morning there will be a penny there waiting for you.'

Jack stared down at the bloody tooth.

'Come,' Aunt Ruth said, 'Let's get you cleaned up and then we'll go and check on your sister.'

. . .

Charlotte was lying on her side in bed with the sheets pulled from her, being as it was such a warm evening. Jack stood at the doorway with his aunt behind him, her hand resting on his shoulder and in the other, a candle. He saw that, though puffy, his sister's eyes were open, glimmering in the light, gazing into some distant place.

'Charlotte?' he asked. 'Are you all right?'

Her eyes slid towards him. 'I'm fine,' she said, sitting up and resting her head against the backboard. 'Though I ... I don't remember much.'

Aunt Ruth softly urged Jack forwards and, cautiously, he approached the bed.

'You had another seizure,' he said. 'Aunt Ruth took care of you. She put you to bed. She made you safe.'

Charlotte's gaze slithered past him. 'Thank you.'

'There's no need to thank me, child,' her aunt replied. 'It's an awful thing that you've endured tonight. You must try and rest and we'll make certain arrangements in the morning.'

'Look!' Jack said, showing his sister his final milk tooth. 'It came out.'

She smiled and there was sadness there. 'It seems you're growing too, Jack.'

'I'll give you some time alone,' Aunt Ruth said. 'But remember, we have a big day ahead of us tomorrow. You must both get your sleep. I'll return shortly.'

Charlotte's eyes followed Aunt Ruth as she left the room, leaving the door slightly ajar. Jack watched the frown form on his sister's forehead.

'She cannot be trusted, Jack!' his sister whispered. 'Her intentions are bad!'

He felt as though he'd been punched in the stomach. 'What? No. No, you're wrong. She's kind and—'

'Listen to me!' Charlotte hissed, clutching his sleeve. 'I can See her halo! It's blood-red, Jack! She is a charlatan and she is motivated by nothing more than greed! She would have me thrown into Bedlam for being mad and you and I will be apart, forever!'

Curling a fist around his tooth, Jack shook his head. 'No, it isn't true! She cared for you when you had your seizure. I've looked into her eyes. She is honest!'

Charlotte rose from her bed so that he was forced to back away. 'She took our father from us, don't you understand?' she said, padding across the floorboards. 'She stole him from Mother. She is not who she says she is or what she pretends to be and you are a fool if you think otherwise!'

Jack's heart was pounding as he edged back toward the door. 'No...'

'She isn't really your aunt anyway,' Charlotte continued. 'If Mother wasn't your real mother then that woman downstairs isn't related to you at all! She's *my* blood relative and she would see me locked up. If she cares so little for me then she cares nothing for you. *Nothing!*'

Tears pricked Jack's eyes once more. 'You don't know her. You don't!'

He noticed then that Charlotte's worried gaze fell towards the gap under the bedroom door and he turned just as the faint light from a candle fluttered on the landing. As though someone had been standing there the whole time, listening.

29

SORE

C rouched and stumbling through the darkness of the sewer, Shanklin flinched as another rat brushed against his water-logged boot. 'Bastard!' he hissed, shuddering. He'd escaped dungeons and demonic dogs of eternal fucking damnation but he was taking little delight in his newfound 'freedom', down here with the vermin of London's underbelly. Yet on he went, groping at the damp walls and pushing through the choking fumes, his mind spinning with the horror he'd witnessed back in Limbo. An impossible apparition, surely? A figment of his imagination. No, it had to have been real. Gripe was dead, torn to shreds by an arcane creature, not of this world, for there was no chance that a dog could have entered that cell and—

A gentle coolness touched his skin.

Air.

Shanklin increased his pace, jogging now, as best that he could, boots slapping through black puddles, sloshing towards the crystal breeze sweeping through the tunnel and teasing him with his first taste of the outside, torn coat flapping, the chill night kissing his neck, sweet and enticing—

He froze. Shouts were coming from up ahead, echoing down the passage. A commotion. Cursing. The riot sounded as if it was in full-swing out there. But there was no turning back. *Back* was where death awaited. So on he went, stomping through slurry, the air turning colder still, the stench becoming less pungent. Onward, toward the amber lights glittering in the fetid pools laid out before him. Toward the ditch he could now see at the mouth of the tunnel, sparkling with fire from somewhere above, and the black outline of a water-pump. On until he exited the sewer and was out in the open, blinking, his eyes stinging.

London burned. Parts of her anyway. Here and there, long, leaping flames were licking at the night sky. Shanklin spun a full circle, trying to get his bearings, no idea as to where he'd just surfaced. He recognised the building nearby though: Christ's Hospital, still in one piece, thank ... Christ. Then the parts began to fall into place. On the north was Little Britain, where a shop was on fire, the cause of the ash and the embers flitting down around him, thick smoke belching from an upstairs window. Blurry shapes hurried past the blaze. Clusters of men and women and children intent on causing mayhem. Groups banded together like savages, nail-tipped clubs and other make-shift weapons in their hands. Shanklin was free, yet his first thought was to get back inside somewhere, fast. He'd been involved in riots himself, as a young man, picking up a stone or two and smashing the odd window, taking whatever was on offer inside. Tonight he'd fled from some unnameable beast but the mob was an animal in itself. Folk acted differently when part of a crowd with a common purpose conjoined to become one wild organism, dangerous and unpredictable. He knew what a monster like that was capable of and here it was, running amok.

'Shit.' The world had gone mad and now James McCabe

seemed like the sane one. But free he was, and right now being free was all that fucking mattered.

He scrambled up the side of the ditch, slipping in the shit and whatever else the sewer spewed out on a daily basis, grappling to reach the top and covered head to toe in human waste. Yet no one raised an eyebrow, too caught up in the unfolding drama all around them. And, for once, Shanklin was glad not to be the centre of attention as he reached the edge and climbed out. Sooner that than the toxic concoction he'd been breathing for a week. On unsteady legs, he rose to his feet and an urchin across the street spotted him, no doubt intrigued by this creature that had just crawled out of a swamp. But in those young, staring eyes Shanklin saw a different boy gawping back.

Harry.

The lad laughed, then spat, and he was off again, whooping and jumping with excitement at what he could break next.

Which way?

Shanklin knew London better than some but not half as well as he wished right now. He had a choice: stick to the main thoroughfares where most of the rioting would be taking place or attempt to navigate his way through back alleys, side streets and slums. The truth was, it wasn't a choice at all, and if McCabe was standing next to him he'd be saying the same. There was less chance of getting lost and more of seeing where he was going if he stuck to the main routes. The streets might've been busy with those of a mind to cause trouble but even the lawless use flares and lanterns and he'd sooner take his chances with a crowd hell-bent on causing property damage than a gang of rakes whose patch he'd just stumbled into.

With the glow of fire to guide him, Shanklin made his way south, cutting through the hospital churchyard, and was soon on Newgate Street, the great, black dome of St Paul's Cathedral looming. A tramp in a tall, feathered hat was attempting to play a fiddle to a small group of drunken bystanders, tapping his foot as he worked them into a merry frenzy. The line between riot and street party was a fine one but the frolics would soon end once the army showed up. And show up they would if the carnage continued.

Heading east, Shanklin felt his tired legs burning but he moved at a pace, thoughts of Sarah and his son spurring him on. *Home.* It was all that mattered now, putting one foot in front of the other till he couldn't feel his feet anymore. Broken buildings blurred past him, looted, destroyed, shattered shards of glass spilling across the cobbles, crunching under his boots, smoke-tinged air singing in his ears.

Revellers or rioters appeared up ahead; it was hard to tell which but they looked a large group, heading towards him, some with flaming torches, others with cudgels. It seemed that this part of the city was bearing the brunt of the havoc and he only hoped that things hadn't spread towards Whitechapel and Brick Lane.

Keep going.

There was no quick or easy way round them so Shanklin went through, thinking that his smell alone might part 'em like Moses crossing the Red Sea. Some moved, some didn't, and he shouldered one or two from his path.

'The party's this way!' cried a drunk, slapping his back as he passed. Shanklin had a mind to slap his jaw, spinning on his heel and grabbing the fool by his collar.

'What's going on here?' he asked.

The man turned up his nose the moment that the smell reached it. 'How the hell should I know?' he slurred. 'Something to do with the silk weavers again, so I hear.' He shrugged Shanklin off and was on his way once more, quick to catch up with his little crowd, too busy chanting to realise they'd nearly lost one of their number. That was the thing with a riot, no matter what the worthy root cause may be – an abhorrent Act of Parliament, a harsh new law passed, a tax levied – more often than not it was simply an excuse for the majority to vent their multitude of frustrations by destroying their own communities. It didn't make much sense to Shanklin but then sense was in short supply when gin was your chosen juice.

Hopping over strewn debris he was starting to doubt if anyone would be going to the gallows in the morning, what with the mess and the amount of clearing up there'd be to do. He was heading in the opposite direction to Tyburn but it seemed that most of the mob were moving that way, and if Snow Hill and Holborn fell foul of tonight's shenanigans there'd be no getting the carts and procession through until the route was cleared. But London had seen its fair share of rioting lately and once the ringleaders of this one were caught, they'd be swinging along with the rest gone before 'em.

He was heading south-east now, down Cheapside, its wide cobbled street populated with more prowling packs of euphoric looters bounding and prancing like they owned the night, lanterns and clubs swinging. Perhaps they did, for a time, but once the soldiers arrived things would take a turn. One lad was banging a drum, a rallying cry to all the young rogues. Shanklin had the brains to keep his eyes from 'em, focused instead on what was in front of him and the next step needed to get him there. That's all that was required, to keep moving. To not stop. Passing King Street to his left, he had a mind to peel off and take his chances in the quieter lanes and alleys. Shit, he missed his pistols, or even a sword for that matter. Just some reassurance that would give him an edge aside from the stink he was carrying.

Don't stop.

Acrid wafts of smoke scratched at his throat as he passed another burning shop. Old Harrington's, the tailor, flames like bright orange banners unfurling from its windows. He'd had his best summer suit fitted there, the one he'd worn to the ball. That got him mad, seeing the place go up like that. Aye, these fools owned the night for now, but their time would come.

Flecks of ash drifted down around him like grey snow. Dogs barked. In the darkness people screamed – out of fright or jubilation, it was unclear. An elderly watchman holding a lantern and a cudgel was trying to quell a little of the disorder, arguing with four men who appeared to be ransacking a residence, one of them carrying a case of what looked like wine under his arm. The silly sod took a crack to his skull for meddling, dropping to the ground as a flurry of kicks followed, bouncing his head like it was a cabbage, stamping till he was a floppy, bloody mess. Another moment of madness that Shanklin felt helpless to do anything about. He was never one to side with the law but some things got him riled worse than others and seeing this old man take a beating for trying to keep the streets safe only pushed him to the brink. Yet his feet had one purpose right now and his mind burned with just one image: that of Sarah and Harry, huddled in their home as the city broke apart around them. So he kept running despite his thighs screaming at him to stop.

Get home, get 'em safe.

In the morning they'd all flee London and head for Sarah's cousin's in the country, leaving this smoking carcass behind 'em. Fresh pastures. He'd been given a chance to start again. Him and his wife, anew. He wouldn't throw this away, not for anything.

When Shanklin reached Poultry the road forked into

three and he slowed to a brisk walk as he spotted a group of Redcoats marching towards him from Cornhill, their kit clacking, muskets ready, probably on the tail of the mob he'd passed. Switching direction he made his way north-east up Threadneedle Street and a young soldier caught his eye. Several Horse Guards were trotting close behind them, an officer shouting orders to fire on any groups that refused to disperse, but with packs of animals to deal with this lot had no time for lone wolves like him. It didn't stop Shanklin from breathing a little easier once he was out of sight though, and he was jogging again. As he passed the stone pillars of the Royal Exchange, musket fire clattered from behind him, echoing from the surrounding buildings.

Move! He had a way to go but every aching step found him closer to his home.

On Bishopsgate the road widened once again and Shanklin decided to cut through Crosby Square leading to St Mary Axe. He turned the corner and his heart almost gave out as he bumped into someone.

'Whoa there!' the old watchman said, holding a lantern up to get a better look at just who was in such a hurry. 'In a rush are we?' He was broad-set and had the look of someone who'd been around a few corners other than this one, a jagged scar running across both lips. Alongside him was another watchman, younger, slimmer, strands of limp, long hair hanging from under his tricorn.

'Ain't everyone?' breathed Shanklin, half-blinded by the lantern.

The older one surveyed him from under a bushy, white frown. Shanklin was conscious of the fact he was still carrying some marks from his fight with four constables but, aside from being covered in cuts, bruises and human faeces, he couldn't imagine what might possibly arouse alarm.

'Well, there's a curfew on, son,' the watchman said. 'So you shouldn't be out here.'

'I'm trying not to be,' Shanklin replied. 'Hence the hurry.'

'And there's no need for any lip,' chimed in the younger of the two, the tip of his cudgel poised an inch from Shanklin's chest. It took every grain of sense left in his skull not to rip the thing from this prick's hand and batter him with it.

'Steady there, Rob,' said the first man, keeping his eyes fixed on Shanklin's. 'There's enough unpleasantness around tonight. Let's keep it friendly, eh?'

The stick was lowered and with it went Shanklin's heart rate, despite mulling on whether to still teach this nipple a valuable lesson.

'Where you going on such an evening as this, then?' questioned the older watchman.

'Home.'

'And where's that?'

'Buckle Street,' lied Shanklin.

'And where you been?'

'Drinking.'

The man scanned up and down the length of him, bruised, shit-covered and stinking to high heaven. 'Looks like it was a good night.'

'You know how it can get.'

'Don't I just.' The watchman held the lantern higher. 'You look familiar. Got a name, lad?'

'Doesn't everyone?'

The younger of the two aimed the cudgel again. 'What did I say about—'

'My name's Robert Knight,' said Shanklin, 'and if you point that thing at me again, so help me I'll—'

'*Night*, eh?' the older one repeated. 'Like the very strange and slightly disturbing one we're experiencing right now or like as in ... *knight* of the road?'

Shanklin sneered, 'I'm no rogue, sir.'

'I didn't say you were, son. Which is it?'

'As in *Lancelot*.'

'Ah, a legend.'

'Not many of 'em left.'

'No.' The watchman stroked at his jaw, surveying the filth-ridden, lice-bitten scoundrel standing in front of him, as though wondering what he should do. 'Plenty thinking they are though,' he said.

The sound of glass smashing somewhere in another street decided his next course of action. 'Get home, lad,' he instructed, moving off in the direction of the disturbance, his worried-looking colleague keeping close behind.

'Oh, I intend to,' said Shanklin, and he was running again.

St Mary Axe; black and eerily quiet. Halfway up the street he lost his footing and tumbled to the ground, his hands taking the force of the fall.

'Shit.' So close to home now that he could almost hear Harry stomping around the house. The last thing needed was to sprain an ankle and have to limp the rest of the way. He climbed back to his feet, moving a little more carefully in the darkness before turning a sharp right into Bevis Marks and the approach to Aldgate.

Almost there. Almost there.

His breath rasped in his throat. He needed water or beer or anything to quench the formidable thirst before he collapsed and died just yards from his home. God could play some cruel jokes but Shanklin reckoned that one would rank quite highly. Onwards to Whitechapel; long and broad and usually so noisy with the clop of horse and carriage during the day, but a distinctly different sound was in the air tonight and that rattled his nerves. Silence; ringing in his ears like the Bellman of St Sepulchre. Drifting sheets of torn newspapers skipped across the cobbles. A ripped poster advertising a circus flapped in the breeze. Anyone not bent on causing chaos was no doubt hiding in their homes. This suited Shanklin, hoping that he'd left the worst of the rioting behind him and that his wife and son were safe indoors. He ran on, ribs sore, muscles spent, ramshackle shops and houses flitting past, until at last he turned left into Brick Lane and could've sobbed to know that he'd made it back. That soon he would hold his wife and his son and he would soak up the look of glee on their faces as he held them. He was home. He was alive.

Standing before his own front door, panting like a hound having chased a fox twenty miles across country, Shanklin was reminded of being back in the dock awaiting his death sentence. His stomach was somersaulting, the faintest glimmer of candlelight peeking through the drawn sitting room curtains. They were in. He sucked in a deep breath and rapped the knocker, hard.

'Sarah, it's me! It's Sam! Open up!'

Another dog was barking somewhere.

Shanklin hammered again. 'Sarah! Harry! Open the door!'

Silence.

Something wasn't right. Yet there *had* to be someone in, being as a candle was lit. Taking a step back, he prepared to aim a firm kick at the door when—

Click. It creaked open, slowly, and, in the dimness of the hallway, was Harry, wide-eyed and as frightened stiff as anyone might be if Bob Creech was standing behind you holding a knife to your throat.

'Well, blow me,' Creech said, creasing up his nose at the smell, 'is that you Samuel? Pardon my rudeness, but you look like shit.' His eyes glimmered and his gold tooth glinted like the bright, long blade he had resting on Harry's neck. 'You'd better come in, quick,' he said, 'it's dangerous out there.'

30

TIME TO COLLECT

'W here's Sarah?' asked Shanklin, sat at his kitchen table opposite Creech who was aiming a pistol at his chest. Harry was standing by his side, shaking like a leaf in the wind. It near broke Shanklin to see that but there was nothing he could do. The only option was to keep things friendly, for the time being. Creech was grinning. Had every right to. It was *him* holding the gun now and every chance that his one worked.

'Now, there's a question, Samuel,' Creech replied. 'And one that I'm sure you're keen to find the answer to. But the truth is, I really don't know. See, I turned up here after hearing the news that there's the mother of all riots taking place. It's pandemonium out there. We've not had anything like this for a while, am I right?'

Shanklin didn't answer.

Creech smiled. 'Gives you a thrill, don't it? A warm feeling inside.'

Shanklin's eyes flitted between that pistol pointing his way and Harry, tears running. *Be calm, son. I'll get us out of this.*

'Let him go, Bob,' he said. 'He's done nothing.'

'Oh, I won't argue,' said Creech. 'And he's *said* about as much too. Hasn't spoken a fucking word since I arrived. I thought the place was empty and then I discovered the back door was wide open. Found him hiding in a wardrobe, I did. Nearly took my leg off with an old army sword.'

Shanklin looked at Harry, tears brimming. 'What's happened, son? Where's your mother?'

'They took her, Pa.'

'Who?'

'I didn't get to see properly. I heard Ma speaking to someone at the door. It sounded like Randall. He came round the other day too. Told her he was here to pay his respects because you were in gaol and soon to be hanged. Said he was here to make sure she was all right.' Harry wiped his eyes with a sleeve.

'Go on, son.'

'Then he got all funny with her,' Harry continued. 'Said things he shouldn't have and she asked him to leave. So he did.'

Randall. Could never keep his fucking eyes off her.

'Then, today,' said Harry, 'he came back. He was standing at the door and trying to talk his way in, telling Ma he should be here 'cause there was a riot going on and it was dangerous for her and ... and I heard her shouting and there was a struggle. I came to help but she screamed that I should run. I was scared, Pa! I didn't know what to do. I made it out into the backyard and I hid and when I finally came back in she was gone!'

'When was this?' asked Shanklin.

'I don't know. Just after lunchtime, I think.' Harry started crying, sobbing. Shanklin longed to reach out to him. To hold him. But that pistol was still aimed in his direction.

'Why did you come here, Bob?' he asked. 'It wasn't to kill me. You couldn't have known I'd escaped.'

Creech laughed. 'Aye, you're a cunning bastard, Samuel, but even I didn't think you'd make it out of Newgate on the eve of your execution.' He scratched at the stubble on his jaw and his expression turned grave. 'No. There was something I needed to know before they strung you up on the gallows and Sarah seemed like the best place to start.'

Shanklin was raging inside. He knew what this maniac was capable of when 'asking' for information. 'And just what's so important that you felt you had to come here and 'talk' to my wife?'

'I need to know why I haven't received my share of the robbery,' said Creech.

'Then it appears that we both need to speak with Randall.'

'That so?'

'Aye, it is. I told him to split the earnings in half with you. I don't want none of it. I'm getting out.'

'Oh, you've done a good job of escaping gaol, but you ain't *out*. Not yet. Not till I've got my money.'

Shanklin leaned forward on the chair as though he mustn't have been talking loud enough before. 'Then speak to Randall.' Slowly, he reached inside his coat.

Creech cocked the hammer on the pistol. 'Steady there, Samuel,' he said. 'We ain't out the woods yet.'

From within his coat, Shanklin pulled out the necklace and held it up, the little tooth spinning. 'This is all I kept from that morning. I kept it 'cause I wanted to return it to its rightful owner. The silver's worth little, but the tooth is worth the world to her.'

'Tooth?'

'Aye. I've had it checked. A poxy tooth belonging to some kid. *Her* kid. A son, a daughter, I don't know and I don't care. Not anymore.' He placed the necklace on the table in front of him and leaned forward again. 'But I do care about my own.

My boy, standing there. My wife, God knows where. You can put a hole in me right now, Bob and I'll say I had it coming, but there's a son in need of his mother and I'm going to call on whatever shred of soul you have in you and ask that you let me find her.'

Creech wasn't grinning anymore. But the gun hadn't moved an inch since they'd sat down, his finger poised on the trigger. Like a crazed dog on a leash, that barking iron had a lead ball in its barrel just itching to be released. Yearning to tear a space in Shanklin so big you could fit a fist in it.

Harry was given a gentle shove towards his father and the boy sprang into his arms. It seemed that even human shit couldn't keep them apart and Shanklin hugged him tight, pressing his cheek to his mop of messy hair and breathing in his smell. It was the best smell he'd come across in as long as he could remember.

'It's all right, son,' Shanklin whispered. 'We'll find her. We'll find your ma.' But he knew it was far from all right and that rage swirled like a tempest in his stomach. Why would Randall kidnap Sarah? Why would anyone? Then his mind spun with the words of Eliza Torne: *I will give my personal condolences to your wife and son.'*

'Seems you've got a serious problem on your hands, Samuel,' Creech said.

'I have to find her,' said Shanklin.

Shuffling in his chair, Creech found himself a more comfortable position. 'I'm gonna level with ya,' he said. 'I came here tonight not to offer my respects and condolences to your soon-to-be-widowed wife and fatherless son. I came here to find out if you'd kept my share of the money. Yet, much to my dismay, we now have a situation, and one that I did not see coming. And I can see round fucking corners, Samuel, of that you have my word.' His eyes narrowed. His frown deepened. 'So, in light of the circumstances and given that your son will most likely have no mother to care for him once I've slain you in front of his eyes, well … Let's say that might be pushing things too far, even by my standards.'

As he held Harry to him, trembling, Shanklin was left wondering what this man's next move might be.

'I'm willing to give you an opportunity,' Creech added, 'one the likes of which you shan't encounter again.' He leaned across the table, the pistol still poised, his voice dropping to a hush. 'But know this, Samuel: I am arm's fucking length from you at all times. I am your shadow now. I'm watching your every move. I'm listening to your every breath. And it will be that way for some time, until we get a few things straightened out.'

Uncocking the pistol, Creech lowered it. 'And now it seems we have a common interest in speaking with Mr Randall.'

Shanklin nodded. Swallowed, releasing the breath he'd been holding. But the time for fear was done and the time for thinking was upon him. Whatever Randall's motives were with Sarah, he couldn't imagine him being stupid enough to hole up in *The Lion*. But then again, where else? It made sense. There was a riot happening and it would be the one place he'd feel safest. Drinking. Drowning his conscience of whatever he'd done. He was a fool at times and, like Shanklin, he'd made many mistakes but this was the biggest one yet and a one-eyed drunk needs all the eyes around him he could muster. A crew of his own. A gang of rats with a point to prove. Besides which, the tavern was on the way to Randall's current lodgings. It seemed only right to call in for one last drink. One for the road.

'Then it's time to collect,' Shanklin said to Creech. But he knew that time was borrowed.

He rose from his chair, his hands on Harry's shoulders. 'Listen to me, son. I'm gonna find your mother. I need you to stay here and wait for us to get back, y'understand? Stay here and stay hidden. Keep the doors and windows locked and don't move. If anyone breaks in, leave 'em to take whatever they want. You listening?'

Wiping more tears away from his dirt-smudged cheeks, Harry silently agreed.

Shanklin turned to Creech. 'I need my guns.'

Creech nodded. 'Just remember: I'm right behind ya.'

The weight of the two pistols felt good in Shanklin's hands. Solid. Reliable. There'd be no misfires tonight.

'I'm almost offended, Samuel,' Creech said, leaning against the doorframe of the sitting room. 'You might've used one of those on me instead of that antique piece of shit.'

Shanklin slung a powder horn over his shoulder. 'Maybe next time, eh?' he said, priming the first gun.

Creech held up his throwing knife for Harry and his father to get a look at, candlelight flashing on a blade sharp enough to shave with. 'Well, just remember; I'm faster with this than most are with one of those. But I've got me a couple of *them* too.' He opened his coat, showing off the handles of his pistols, like anyone needed reminding.

Using his teeth, Shanklin plucked the cork from the narrow end of the powder horn and poured a measure down the muzzle of his own gun.

'There a plan?' asked Creech.

'No.' Shanklin was pumping a lead ball into the barrel with the ramrod.

'Oh, good. Overrated anyway, ain't they? Plans. Fly right out the fucking window when things get a bit warm.'

Shanklin tapped another dose of powder into the pistol's pan, snapping the frizzen closed. 'If he has Sarah with him, I don't want any shooting till I say, that clear? I'm not risking her getting hurt.'

'I'm not so sure you get to choose, Samuel,' Creech replied. 'If we go barging in there with our bollocks hanging out then Randall and whoever else he likes drinking with these days may have other ideas.' He shrugged. 'But listen, you're the boss, right?'

Shanklin was priming his second pistol; same routine, well rehearsed. The sweat he'd worked up from running here was tickling his back again. He'd loaded many guns down the years. He could do it in the damn dark. It was just the bit where you pulled the trigger that he was a little rusty at, and the last time he'd tried, it hadn't gone so well.

'Let's just keep things tidy,' he said, tucking them both into his belt, though he knew that turning up at *The Lion* bristling with pistols had every chance of being anything but.

Creech was grimacing, rubbing at his chin. '*Tidy* is not how they will describe me on my gravestone but, for you, I'll try my best.'

'That's what bothers me,' Shanklin said as Harry's worried eyes followed him around the room. 'Where the hell is it?'

'Looking for this?' Creech tossed the old military sword to him and Shanklin caught it with one hand. It hissed as he slid it free of its sheath and inspected the blade.

'You sure you don't wanna bring your lad along?' Creech asked. 'He almost knows how to use that thing. I'm lucky to still have both legs.'

It could've done with whetting but there wasn't time for that now. Slipping it back into the scabbard, Shanklin hooked the strap across him. 'This is *my* fight, Bob,' he said, tightening his belt up a notch. 'You don't need a part in it. You could wait here. Keep an eye on my boy.' It pained him to even consider suggesting it but there was a riot going on and Shanklin was out of child-care options.

'Oh no, no, you're forgetting something, Samuel,' said Creech, wagging his knife like it was a long, very sharp finger. 'That night you were arrested, I knew nothing of those constables being there, so don't you go feeling all sorry for yourself now. Aside from lacking the money I'm owed, I've got unfinished business too.'

Shanklin wasn't sure what was better or worse: having this lunatic accompany him or Harry being left on his own.

'You ever killed a man, Samuel?' Creech asked. 'Now would seem an appropriate time to ask.'

Images of McCabe choking to death flashed through Shanklin's mind. 'Aye,' he said, before fastening the strap on his pouch of lead shot. 'I've killed.'

'Good,' said Creech. ''Cause I don't want to be the one doing all the work tonight.'

It was then that Shanklin felt inclined to ask a question of his own – something that'd been bothering him since the start of all this. 'Randall told me you were looking to mill Rousingham House. That you were gonna hurt 'em up there; Lady Torne and her husband. That true?'

Another frown formed on Creech's heavily creased face. 'Where the fuck is Rousingham House?' he said. 'That good enough for ya?' Sheathing his knife, he added: 'Seems to me like our Randall has some explaining to do. Seems that he's been telling tales of late. Trying to stir some things up between us. Reckon he set us both up for a fall, don't you?'

Shanklin couldn't tell if he was lying or not, but it would have to do for now. The situation was already stirred up plenty. It was answers that were needed. He brushed past Creech, back into the kitchen, swiping the necklace from the table. 'I'd offer you this as compensation,' Shanklin said to his new 'shadow' who'd followed on behind. 'But it might be the only thing I can use to get my wife back.'

'No, you keep it, Samuel,' Creech said, a glint of gold in his mouth. 'I prefer my teeth with a little more bite.'

If Creech was Shanklin's shadow then Harry was his second skin, sticking to his every step. 'Go wait in your room till I'm back, son. I won't be long.'

Harry lunged forward, throwing his arms around his father's waist. They embraced one more time. 'Go,' Shanklin whispered.

The boy left the room and the two men were finally alone. Their stares met. If Creech wanted to level things up between 'em, then now was his chance.

'You look like you're just about ready for a war, Samuel,' he said. 'You didn't come for me all dressed up like that.'

'Maybe next time, eh?' said Shanklin. 'You got a horse?'

'Well, I didn't fucking walk here. Round the back. You?'

'Stable Yard, close by.'

With a loud clap, Creech rubbed his hands together like he was off out for a relaxing country walk. 'Right, well, nothing like a riot to work up a thirst, eh?' he said. 'Let's get going then. I could kill for a drink.'

31

WHISKY AND BLOOD

Randall slammed the empty whisky tumbler on the bar and a candle wavered. 'Another!' he ordered.

Fat Tom waddled over with a new bottle, popping the cork and filling his glass for the third time in five minutes. Randall watched it being poured – that glittering, liquid gold. The one thing he could rely on to save him from the world. From himself.

Tom moved to take the bottle away.

'Leave it there,' Randall said.

The inn-keep did as he was told, setting it back down and slinking off somewhere while Skim's still somewhat blackened, imp-like eyes followed him the length of the bar, till he was out of earshot.

'Drinking ourselves into oblivion doesn't solve things, Mr Randall,' the young thief said.

Randall's eye was closed, the warmth of the liquor surging through his veins and soothing his heavy mind. Just what was this persistent buzzing in his ear? This continuous, unpleasant noise, like a wasp that wouldn't fuck off.

'Meaning?' he replied, staring at the bar straight in front

of him. So many bottles. So much drink. This could be a long night, what with the chaos outside. Best get settled in.

Skim leaned closer. '*Meaning* that you're beating yourself up over nothing in my opinion. Samuel Shanklin *used* me to get close to that beau monde crowd in Vauxhall, for whatever ridiculous reason only known to him, and all I got was a broken nose for my part in his plan! Oh, I'm sure you two are old friends an' all, but how long was he sneaking around behind your back and you wouldn't have known it?'

How long indeed? Randall mused, swilling the whisky round in his glass, mulling on quite why Shanklin would've kept such secrets from him. It wasn't their way. Never had been. And now it cut deep, knowing what he did, or did *not* know, such was the case. But he didn't need this little prick next to him to point it out over and over. What he needed was some quiet drinking time while the streets burned outside. Some time to reflect on his old friend, soon to hang. A friend whose wife he'd just kidnapped and given over to an insane woman in return for a fat purse. A woman he loved but would never love him.

'I was out of that ball faster than a rabbit with one of those fireworks up its arsehole,' Skim was bleating on. Still. 'I'm lucky to be alive!'

Aye, you are, but if you keep talking …

'Don't punish yourself over this, Mr Randall. Shanklin was washed up. He's better off out the way. But we need you straight if you're gonna run this crew.' Skim was glancing around the tavern but Randall had seen enough of their ugly faces. Half a dozen of 'em so far. Jonah Oakes and the rest. Green as a summer meadow but ripe for learning what it takes to rob a coach. And they'd learn under his expert tuition.

But first there was drinking to be done. In peace, if only this fool would close his mouth.

'Shanklin's getting what was always coming to him,' Skim continued. 'He was gonna hang regardless. All you've done is speed up the process. Bob Creech is a matter for another day, but look at us; we've got numbers now!'

Numbers? Is that what this tit thought it took to make a gang?

Skim leaned towards his ear further still. 'And the best part? It's made all the sweeter when Shanklin realises his wife ain't there to say goodbye as he stands in that cart. She's another one who deserves what she's getting if you ask—'

Randall spun, grabbing Skim by the collar, the stool he'd been sat on clattering to the floor. 'If I hear you so much as *think* that of Sarah Shanklin again, I'll tear your fucking tongue out with my teeth, you pointy-eared, snot-nosed little cunt. That clear?'

A silence fell on *The Lion* as the others watched on, twitchy, but who could blame 'em? Whilst still holding Skim, Randall looked around him. Shanklin had been right – little stains like this lot knew nothing of life, though their friend here would soon find out about death if he didn't shut up.

Pushing the rat away, Randall picked up his stool and poured himself another whisky.

Skim straightened his shirt, keeping a somewhat safer distance now. 'Well, pardon-*fucking*-me, Mr Randall,' he said, 'but might I remind you that, thanks to us *both* his wife is now in the capable hands of a lunatic, blue-stocking bitch and her bodyguard?'

Randall had sat back down and was watching his hand tremble as he brought the glass to his lips. Hadn't done that before. Not like this. But then he'd never sold a dear friend down the river, only then to steal his wife for a large sum of money. Funny how a thing like that can get to you. 'I'm warning ya, Skim,' he said. Then he glanced at 'em, all of 'em; fresh as daisies and no idea what it took to make a living as a villain. 'I'm warning *all* of ya! Barely off your mothers' nipples and you think you have the right to be here?' Randall was slurring now, the whisky well and truly in his blood. Blood that boiled as he recalled his past. 'This is *The Lion!* This is where legends are made!' He was glaring at the lot of 'em. 'But *you* ... you lot belong out *there*, running with *them*! Them opp ... opportunistsists! Pond-scum, looting from their own kind instead of those that deserve to be robbed. You don't have the privilish of being *here*. Of treading the same floor Samuel Shanklin once trod.'

Skim was sniggering, shaking his head in disbelief as the others fidgeted, unsure of what they were supposed to do but looking like they'd heard enough of this nostalgia.

'Where you going with this, Mr Randall?' Skim asked, no doubt feeling a little braver now that his 'boss' was heavily inebriated. ''Cause this is sounding to me like a cry for help and, though I don't speak for everyone here present, I'll wager that this ain't the way to make friends, let alone build a crew.'

Standing up, Randall brushed him aside with a wave of his hand, turning his attention instead to Tom, wedged behind the bar, shirking his responsibilities as a human being, let alone a landlord. 'And you,' he went on, two blurry, fat bastards seen through one bleary eye. 'You couldn't run a race let alone a tavern. This was a fencing house once! This place had a ... a reputation. You wanted something that was stolen, you came here. You wanted someone killed, you—'

'Let me guess, Horatio,' interrupted Tom, 'you came *here*? Well it isn't *The Lion* you once knew so the sooner you get your head around that the better.'

Skim was laughing. 'Horatio? That's your name?'

The floor wobbled under Randall. 'Got a problem with that, boy?'

The others were making faces too. Like something was mildly funny.

But Tom was in no mood for jokes. 'I'm cleaning this place up, y'hear me?' he said. 'The lot o'ya best be listening! I'm not standing for it any longer. This is a decent inn for decent folk!'

An old man watching from his spot in the corner raised a tankard to his crinkled lips and farted.

'You're a poor excuse for a person, Tom,' said Randall. 'You set Samuel Shanklin up. My partner. My friend!'

'Listen to yourself, *Horatio*,' Skim said. 'You're deluded! You wanted Shanklin gone along with the rest of us, so that you could finally get your hands on his wife! And when she rejected ya, what did you do? Turned her over to the woman you all robbed to save your own neck from the noose!'

Randall's glass smashed into a hundred tiny pieces on the floor and he fumbled for his pistol. 'Shut your mouth or I'll kill you where you stand—'

One of the candles on the bar was blown out by a gust of wind as the tavern door swung open, and all eyes were turned towards the dark shape standing before them.

Shanklin stepped into the dimly lit tavern, his coat unbuttoned, eyes flitting around the gloom, counting heads. Seven, from what he could tell, though with the poor light and several timber columns in the way it was difficult to know for certain. Randall was in the centre of the little gathering, Skim just off to his left. There were two others next to *him* – a tall one with a nose you could prise open crates with and Jonah Oakes being the other, wearing that fake frown again. To Randall's right, there were two more — just shapes in the shadows but you didn't need much light to spot the glint of weapons. One of them was the size of a mountain, tricorn pulled low. No problem. Just a bigger fucking target was all.

Tom was hovering behind the bar, wiping a squeaky glass and looking about as pale as a fat, thief-taking bastard might look if the man he'd tried to put in gaol turned up. Back from the dead.

Bad odds then, but Shanklin had Creech at his back now and that evened things up a touch. It was worth the ride here just to see the look on their faces when they spotted the pair standing side by side.

'Shank!' cried Randall, his arms open. 'Well, Jesus Christ, is my eye deceiving me? How'd ya make it out of Newgate?'

'Where's Sarah?'

That stained smile slipped from Randall's lips. 'Sarah? I dunno. She not at home?'

Shanklin's teeth were grinding like a millstone on grain. 'If she was then I wouldn't be standing here now, would I? So where is she?'

Randall was looking around him like he was missing something other than an eye. 'Well, she ain't here, Shank, you can see that. You two had another falling out?'

'I'm giving you ten seconds, Randall.'

Creech had his glare fixed on the two twitchy pricks to Randall's right.

'Till what, Shank?' Randall said, scratching the back of his scalp. 'You wanna tell me what the fuck this is about?'

An old man who'd been sat on his own in a quiet corner was edging along the wall, making for the door. Shanklin let him pass without a glance. The gang began to fan themselves out.

'Stay where you are!' Creech ordered. They did, every one of 'em, ugly statues in the low light.

But Shanklin hadn't taken his stare from his oldest friend

and long-term associate whose back was up against the bar like a cornered dog.

'You've got five seconds, Randall.'

Skim was licking at his dry lips while Randall's voice squeaked like that damn glass Tom was still rubbing for all his worth. 'Shank, I've got no idea what—'

'Where's my wife?' screamed Shanklin, and the whole tavern seemed to shake.

It was Skim who was first to the draw. At least he would have if his pistol hadn't snagged on his belt. And now he was floundering, desperately tugging to free the gun just before the handle of a knife appeared in his chest with a sickening *Thap!* Creech's knife; buried to the hilt. The medal for the most surprised looking man in the room went to Skim, right before his legs buckled from under him and he dropped to the floor.

Six left.

Time slowed to a crawl then as pistols were pulled and a chorus of guns being cocked rattled through the alehouse. But Shanklin's was already raised, aimed, sparks fizzing as flint met frizzen. *Phoosh-crack!* A plume of smoke followed and the tall one with a nose for opening crates was thrown backwards into the bar, blood spraying from his throat.

Five.

Randall spun, face and beard all spattered red, hurling himself over the counter as Shanklin lunged sideways just before the room lit up like lightning amid clouds of spewing smoke, hot lead zipping across the tavern, smashing holes in walls. Creech's aim was keener than that of these amateurs though – his shot catching the mountain-sized one in the stomach as he came lurching forward, stumbling, crashing face-first into a table.

Four.

Behind the protection of a thick column Shanklin drew

his second gun, bringing it round on the youngest of the gang, panic plastered all over the lad's face as he flustered to find cover. He paid the price for his hesitating too; Shanklin's shot punching a hole in his head and smothering his brains all over the bottles lining the back shelves. Skull ripped open, he dropped like a stone, glass tinkling on the flagstones.

Three.

Thack! The column Shanklin had ducked behind sprouted splinters while he pummelled another shot into his pistol. It was strange that, now he was in the thick of it, things weren't so frenzied. He was thinking clearly enough, going through the motions: powder, ball, more powder in the pan, hands as steady as rocks. The only problem he could see was that every other bastard was doing the same, rods *snicking* in barrels as guns were primed for the next round.

While Skim gargled, clutching the hilt of the knife in his chest, Shanklin glanced across at Creech through the haze of gunsmoke, crouched behind an overturned table and his pistol pointing at someone making for the staircase leading up to the rooms above. *Boom!* The shot missed, splitting the bannister and not much else, while the shape whipped round, shooting back, Creech's gun spinning from his hand and a couple of fingers right along with it.

'Aaaagh! Ffffuuuck!'

Shanklin took his turn at the same lad now as he fumbled to reload with all the grace of a newborn foal attempting to stand, but all he managed to hit between the eyes was a bad painting of King George II, sending it clattering to the floor in a cloud of dust.

Thack! Shanklin flinched as another piece of the column was frayed, slivers of wood spinning. He'd need to switch position soon or there'd be nothing left of the damn thing. Peeking out, he caught sight of a blur ducking behind the bar. It looked like Oakes but he couldn't be sure.

Ting! Another shot piped plaster from the wall near the front door. With his teeth, Shanklin popped the cork from his powder-horn and began reloading once more. Creech was lying low behind the table, signalling towards the staircase with the hand that still had all its fingers. There was another beam to his left but given that there were ten yards of ground to cross in order to get there Shanklin didn't fancy his odds. The thick fog of curling smoke would provide some cover but the prospect of leaving his beloved beam behind didn't fill him with joy.

Crack! 'Agh, ssshhhiiit!' The shot caught Shanklin's thigh and he dropped his pistol, clutching at his leg, blood seeping through his fingers. Man-mountain was lying on his side, holding his stomach with one hand and a smoking gun in the other. Knowing he only had a small window, Shanklin pulled his sword from its sheath, whirling round to finish the fucker but Jonah Oakes had finally found his bollocks somewhere and having vaulted over the bar was now running full-pelt, screaming: 'Baaaastaaaarrrrd!'

Shanklin swerved the blade as it came slicing through the smoke-swirling air, but the lad had the look of someone whose heart wasn't in this fight. Another wild thrust from Oakes was easily parried, steel flashing on steel and, with a firm kick, he was sent stumbling backwards, giving Shanklin enough range to slash a deep gash in the lad's cheek. Screaming, Oakes's sword clanged on the floor and Shanklin plunged his own into the first spot he found, toppling him backwards over the body of the now dead Man-mountain. There he remained on the bloodied floor, gazing up at the ceiling until the life was gone from him.

Two.

To his left Shanklin heard the unmistakable click of a pistol being cocked – a sound that'll send a chill through you when all you have is a sword in your hand. A dark shape in the gloom: the shot-dodging, gun-fumbling 'foal' near the staircase. He wasn't fumbling now though; he was aiming straight and true and Shanklin's blood turned to ice.

Boom!

The lad was flung crunching into a wall, dropping his gun and gripping a curtain as he slid to the floor, hooks pinging from the rail.

Creech was hunched over the edge of his upturned table, smoke curling from his pistol and a look in his eye that told Shanklin: *'I said I was your shadow.'*

One.

He glanced down at his leg, breeches soaked red. Needed fixing that did, and soon. But something else required his attention first.

'Randall!' Shanklin called out. 'Where's Sarah?'

Drip. Drip. Drip.

Warm blood trickled down his leg and he gripped the sword a little tighter. 'Answer me, ya coward—'

'I didn't want for this, Shank!' came the reply from behind the bar. 'I thought you were as good as hanged!'

'What have you done with her, ya stupid bastard? Where's my wife?'

'Your *wife?* That's rich! You ain't treated her as such in as long as—'

'Tell me where she is, Randall!'

The sound of sobbing could be heard now. 'I had no choice. That ... *bitch* we robbed ... she knew it was me with you that day on the road! She found me! Dunno how but she fucking found me! Had some big cunt with her too. She wanted Sarah or she'd have me arrested, Shank. I had no choice!'

Eliza? Shanklin's chest was pounding. His head spinning, foggy as the smoky room.

The floor tilted and he leaned against the column for support, his legs firm as jelly. 'She's ... she's got Sarah?'

Through the haze, two sets of fingers appeared on the bar, followed by a blood-speckled bald head and one beady blinking eye. Slowly, Randall stood up, glistening with sweat and dripping with liquor from the shattered, brain-spattered bottles above. There was no weapon in his hands from what Shanklin could see.

'They took her to Tyburn,' he said, tears running. 'That tart wanted her more than you or I ever did. Wanted her so badly, Shank. But most of all, she wants that necklace you stole. That's what she wants.'

Tyburn? The gallows? Shanklin's stomach churned and rolled and he felt sick like he'd been at sea for a week. 'When?'

'Couple of hours ago.' Randall was shaking his soon-to-be-removed head. 'I had no choice.'

Drip. Drip. Drip.

The room swayed. Shanklin's hands were numb. He could hardly feel the sword in his wet grip. His leg had lost some feeling too and he was wobbling now. Dizzy. He glanced to his left and saw that Creech was gone. Not that he could blame him. There could be soldiers swarming this place any minute.

Tyburn? Miles from here. Could Jess make it? Maybe. Could *he?* Perhaps if he just got himself straight—

Everything tipped as Shanklin staggered towards the bar. He dropped the sword and his hand caught the counter just in time to stop himself from falling. Randall stepped back, bumping his head on a shelf and knocking a bottle over where it smashed on the floor. Another waste of good whisky.

Shanklin tried to steady himself. *Harry. Sarah. Christ.*

Boots crunched on broken glass. Shanklin looked up and saw Tom, standing there with a musket aimed straight at him.

'This is my tavern, Shanklin,' he was saying. 'What's left of it anyways. It's *mine* and it's staying mine, y'hear me?'

There were two of him; two fat, blurry landlords and Shanklin gripped the edge of the bar with both hands. 'I, er ... I'll just ... I'll be going now then— '

'No, you won't,' Tom replied, his jowls quivering, the musket trembling, a chubby finger poised on the trigger. 'You'll wait right here till the constables come. You'll hang this time, Samuel, I'll see to that. I'll not have any more troub—'

Shanklin wasn't sure what surprised him most: the fact there was the point of a knife sticking out of Tom's throat or that his musket hadn't fired.

'Ggguuuurrrrraaakkk,' was about all he could manage as the gun slipped from Tom's hands which then clasped themselves to his neck as the knife slid back out. The inn-keeper fell to his knees, eyes wide, blood squirting through his fingers in pulsating streams. And there was Randall, standing with a dripping knife and gazing blankly down at the man he'd just killed. He looked back up at Shanklin and his eye had an emptiness to it. Like he wasn't really there. Not anymore.

Shanklin's legs finally gave out and he dropped to the floor, one hand still holding onto the bar.

Stepping over Tom, Randall stood above his old friend, blood dripping from the long knife he held. 'I always thought it'd be me that saved Sarah, Shank. Saved her from you. Saved her from a life she didn't deserve. I just didn't know how. And even if I did, she'd never have wanted it. She loves you. Always has. Always will.'

Shanklin blinked up at him. If that knife was coming then he'd better make it quick.

'Get up, Shank,' Randall said. 'There's still time. Eliza Torne; she's waiting for sunrise. Told me so herself. Said there's never a better sight than that of a body swinging up there when the sun comes up over the horizon. A *ritual*, she called it. She's crazy, Shank. You can save Sarah. You can do what I never could.'

Hooking an arm under Shanklin, he helped him stand. Then he held the knife out for him to take.

'I don't deserve the gallows,' Randall said. 'That's where *men* die and where legends are born.'

The surface of the bar was slippery wet. Shanklin straightened himself up and took the knife, greasy with Tom's blood.

'The throat,' said Randall. 'Make it fast, eh?'

For once in his life Randall was right on something.

'Aye, you don't deserve the gallows,' Shanklin said. 'Fact is ... you don't deserve death at all.'

He dropped the knife to the floor and turned, limping away, making for the door.

'No!' Randall called out. 'Don't you dare, Shank! Don't fucking do this to me!'

Wincing, Shanklin picked his way through the carnage, stooping to tear a sleeve from a dead lad's shirt, wrapping it round his ruined leg, sucking in air as he tied it off. He didn't fancy his odds on not bleeding out before the night was done with, but he'd take what he could right now.

'Wait!' Randall said as Shanklin collected his two pistols and the sword he'd dropped before limping for the door. 'Don't leave me here,' he pleaded. 'I ain't got the bones to do myself in, Shank. It's gotta be you! You've gotta do it!'

Shanklin paused to take a last look at his friend. Then at the mess he was leaving behind. Broken stools. Shattered glass. Dead bodies. There'd been some wild nights in here but this would take some beating. It looked as though *The Lion* had finally been tamed.

'That's not my problem now,' he said and he pushed open

the creaky door, letting it slam shut behind him as he staggered out into the night.

Jess was still tied to the post where he'd left her, now without the company of Creech's horse. His leg throbbed like nothing he'd ever known and he reckoned climbing into the saddle might prove a challenge. But then he'd lived with Sarah for long enough, how hard could it be?

Groaning, Shanklin stuck a boot in a stirrup and swung his wounded leg over his horse, gripping the reins tight. The world tipped and swayed and he fought against the pain, teeth clenched. A distant grumble of thunder could be heard. Or was it musket fire from the army? Hard to tell which. He turned Jess in the direction of Tyburn and they set off, leaving behind them Randall's screams coming from inside the tavern.

THE TOOTH FAIRY

I t wasn't the growl of thunder that had woken Jack from a fitful sleep, it was the noise from downstairs. A scream? He couldn't be sure. Now he was sitting up in bed with the sheets pulled to his chin while his heart hammered and he stared at his bedroom door, wondering if he'd only imagined it. The room was deep in darkness. The kind of darkness that makes you wonder if you actually have your eyes open or not. Jack strained his ears to listen and he dared not breathe, there in the gloom, alone. His tongue pressed at the tiny stump of new tooth and he remembered that his old one was still under his pillow awaiting the Tooth Fairy. He hadn't been sure if she was even real or just some silly folk tale that mothers told their children. But *now*...

A floorboard creaked just outside his door and Jack flinched. Someone was on the landing.

'Charlotte?' he whispered, his voice sounding so feeble in the blackness.

Silence.

He swallowed.

Another creak.

'Aunt Ruth?'

A white flash lit the room through the threadbare curtains, just enough for him to glimpse a shadow in the gap under the door. Terror now; tearing through him as a clap of thunder followed, louder than before, the storm creeping closer.

'Charlotte, if that's you, then say something!'

Rain began to tap at Jack's window. He thought of Mother lying in her room just yards away and his skin prickled with goosebumps despite the warm night. Was she risen from the dead? Had she come back to haunt him? To torment him one final time...

Another flash of lightning and he saw that his door handle was slowly turning. He pressed his back up against the wall, gripping the sheets even tighter to his chest. 'Aunt Ruth? Is that you?'

The inevitable boom of thunder followed, rattling the glass in his window. He heard the door whine open but he couldn't see a thing, his eyes still quite unaccustomed to the dark.

'Charlotte, answer me!' He was flushed cold with fear, sweating, his hands clammy, his mouth dry.

Another flash and the shape of a young girl was revealed there in the middle of his room. Jack's relief was vast and sudden. It was as though he'd just received the best Christmas present he could ever wish for. His sister was walking in her sleep.

'Charlotte!' he said, as the thunder groaned and his room was plunged into darkness again. 'I was frightened! I didn't know—'

The next flash of lightning revealed her standing directly at his bedside, smiling. He noticed that her nightdress was heavily stained with red and she held a carving knife in her hand, dripping blood.

It was Mother's voice which spoke to him.

'Hello, boy,' it said.

Aunt Ruth lay dead on the study floor, her eyes wide open and a deep cut across her throat. Fascinated, Charlotte gazed down at her, Jack's blood now also on the knife she held. She had no real recollection of killing her aunt, just the vaguest sense that she had. Like the memory of a dream from which one awakes, hovering in the mind for a moment before it's gone. And already her brain was beginning to concoct a story that would ensure no accusations were aimed towards her. The blaze that she would soon start would engulf the house and the bodies along with it. The authorities would discover that Charlotte's aunt had been gripped by madness following the death of the childrens' father and that she had attempted to kill the siblings before cutting her own throat in desperation.

Charlotte sighed. Mother's body would burn also, of course, except that ... it was her *own* body lying dead upstairs. That's how it felt anyway. She was ... disconnected. It was all so strange and surreal. Her head hurt.

Picking up the candle from the mantelpiece, Charlotte began to drip wax onto Aunt Ruth's face, watching as the white blobs hardened on her cheeks and blue-tinged lips. When she grew bored of this, she turned, tossing the candle onto Mother's rocking chair where she had left the book she'd been given. A blanket began to smoulder, flames catching the tassels. Charlotte gripped the carving knife firmly and she breathed in, pressing it to her forearm, screaming through gritted teeth as the blade sliced into her flesh. Then she cut herself some more, small nicks and slashes to her legs and hands, groaning all the while. She had to make it look as though there had been a struggle.

She dropped the knife next to Aunt Ruth and staggered from the study, turning just once to see the that flames had already smothered the chair and were spilling onto the rug upon which her aunt lay.

Down the hallway, Charlotte walked and, once out on the porch, she waited there, covered in blood, watching the rain pour down, black clouds lit from beneath by white flashes. Thunder crackled across the heavy sky. The rain would not dampen the fire she'd begun, not for some time and, looking towards the silhouette of Tyburn gallows illuminated by the lightning, she closed her eyes. Charlotte smelled the wet earth rising to meet her. She could *taste* the sound of the thunder on her tongue, bitter as chalk. She could *hear* the colours of the flames, gold and green and amber, a sweet lullaby to her ears. She wanted to stay on this porch forever. She never wanted to leave. She wanted to burn along with the house and her family.

Her family!

A crash came from the study, snapping Charlotte to her senses. She glanced down at her arm to discover that she was bleeding. *How?*

She began to panic. There was blood all over her! So much of it! What had happened? Then she remembered that she'd left the grimoire on Mother's rocking chair and she ran back down the hallway and into the study, shielding her face from the raging fire now clawing up the walls and across the ceiling.

'No!' Charlotte cried, lunging for the book and patting at the flames curling around it, the skin on her hands blistering from the intense heat until she could bear the pain no longer and, realising her efforts were futile, she backed away from the chair. She shook and coughed as the room blazed around her, the choking smoke forcing her to retreat.

'Jack!' she screamed, making her way to the staircase, but the fire had spread so fast and the bannister was already covered in flames, smoke belching up towards the landing. With no option but to flee, Charlotte escaped through the front door, stumbling out into the night, turning to watch her house burn.

'Jack! Jack! Someone help us, please!'

Her hands felt as though they were still on fire even as the rain beat down, plastering her hair to her face. *She* had done this yet she knew not how!

The sitting room window burst outwards, showering glass at the precise moment an arm hooked itself round her waist, snatching her up, and then she was being carried away.

'Nooooo!' Charlotte screamed, bouncing in the stranger's arms, her blistered hands reaching back for the house. 'My brother is in there! My brother!'

She was lying on the wet grass now, more hands pressing on her as she fought and squirmed in an attempt to stand, black shapes towering over her.

'Child, be calm! Be calm!'

'She's bleeding!'

'How badly?'

'Her hands are burned something terrible!'

'Good God, what's happened here?'

'Lord, have mercy on their souls!'

But Charlotte's strength was spent. She could no longer resist those restraining her. She blinked as the rain washed the tears from her eyes and she watched as a section of the roof crumbled inwards, sending a shower of embers sailing upwards into the night. Jack's bedroom, destroyed.

'We need to look at those wounds, girl!'

A woman came into focus, looming over Charlotte, wet

hair stuck to her cheeks. Her halo shimmered so brightly, sparkling gold in the glow from the blaze. 'You'll need a physician's attention,' she said.

Someone was pressing a thick cloth to Charlotte's arm.

'What's your name, child?' asked the woman as she dressed the cut on her leg. But Charlotte couldn't remember. Her mind was blank.

'I know who she is!'

It was a young girl's voice. One that she recognised. Charlotte looked across at her, standing there; small and soaked to the skin, her blonde locks hanging limply. She knew that face too. It was Tilly Jones! She owned a cat called Acorn. Her mother was standing next to her with a hand on Tilly's shoulder and the other to her mouth, sobbing as she gazed at the inferno.

'Her name is Charlotte,' Tilly said. 'Charlotte Eliza Hunter.'

The pretty woman fastened the bandage and wrapped an arm around Charlotte, helping her to stand before gently leading her away. 'You're safe now, child,' she said.

As she limped away, Charlotte had one final look back at the burning house, the heat of the flames still pressing at her face and the smell of burning timber in her nose. She recalled having picked something up before she'd fled and she reached inside the little pocket of her wet nightdress. A tiny lump was in there. She pulled it out.

And she saw that it was a tooth.

33

EMBERS AND MEMORIES

Eliza's eyes were closed, the heat from the torches wedged into the ground warming her cheeks. She listened to the crackle and the hiss of the flames and she remembered her brother, Jack. Remembered how the sun would feel on her skin on those days when they would run through fields together. Remembered how he had only wanted the best for her and how he'd tried his hardest to save her from this madness.

And she remembered how she'd murdered him in his bed that night, long ago.

Opening her eyes, a tear slid down her pale cheek while the wind flicked long strands of greasy, auburn hair across her face. She had no need of wigs now, such was her desire to be free of the charade she had been so wrapped up in all these years. Her long flowing dress was black and she wore a shawl around her shoulders with black silk gloves reaching elbows. The three torches in front of her burned hot and fierce as she gazed up at Tyburn gallows while George, her bumbling bodyguard, was sitting perched astride one of the beams, securing a noose.

Nearby, shivering in a horse-drawn cart in the centre of the *Triple Tree*, was Sarah Shanklin, wearing a thin nightdress, her hands tied behind her while she whimpered into a gag. Eliza saw how her halo burned so bright and so clear about her shoulders, shimmering gold, despite the hatred she must have harboured for her captors. She sighed. Jack was gone. He'd been gone a long time and he wasn't coming back. Charlotte was gone too and someone new had been born from the ashes of that dreadful night. His tooth had been the one thing she had to keep his memory alive within her. And now that was gone also, like embers in the wind.

George lowered himself down to the cart below and Eliza giggled, child-like. She found it most amusing that he could not bring his eyes to meet those of Shanklin's wife.

'Relax, man, we are almost done,' she said, as he made to climb down to the bone-dry grass. 'But not so hasty!' She glanced across at Sarah, sobbing. 'There is one more job for you to do.'

Standing in the cart, George frowned. 'Lord Torne would not approve of this, my lady! There are procedures for criminals! This is murder!'

Eliza took a step towards him. 'It is only *murder* if the person is *innocent!* This woman is the wife of an infamous highwayman. His crimes are wicked and she is guilty by association!'

Sarah screamed a muffled cry into the gag.

George was shaking his head as he moved towards the prisoner. 'It still don't feel right,' he mumbled as Shanklin's wife backed herself into the corner of the cart, sobbing hysterically. Eliza was happy that no one would hear her pathetic moans out here in the dead of night as London burned in the distance. Every good man with a musket would be doing his best to regain control of the city as the mob rioted. Even Jasper, the fool, taking up arms and doing his bit for King and country. She'd encouraged him, of course. *Go, husband! Be my hero! I hope no one clubs your damn head in while you're at it.* The timing of the disturbance could not have been more perfect. A window of opportunity had opened, giving Mr Randall and his merry men the chance to bring Shanklin's wife to her. George had not been happy with the arrangement, but then George wasn't paid to be happy. He was here to serve and not ask questions.

Sarah kicked out at him, thrashing her legs wildly at his shins while he attempted to grab hold of her. 'Keep still!' he barked. 'The sooner this is over, the better for both of us!'

'It seems she has a little fight in her!' Eliza called out. 'If I had known it would be this difficult, I'd have paid someone else to help you.'

Gripping Sarah in his large hands, George forced her to her feet, slipping the halter over her head. She coughed and spluttered as the rope tugged at her throat and he jumped down from the cart, wiping sweat from his brow.

'Well done, George,' Eliza said, clapping. 'You may sleep soundly in the knowledge that you are helping to rid the world of a *terrible* woman.'

To Eliza's left, rising up from the earth, was the seating gallery with the greatest view of the executions for those willing to pay. She spun full circle, sweeping her arms theatrically.

'Observe, Mother Proctor's pews! Such craftsmanship! Look at the crowds all around us. Listen to how they cheer! They have flocked here for this moment. Hear them roar their appreciation for the entertainment forthcoming. They demand justice. They desire vengeance!'

Worriedly, George shook his head.

Eliza closed her eyes and filled her lungs with the rich smell of this place. Too long had it been since she'd come; too many months had passed without watching anyone hang,

269

without claiming a single soul. And yet those souls she had stolen in her youth had been the very catalyst of her corruption. Vile and stained. Broken and twisted.

She turned back towards Sarah Shanklin, standing shivering in the cart with a noose round her neck. But now, here, in front of her – here was a creature as pure as she'd ever laid eyes upon. Untainted by the evil that resides in men's hearts. Here was a spirit that would serve to atone somehow for all those wretched ones she had taken throughout the years. That harvest which had turned a once innocent child into a monster. *Here* was her redemption.

Far beyond the gallows rose the grey shape of a hill, the first pink light of dawn peeking above it. Eliza's eyes glistened as she stared off towards it.

'There once stood a house over there,' she said. 'I lived there with my mother and my younger brother.' Jack's death scratched at her tortured mind, stabbing and cutting like she'd stabbed him that night, fifteen years ago. Painful memories, slicing like shards of glass. George said nothing, shifting from one foot to the other, clearly keen to be as far away from here as possible. But there had been no one Eliza could ever tell her story to, and so, he would listen, whether he liked it or not.

She pulled her silk gloves off and gazed at her scarred hands. 'I razed it to the ground,' she said, 'after killing my aunt and my brother. Except that ... it wasn't *me*. I ... was not in control, you see. It was as though ... Mother wasn't really dead. Not *really*. And for many years I wondered why she'd wished it so, but now I understand. The book she'd given me had to be destroyed so that my *Gift* would not be discovered. So that I could be safe, always. Because people don't understand. I think that was Mother's final gift to me.'

'Forgive me, my lady,' said George, 'but what are you talking about?'

'A family took me in,' Eliza continued, staring at the distant hill. 'They cared for me as best they could. But they were poor and we struggled. I became a burden on them. So I ran and I lived on the streets for a time. Until I was introduced to our very own Lord Jasper Torne. A man who took a … *special* interest in me, despite my poverty. A pact was made between us: we agreed to lie about my situation and social class to those who would disapprove.'

Sarah Shanklin's muffled cries pulled Eliza from her thoughts. She realised that George was climbing onto his horse, a manoeuvre which had very nearly gone unnoticed. But then this place did tend to do that to her: to wrap her so deeply in darkness that she could not see what was directly in front of her.

'Where are you going?' she asked him.

'I've heard enough, my lady,' George replied while his horse fidgeted. 'I want no more in this!'

'But you will miss the show!'

He shook his head at her once more. 'Perhaps I shall read about it in the papers,' he replied. 'Or perhaps we will give the judge our accounts before they sentence us!'

Eliza smiled at him, pitifully. She cared little whether he was here or not now. She had no more need of him.

'You bitch!' Sarah had somehow managed to spit the gag from her mouth. 'Cut me down from here!'

Eliza tutted. 'Do calm yourself, dear,' she said, approaching the cart-horse, stroking its mane. 'If you frighten him then you will go to your death somewhat sooner than we would like. The sun is not yet fully risen.'

'Why are you doing this?' sobbed Sarah. 'What have I done to you?'

'Oh, nothing whatsoever! But your husband; now he took something very precious from me.'

Sarah coughed, the noose biting at her neck. 'I mean

nothing to Sam Shanklin! Killing me won't change a damn thing!'

'You mean more to him than you know, dear. More than even *he* knows. Besides, it is sometimes only when we lose someone that we discover quite how much we loved them.'

The sky began to burn amber above the black hills surrounding Tyburn. The dawn had come. But George had not left for the hills quite yet. He was staring off into the hue, the glow from the torches casting worried shadows across his face. 'Someone's coming!' he said. And he was right.

Eliza turned, her gloves dropping to the ground when she saw the black shape of a horseman riding towards them. Riding like the devil was at his back.

34

ENTWINED

Yah!' Shanklin's uninjured leg kicked at Jess as they thundered toward the lights – three orange beacons shifting in the thick gloom, guiding him in like a lantern helps steer a ship safely to the shore. He only hoped that he wouldn't be crashing against rocks anytime soon, having no idea who or what awaited him when he reached the gallows tree itself. He rode hard and fast, the wind singing in his ears, two loaded pistols in his belt and the old army cutlass bouncing at his side. The black outline of the Deadly Nevergreen loomed closer and he saw that a woman was standing in a horse-drawn cart in its centre.

It was Sarah and she had a noose around her neck.

'Yah! Yah!' The wound in Shanklin's thigh screamed with every jolt but he urged his horse on, faster, faster, hooves thudding at the dry earth. He now recognised the figure standing beside the cart-horse: Eliza Torne, her hair trailing in the breeze. She had her bodyguard with her too and he was pulling a pistol from inside his coat as Shanklin gradually slowed Jess down, drawing his own gun as he approached.

'Don't shoot, Sam!' Sarah cried from the cart, the horse nervously moving from one hoof to the other.

Ghostly pale in the torchlight, Eliza was smiling, the skin around her eyes red and raw. 'Well, well, what a surprise!' she said. 'It seems that your wife is the sensible one in this marriage though, Mr Shanklin.'

'How's Harry?' Sarah said, sobbing. 'Is he safe, Sam? Please tell me he's safe!'

Shanklin's eyes didn't leave those of the bodyguard, their pistols aimed at each other as they sat astride their horses. 'He's safe, Sarah! Now someone needs to tell me just what the hell is going on?'

'A most unfortunate situation is what,' Eliza replied. 'At least it is now that you have shown up, sir.'

'You'll have an unfortunate hole in your fucking chest unless you cut her down!' said Shanklin, Jess fidgeting beneath him. 'The first shot is for this bastard here, but I've another primed just for you, *my lady*.'

The guard's piggy eyes were flicking between his mad employer and the mad bastard pointing a gun at him.

'I do not advise pulling that trigger, Mr Shanklin,' Eliza said, patting the cart-horse. 'This one is particularly frightened of loud bangs.'

'Why are you doing this?'

She seemed deep in thought. 'Because I have no choice,' she muttered.

Shanklin's gun remained on the guard but his eyes shifted towards her. 'We *all* have a choice,' he said. 'Let her go.'

Eliza Torne clasped her scarred hands behind her. 'A little late for philosophies, Mr Shanklin, but I admire the effort. Do you know, when I was much younger, I could not quite understand my Gift—'

'For being such a *cunt*?' asked Shanklin. 'I'm sure you were a talented child.'

A devious smile struck her lips. 'No, sir, I inherited *that* particular skill from my mother. I speak of something far more profound.' She looked off in the direction of Mayfair. 'They huddle in their coffee shops and they talk of Enlightenment and reason and logic, and they speak of science, but they know little of the rich tapestry upon which we all tread. We are one, Mr Shanklin. Connected. Entwined like the fine threads of a noose; each in itself fragile but when joined ... *so* strong.'

The pistol was growing heavy in Shanklin's hand. 'Aye,' he said, 'but this thread is unravelling fast so I suggest you make your farewell speech very quick. What is it you want?'

'Oh, I think you know,' replied Eliza. 'You thought that you could steal from me and expect nothing stolen in return? That you could go *unpunished?* Please, you must behave. An eye for an eye, sir, this is only fair.'

With his free hand, Shanklin pulled the necklace from inside his coat, his eyes still fixed on the bodyguard. 'A tooth for a tooth?' he said, holding it up.

The wind stirred more whirling embers from the torches. Slowly, Eliza began walking forward, transfixed by the tiny, twirling tooth. 'You claimed it was lost.'

'And you said you were good at reading people,' Shanklin replied, cocking the hammer on his pistol. 'Cut my wife down.'

George swallowed.

Sarah screamed.

The cart-horse flinched.

Up in the saddle, Shanklin felt his world tip and sway. His leg burned, warm blood trickling down his flesh, the heavy weight of the pistol pulling his arm down.

'We ... have a son,' he said, as Eliza came closer. 'Please ... leave us be.'

'Give me the necklace,' she said, reaching up.

Shanklin's eyelids were heavy. He was weary, fighting to stop himself falling from his horse. The bodyguard was becoming blurry. Eliza Torne pulled his gaze towards her. His eyes met hers and in that moment she appeared to him as beautiful as she was the day he'd robbed her. Her lips were just as enchanting, small puffs of breath coming from her mouth. A mouth he'd once longed to kiss.

'Give me the necklace,' she whispered.

Shanklin felt the chain begin to slip from his grasp. Another voice was calling his name from somewhere distant. A woman's, though he couldn't be sure who ...

His eyes closed and the necklace fell from his hand as a warm cloak of darkness wrapped around him and slowly he began to tip from the saddle—

A yelp startled him and he sat upright again. Sarah: silently flailing her legs as she dangled from the noose, taut round her neck, nothing but empty air beneath her while the horse and cart trundled off into the early morning mist.

Kicking at Jess, Shanklin spurred her into action and she sprang forward, knocking Eliza from her path as they raced for the gallows. Pig-eyes turned his own steed around to flee but Shanklin fired his pistol, the shot striking the horse in the neck, toppling it sideways, throwing its rider as it crashed to the ground, crushing him before knocking one of the flaming torches into the gallows amid a shower of sparks.

Dropping his gun, Shanklin drew his sword from its sheath as he rode, the full terror in Sarah's eyes now as she gasped for her last breath. With one fluid motion, the blade sliced through the rope and she fell to the grass, choking, the noose still tight on her neck.

'Aaaaghh!' Pain tore through Shanklin's leg as his boots met the ground and he dropped to one knee. Sarah's lips were blue, her mouth opening and closing but no sound came out. He staggered to her side and loosened the halter gripping her throat. With his knife, he cut the rope from her wrists and her shaking hands rubbed at the burn marks on her neck. Then she was sick on him. Sick and more pissed off than he'd ever seen her, but she was alive.

Shanklin collapsed on the ground beside her.

Crawling around on her hands and knees, Eliza desperately searched for the necklace she'd dropped when Jess had barged her aside. Scorching flames from the fallen torch licked at one of the timber struts. The bodyguard lay crushed beneath his own dead horse, his face as white as fresh linen. He wouldn't live long.

Sarah knelt beside Shanklin. 'Get up!' she croaked. But he could not, the pain in his leg was too sharp and too terrible, the makeshift bandage and his breeches were sodden with blood. He lay on his back, blinking up at a pink dawn and the crackle of fire was in his ears.

A piercing scream brought him once more to his senses, but it wasn't Sarah this time. He turned his head to see Eliza Torne, stumbling towards the stricken gallows, her long black dress billowing. 'Noooo!' she was crying into the unforgiving wind which fanned the flames, clawing their way up the timber, waving her arms in panic and desperation, the bright necklace still in her grasp.

Shanklin realised that his head was now in Sarah's lap as he watched Eliza approach the burning strut, making vain attempts to douse the flames with nothing but her already scarred hands. He watched her as though he was someone else, detached from the scene playing out before him. It was as if he was a member of an audience in a theatre-house and this would be the final performance. And the world became so deathly quiet as he observed; as he saw Eliza's dress brush against the flames now spreading further up the gallows, urged on by the bitter breeze; as he noticed the hem catch and the fire claw upwards while she spun in frantic circles. He wanted to call out to her, to warn her that she was in grave danger. To warn her like he had that night at the spring ball. But he hadn't the strength, and he hadn't the will; he could watch no longer.

He turned his head the other way and saw that Jess had buckled too, lying on her belly with her legs folded beneath her, exhausted from the long ride here. He'd pushed her too hard, too fast. She hadn't drank water. He'd mistreated her the whole time he'd owned her, just as he had all those around him. And now she was paying for it.

Sorry, Jess.

His palm was covered in blood from the gunshot wound in his thigh. But it didn't hurt anymore. Turning his face to the brightening sky, Shanklin closed his eyes. And so it seemed that he *would* meet his death here at Tyburn, just not how he'd quite imagined it. But then life is full of corners, some sharper than others and, as Randall once said, most often you don't know what's around 'em.

'Wake up, Samuel!' said Sarah, shaking his shoulders, hard. He could hear her sobbing again. It seemed like all he ever did was make her cry. Better this way then, him being dead. Better for her and for Harry. For everyone.

'Get up!' she was screaming, though her voice sounded thin and far away.

He opened his eyes, half-surprised to find she was still there. She looked younger. Beautiful, like she had when they'd first married. When they were in their youth. When they were in love.

'Get up, Samuel Shanklin!' Sarah was saying, laughing, leaning over him, her tumbling, chestnut-brown hair tickling his nose.

'I just … need … a minute,' he said, blinking up at the blinding brightness.

'We don't have a minute,' said Sarah. She appeared almost

angelic as the morning sun blazed through their bedroom window, a golden glow of light around her head. He suddenly felt safe here. Safe and warm in the bed they shared.

'Get up!' She was laughing while she shook him. 'Get up Sam or we'll be late! Your mother's coming over for breakfast, remember?'

The sun felt so warm on his face now. *This* was living. Not long married and another day of bliss with the woman of his dreams.

'Samuel Shanklin, get up this instant! She's coming!'

The room was growing warmer by the minute. Very warm.

'She's coming, Samuel!' Sarah kept saying, no, screaming at him, violently shaking his shoulders and he blinked seeing then that her face was twisted with panic. *'She's ... fucking ... coming!'*

And then Shanklin heard another scream unlike any he'd heard yet and he realised that it was coming from *him*, and that he was now sitting upright as Sarah pressed a finger to the wound in his leg. On instinct, he shoved her aside and he saw then what his wife was gazing at with such a horrified look on her face: a fireball. A walking, raging, human fireball coming straight towards them. It didn't take long for Shanklin to understand that it was Eliza Torne, engulfed in flames, her arms outstretched towards him, the necklace still in one hand. She was wailing and gurgling as she boiled, her eyes now flaming black holes, her tongue a charred flap of skin and the flesh sagging from her face like candle wax.

Scrambling for his pistol, Sarah pulled it from Shanklin's belt and she aimed, both hands gripping the gun.

'Shoot,' he said.

She cocked the hammer with two trembling thumbs. So close was Eliza now that he could smell her burning flesh and feel the heat from the fire. But Shanklin couldn't comprehend what he saw inside those flames. Her ruined face had become many faces, each one different, stretched and warped and switching from one to the next like the head of a doll that can be spun to show different expressions, each expression stricken with anguish. Each one a tormented soul.

'Shoot, Sarah,' he whispered, as it approached, whatever the hell it was.

Sarah shook. The gun shook. Shanklin reached across and his hands wrapped around hers, steadying the pistol. Eliza was five feet from them now, the heat pressing against his skin, her blackened hands reaching down for him, the necklace melded to her fingers.

'Shoot!'

The *crack!* echoed across the fields and the shot put a hole in the skull of the monster. There it stood, for a moment, blistered and burning, before it dropped to its knees and sloped to the ground, dead.

Holding his head in her lap once more, Sarah sobbed as they watched Eliza burn and the gallows burn along with her. The grass beneath him now felt damp and Shanklin noticed that his palm glistened red.

'Look, Sarah,' he whispered, 'even the ground here bleeds.'

'Hold on,' she said, cradling him. 'Help will come.'

Shanklin saw him then – a boy standing right next to the blazing corpse. He was no older than Harry, unscathed and unafraid of the flames whipping around him. He was staring down at her when there appeared behind him a man who placed a hand on the boy's shoulder. Holding the man's other hand was a woman wearing a cream-coloured dress. She was pretty. Her face was kind and her hair was pinned up in a bun high at the back of her head. The boy looked up at them both and they smiled at him with so much love in their eyes. The boy smiled back.

'Look, Sam!' said Sarah. 'Riders!'

Beyond the flames and the belching smoke, Shanklin saw

them: four horsemen, their silhouettes rippling in the heat haze. He'd seen a glimpse of heaven earlier; a much happier time when he and his wife used to laugh and tease. When they'd play like lovers. But now that time was passed. Heaven was gone and now hell was coming to claim him.

'Tell Harry ... I love him,' Shanklin said, gripping Sarah's arm.

'I told you once before that you can tell him yourself,' she said. 'Don't leave me!'

The ground shuddered with the thud of hooves as the horsemen drew closer, smoke swirling around them. The boy and the family that Shanklin had seen were gone and only the burning body of Eliza remained. As the riders slowed to a stop, he saw a flash of gold in the mouth of the one leading them.

'Reckoned I'd find you here,' called out Creech, his arm in a sling and his hand all bound up with brown-stained bandages. 'You wanna try lighting a fire next time; you might attract more attention!'

The other three men swung down from their horses and came running over. An African, shoulders as wide as a ship's bow, his face scored with tribal scars. Another one Shanklin recognised as Nathan Baines, his short ponytail flapping. The third man he hadn't seen before. Two of them pulled Shanklin to his feet and the African man assisted Sarah.

'Let's get back to civilisation, eh?' Creech said from up in the saddle. 'What's fucking left of it anyway.'

35

HAUNTED

Rivulets of rain streaked the carriage window as Sarah gazed out at the grey morning and at what had once been her home. A dripping wet shopkeeper swept broken glass from his doorway as people hurried past, dashing for shelter. The rain had been well received, helping to douse the fires that had still burned from the night of rioting. She watched as a body wrapped in a sodden blanket was carried to a waiting cart by two men and tossed into the wagon without a shred of dignity for the person it'd once been. She swallowed, wincing, placing a hand to her throat, the raw marks left by the gallows rope now covered by her high-necked blouse. It seemed that while she'd been hanging from a noose London had picked up a few bruises of her own. There were rumours of why the riots had begun, but no one knew for sure. What was absolutely certain though was that folks would hang, regardless.

Sarah's stare slid towards the huge African man sitting across from her and Harry, silent and sour-faced. A face carved with tribal markings and about as grim as any she'd seen in all the time she'd been married to Samuel Shanklin. A pistol was holstered in a belt across his great chest and the hilt of a knife peeked out from inside his coat. She placed a hand on Harry's knee as he gazed at their new protector. The military sword that Samuel had used to cut her down from the gallows now lay sheathed on his lap. She could hardly bear to look at it, but it was *a gift*, so Creech had said; her husband's dying wish that his son should have it. And what of *her* wish that none of this had ever happened? What of how *she* felt? A lump formed in her tight throat but it was too painful to cry, too sore to shed yet more tears. And she was too numb to even allow it.

Creech slid the last of the bags into the coach with the one arm he still had use of. The rest of her belongings had been secured to the roof by the man sat opposite, tasked with accompanying her and Harry as far as her cousin's house in the country.

'That's everything,' Creech said, leaning in, one elbow propped against the carriage, his bandaged hand tucked inside his coat. He sniffed, wiping at his nose as he glanced her up and down. 'You all right?'

Sarah hardly had the strength to frown. *All right?* Aside from having her neck wrung like a chicken's, aye, she was fine. Besides having to abandon her home, snatching what she could and flee before the authorities came knocking, she was just great. *All right?* Far fucking from it. She said nothing in reply though, mainly because it hurt so much to speak but also because she had not the will to. All trace of energy had left her. She felt as though her soul had been sucked from her body leaving only a walking, hardly-talking shell. Perhaps she'd heal in time. Physically, there was little doubt. The rest was up to God.

'Listen,' Creech went on, 'I ... er, I know you've been through a lot. But you're safe now. Bagpipe'll see to that.'

Safe. Funny how she felt anything but.

'Bagpipe?' Sarah whispered, glancing at the monster of a man sat opposite.

Creech grinned. 'On account of the fact that he don't say much. But I get the feeling that's gonna suit you just fine.'

It would be a quiet trip, he was right about that. Harry hadn't spoken since she'd returned to find him hiding in his wardrobe, and he showed no sign of starting anytime soon. He'd closed up like a clam when she told him his father wasn't coming home.

'The surgeon did what he could,' Creech said, as though reading her thoughts. 'There's none more skilled in London.'

'Right,' whispered Sarah.

Creech sniffed. 'Well, anyway … hang in there, eh?'

Blinking, Sarah stared at him as he closed the carriage door and whistled to the driver. A whip snapped and the coach began to move. She closed her eyes and breathed. When she opened them she found herself gazing again at the man they called Bagpipe. Staring at the guns and the knife and the scars scored into his dark skin. Sam had carried a few marks himself but they weren't arranged quite so neatly as these.

'Were you a slave?' she asked, her hand on her throat.

Bagpipe said nothing as he looked out the window.

'And you fled?' Sarah added. 'Joined the mob?'

Silence.

It was sore to speak but she wasn't giving up. 'So, how's that working out for you?'

The man looked at her briefly. 'It beats being a dog.'

It might be that she and Bagpipe had something in common. He'd run from an oppressor too.

The coach rocked and rattled over slick cobbles. Harry's eyes remained fixed on the stranger.

'Did you know my husband?' Sarah asked.

'Not too well,' replied Bagpipe while rain streaked down the glass.

She watched a young couple walking, laughing while the man attempted to wield a cumbersome, oiled parasol above their heads.

'Better than I,' she mumbled.

The carriage trundled on through the broken streets, past blackened, burned-out shops and buildings. A child's soggy rag doll lay in a puddle. Sarah wondered where its owner was now, perhaps having dropped it in their haste to run as angry crowds had come this way. They turned a corner and she saw then the great hulk that was Newgate gaol. Harry gazed up at it and Sarah knew he'd have questions, if not today, then soon enough. She had a few of her own but she wouldn't be getting the answers now and that hurt as much as anything.

It was with some horror that she realised the coach was taking the route which those condemned to hang at Tyburn would travel, and she pushed back the panic rising in her, not wishing for her son to feel her distress. He'd felt enough.

Along Snow Hill they continued, further west towards Holborn. It wasn't hard to imagine the solemn journey those destined for their deaths would take, sitting on their coffins in carts with halters around their necks. In her mind's eye, Sarah saw the crowds lining the procession, cheering and chanting and raising their tankards as the wagons rolled past, the City Marshall and his horse-mounted guards surrounding them. She pictured girls blowing the condemned men kisses while others threw rotten food. Many onlookers hanging out of windows, all trying to catch a glimpse of the soon-to-be dear departed. Sarah massaged her neck again. It wasn't hard to imagine it at all.

They passed Lincolns Inn Fields and then through the slums and rookeries of St Giles, one of the worst parishes she'd ever seen. Lepers roamed like the dead were risen and walking freely, and Sarah shuddered as a hooded woman draped in rags caught her eye, sores covering her half-concealed face. She was glad when they left that place behind them and entered Oxford Street, but her relief was short-lived as she braced herself for a worse sight still.

They came to Tyburn Road and buildings gradually gave way to grey fields cloaked in the rain that tapped softly at the carriage window. In the distance she saw it, or what was left of it: the Triple Tree, in the process of being pulled down by half a dozen or so men while several drenched constables kept watch. She watched a blackened beam collapse to the ground but she gave no thanks to God. Another gallows would soon take its place. Another factory of death, harvesting souls for evermore.

'Ma,' Harry whispered, his face contorted in pain.

Sarah looked across at him. She was gripping his knee so tightly her knuckles were white. 'Sorry, son,' she said, pulling her hand away. He smiled up at her, though it wasn't really a smile at all.

The gallows slowly drifted from view. Sarah wondered what had happened to the burned body of Eliza Torne. She'd seen some things there was no explanation for. Things she could never un-see.

A meadow came by the window, no different to any other except that two children were running through it, a young boy and a girl, a little older than he was. This struck Sarah as strange, not least because it was raining but because they appeared dry and dressed in thin clothes as though it was a fine summer day. The boy was having trouble keeping up with the girl, laughing and shouting, yet no sound could be heard coming from them. They looked happy, both of them, their arms outstretched like the wings of two birds in flight. Harry and Bagpipe appeared oblivious they were there and when Sarah looked back out of the window, the children were gone.

~

A thick fog had rolled in from out of nowhere and a fine drizzle smothered the fields. Through the haze of the spyglass, Shanklin saw only a wall of grey; a dense veil that no sound or light could penetrate. No bird chirped. No breeze stirred. The world had become silent and still and blank. Haunted.

Groaning, he snicked the telescope shut and slipped it back inside his coat as he sat astride Jess. From here, at the edge of the wood, he'd have no chance of spotting an approaching stagecoach. He'd have to move nearer to the road which snaked alongside the slippery bank, yet he ran the risk of being seen if he drew too close.

Shanklin patted Jess's coat, shimmering wet from the drizzle and the fat drops falling from drooping leaves above. With his heel, he nudged her on, grimacing with the sharp pain in his stitched thigh. He'd lost consciousness during the procedure and he couldn't remember much about the next day either, except for lying in a strange bed overcome by delirium and the worst fever he'd experienced in his life, sheets clinging to his sweating skin. It all felt surreal, like a nightmare he couldn't wake from. And now ... now he was here, with the strangest sense of separation from the world.

Beyond the fog, Shanklin could just make out the black road, pocked and full of puddles. Puddles that rippled now, not from the rain but from tremors in the ground — hooves drumming the earth.

Coach wheels whined and Shanklin sat up straighter in

the saddle. 'Here it comes, girl,' he said, as Jess fidgeted under him.

He pulled his black scarf up over his mouth and nose and drew in a long breath. With the hand that wasn't gripping the reins he checked for his pistols. Again. Checked for his knife. Again. Old habits and that niggling feeling they'd abandoned him. As if they'd just disappear because he hadn't felt their presence every two fucking minutes. Vanished like everything else he'd ever known, leaving nothing but the trace of a memory.

Shanklin tensed, every nerve and muscle taut, preparing himself for the biggest challenge he'd face yet; a final glimpse of the family he'd left behind. *His* family.

Then, and not for the first time in his miserable life, the moment slowed to a crawl as two horses appeared from the swirling mist, mud-spattered legs moving in unison, rain-slick manes clinging to their oily necks. The harnesses chinked and the buckles rattled, the driver's whip snapping as he drove them on, fear in his eyes when they met Shanklin's. The kind of fear every driver knows when they encounter a highwayman on a lonely road. Or the ghost of one.

But this was no ambush and there'd be no robbery today, so the coach continued on, sloshing through black puddles, creeping past Shanklin, dream-like. He saw Sarah through the window, looking tired. So tired. But worse, she looked numb, looking towards some further place. And Harry – oblivious, sat opposite the huge bastard who'd get them safely to Sarah's cousin's.

Safe. Something Shanklin hardly managed to have ever done for them.

Then the coach was gone, swallowed up by the curling fog and he was left alone knowing that his family were better off without him hanging round their necks like a damn noose. At least for a while. Perhaps it was the excuse Sarah had been looking for: a chance for her and Harry to start afresh. Yet, in her wet eyes he'd seen the truth of it, the answer they both knew; that, even with a damaged leg, he could run faster alone. That when the lawmen came for him, like they did before, he should be nowhere near her or his son.

Right before he'd left she'd asked him what he wanted most in life, and he'd said that he wanted nothing more than to not have to look over his shoulder forever. She then asked what it was he needed, and he'd told her it was a good pistol at his side. After quickly grabbing his gunpowder, he'd opened the door of their house to limp outside into the rain. Sarah had called out to him with tears in her eyes and she'd said:

'And what is it you can't live without, Sam?'

He'd paused before turning to her and he'd replied: 'I'll come back for you both, I swear it.'

Wincing from the pain in his thigh, Shanklin turned Jess round and they headed back into the wood.

THE END

JOIN THE GANG

By signing up to my newsletter, you'll receive exclusive updates on my forthcoming books, cover reveals and other cool stuff. You will also get the novelette ebook, ***Supply And Demand*** delivered directly to your inbox.

You can unsubscribe at any time, I won't bombard you with pointless emails that offer no value whatsoever, and I'll never send you spam. Promise.

Pull the trigger!

YOU CAN MAKE A DIFFERENCE

I hope you enjoyed reading this book as much as I loved writing it. If you did then I'd really appreciate you leaving me a quick review on whichever platform you prefer.

Reviews are extremely helpful for any author, and even just a line or two can make a big difference. I'm independently published, so I rely on good folks like you spreading the word!

Thank you,

Cheynne

the pair soon find themselves tasting a little of their own foul medicine.

Get Supply and Demand

ACKNOWLEDGMENTS

This book began as a short story, which grew to become a stand-alone novel, which is now the first in a series. Funny how you can get carried away once the writing bug bites. But even though it became somewhat bigger than was originally intended, it wouldn't be half of what it is without the input and support from a number of people; chiefly, my editor, Emily Cole, an amazing historian and equally outstanding human being. Reading her comments for the first time after I'd shakily handed the manuscript over to her will stay with me for all the right reasons. Thank you so much for your expert guidance and no bullshit approach, Emily. You proper rock.

A big thanks also to everyone who gave me encouragement along the way: work colleagues, friends and family (too many to name them all.) To those lovely folks who tapped on the window when they saw me sitting in Pret during the early hours, nursing a coffee and wearing an expression of utter dismay as I stared hopelessly into the glare of my laptop. I'm still staring as I continue to write this series.

For your love and faith: a huge thanks to my own ma and pa. Looks like this writing lark is in our blood, Pops, cheers. And a big thank you to my loving, supportive and long-suffering wife, Donna. I look forward to discussing more plot twists with you on country drives. (I can hear your groans even now.)

I want to also give a big shout out to the indie author community, especially to those die-hard pioneers who are paving the way for newbies like me. Indie gurus like Mark Dawson, Joanna Penn and Nick Stephenson. I don't know if I'd have made it to THE END without such solid and easily accessible advice. Their knowledge of this fast-moving industry is incredible and the support and encouragement from the like-minded, self-published authors I've met in the online groups we are a part of is nothing short of awesome. I'm bowled over by how much everyone helps each other out and I'm proud to be a small part of it.

Finally, a massive thanks to you, the reader, without whom I'd still only be reading this to my six year old daughter every night. I'm joking of course ... she's far too grown up for guns.

Emberlake Publishing, Unit 25002, PO Box 6945, London, W1A 6US

www.ccedmonston.com

Printed in Great Britain
by Amazon

86194244R00178